D1527575

ANTIQUES FOE

ANTIQUES FOE

Barbara Allan

SEVERN
HOUSE

First world edition published in Great Britain and the USA in 2023
by Severn House, an imprint of Canongate Books Ltd,
14 High Street, Edinburgh EH1 1TE.

severnhouse.com

British Library Cataloguing-in-Publication Data
A CIP catalogue record for this title is available from the British Library.

ISBN-13: 978-1-4483-0962-7 (cased)
ISBN-13: 978-1-4483-0963-4 (e-book)

All Severn House titles are printed on acid-free paper.

Typeset by Palimpsest Book Production Ltd.,
Falkirk, Stirlingshire, Scotland.
Printed and bound in Great Britain by
TJ Books, Padstow, Cornwall.

Praise for Barbara Allan

"Humorous asides and loads of antique lore . . . Allan delivers the cozy goods"
Publishers Weekly on *Antiques Liquidation*

"Best for readers of cozy mysteries who enjoy small-town living, humor with a side of murder, and cute canine companions"
Library Journal on *Antiques Liquidation*

"Amusing mystery chockablock with antiques lore"
Kirkus Reviews on *Antiques Liquidation*

"Allan consistently entertains"
Publishers Weekly on *Antiques Carry On*

"Delightfully quirky . . . For those fond of feel-good cozies, Allan delivers"
Publishers Weekly on *Antiques Fire Sale*

"One of the best in Allan's long-running series"
Kirkus Reviews on *Antiques Ravin'*

"This humorous cozy – with its well-drawn, quirky characters – is a hoot"
Booklist on *Antiques Ravin'*

About the author

Barbara Allan is the joint pseudonym of husband-and-wife mystery writers, Barbara and Max Allan Collins. Barbara is an acclaimed short-story writer, and Max is a multi-award-winning *New York Times* bestselling novelist and Mystery Writers of America Grand Master. Their previous collaborations have included one son, several short story collections, and twenty novels. They live in Muscatine, Iowa – their Serenity-esque hometown – in a house filled with trash and treasures.

www.barbaraallan.com

For our granddaughter
LUCY
in hopes she'll read (and enjoy)
this one day.

Brandy's quote:
Heat not a furnace for your foe
so hot that it do singe yourself.

— William Shakespeare

Mother's quote:
Believe nothing you hear and only half of what you see.

— Edgar Allan Poe

To: The *Serenity Sentinel* Obituary Department

From: Vivian Jensen Borne

Staff note: letter received from Vivian the morning of her death. Edited for space consideration in print edition.

Vivian Jensen Borne came from humble beginnings, the daughter of Ernest and Esther Jensen of Hackensack, Minnesota. Born in the middle of the last century, Vivian was a lovely, if precocious, child who excelled at everything she did. (*For more on childhood, visit unedited version at www. SerenitySentinel/obit.com.*)

Vivian married Jonathan Borne, a world-renowned war correspondent and photographer, who preceded his much younger wife in death. Left to honor Vivian are two daughters, Peggy Sue Clark (Senator Edward) and Brandy Borne (soon to be Mrs Tony Cassato) (NOTE from VJB: Hope it's all right to mention that!); grandson Jacob Bramhall (parents Brandy and ex-husband Roger); and goddaughter BeBe Richards (parents Tina and Kevin). Finally, a shout-out to Sushi, an adorable (if somewhat spoiled) shih tzu, who upon more than one occasion assisted Vivian in her celebrated sleuthing.

Vivian, along with Brandy, owned and operated Trash 'n' Treasures, a thriving antiques store in Serenity, which became the setting of the reality TV show *Antiques Sleuths*, on which collectors brought in unusual items to be identified by the duo. Although short-lived (one season), the popular series was cancelled when a key member of the film crew (who shan't be named, else spoil the book *Antiques Chop* written by Vivian, with the assistance of Brandy) was cancelled himself (or herself!), shutting down production. Nonetheless the show left an indelible mark on the psyche of the viewing public, many of whom (including a *TV Guide* critic) claimed to have 'never seen anything quite like it.'

Vivian is perhaps best known for her aforementioned sleuthing activities, having solved – with minor but appreciated assistance from daughter Brandy, grandson Jake, and bloodhound-in-spirit Sushi – over thirty murders in and around Serenity, which thrust her hometown of twenty-five thousand inhabitants into the pages of *The Guinness Book of World Records* (Most Unrelated Murders Per Capita), a point of pride for the acclaimed amateur criminologist. *(For more on sleuthing visit www.SerenitySentinel/obit.com.)*

For three productive months, Vivian was sheriff of Serenity County, taking early retirement (with bennies) after solving one of the most brutal series of murders in the history of the state of Iowa (or many states!) where, at an Edgar Allan Poe festival, a killer reenacted scenes from the works of the venerable author of horror (as chronicled in *Antiques Ravin'*). Vivian consistently denied there being any truth to the rumor that she was fired after taking liberties with legalities in solving the case, citing instead retiring for 'personal reasons.'

Vivian, a staunch protector of historical architecture, founded the Serenity Historical Preservation Society after an entire downtown block of Victorian buildings in Serenity was leveled and turned into a vast parking lot. A photo of her having chained herself to the wrecking ball to stop the destruction appeared in an issue of *Architectural Digest*, back in the day, with the heading, 'Lengths To Which We Cannot Endorse Going.'

Antiques dealer, sleuth, reality-show celebrity, former sheriff, preservationist, and reincarnate – whose past lives include Iras, handmaiden to Cleopatra, and the Egyptian queen's asp handler *(for more on past lives visit www. SerenitySentinel/obit.com)* – Vivian Borne was truly one of a kind. But of all Vivian's extensive accomplishments, treading the boards (theater, for the non-thespians among you) was her first love.

Vivian began her theatrical career at the tender age of three when she ran au natural onto the stage during a local production of *Carousel*, upstaging her mother, who was singing 'You'll Never Walk Alone,' the spunky child refusing to leave until she could join in. The duet performed by mother and daughter was perhaps the only time the emotional song brought tears of laughter to mingle with those of sadness in theatergoers' eyes. *(For more on childhood acting visit www. SerenitySentinel/obit.com.)*

In later years, Vivian became a staple at the Serenity Playhouse, starring in or directing (often both) hundreds of plays, including *Everybody Loves Opal, Opal is a Diamond, Opal's Baby, Opal's Million Dollar Duck* and *Opal's Christmas Goose* (unauthorized) *(for further listings of plays in which Vivian performed visit www.SerenitySentinel/obit.com)*. Vivian broke new ground when she produced, directed, and starred in a one-woman musical version of a Shakespearian play that cannot be named due to theatrical superstitions (the title can be assembled by combining the final word of McDonald's Big ___ with the last syllable of the feminine name Eliza____). In this production (later performed at the theater in Old York, Iowa, as described in *Antiques Fate*) Vivian portrayed all the roles by wearing different hats.

As a director, Vivian brought bold new innovations to her productions, incorporating pyrotechnics on stage long before rock groups thought to do so, and frequently using live animals on stage (never dead ones). While there were a few mishaps – such as the curtains igniting during the fireworks scene in *You Can't Take It With You*, and a horse galloping off the stage into the orchestra pit in the Ascot scene in *My Fair Lady* – thankfully no one was hurt, even the horse (lawsuits were settled out of court to everyone's satisfaction, and damaged curtains and dented musical instruments replaced by an insurance company who thereafter dropped the Serenity Playhouse from their coverage) (sore losers!).

While incarcerated in the county jail on a charge of first-degree murder (later dropped after the esteemed sleuth uncovered the killer's true identity), Vivian organized a women's theatrical group, the Serenity Jailbird Players, which put on plays for fellow inmates. The group became so popular it began performing in other prisons throughout Iowa, until two women in the troupe escaped while on tour at the Fort Dodge Correctional Facility, bringing an abrupt end to Vivian's dream of expanding their Midwest circuit to the Big Time (Big Houses?) – Sing Sing, San Quentin, Folsom, and Leavenworth.

Modesty prevents Vivian from enumerating her many other accomplishments – and money, as this newspaper charges 50 cents a word for print (which at 968 words thus far equals $484). (Oh! Now it's 976 words!) (Now it's 981!) Therefore, Vivian Borne would like to bid a fond farewell not just to family but to any friends who ever did her a kindness, including those who did not make it onto her Christmas card list. While she would have preferred to stick around longer on this ol' big blue marble, current circumstances have made that an impossibility, and she finds the only way to protect the ones she loves so dearly is to (reluctantly) take her own life.

Adieu! Who was it said, 'Parting is such sweet sorrow?' (Shakespeare, of course. And, now, Vivian Borne.)

P.S. But look for her in her next life. *(For more post-scripts visit www.SerenitySentinel/obit.com.)*

ONE

Curveball

Six days earlier . . .

On a cold, blustery, overcast Saturday morning in early December, Mother and I were working in Trash 'n' Treasures, our antiques shop, located in an old two-story clapboard house at the end of Main Street in Serenity, Iowa, at the rise of East Hill. We had purchased the house a few years ago after outgrowing several booths in an antiques mall.

Sushi, my brown-and-white shih tzu, was keeping a watchful eye trained in the event that either of her human caretakers should make a move toward the kitchen, where a pan of complimentary cookies cooled on the 1950s stove.

The house, with its wide front wooden porch and compact yard enclosed by a white picket fence, had been languishing on the market for decades due to a bit of unpleasantry that had taken place in the parlor nearly seventy years ago. Most buyers apparently had an aversion to sites of ax-murders, historic or otherwise. But not Mother (or, apparently, me).

When we first moved in, doors upstairs would sometimes suddenly slam shut – *bang!* – and the antique rocker in the parlor often got going on its own – *creak, creak!* After Mother and I solved the long-ago murder (*Antiques Chop*), however, these occurrences ceased, the ghost – or entity – finally finding peace. Anyway, I like to think so.

Each room was stocked to reflect its original purpose – kitchen antiques in the kitchen, bedroom sets in the bedrooms, linens in the linen closet, bath fixtures and paraphernalia in the bath, steamer trunks and old doors in the attic. Downstairs, formal furniture was arranged in the parlor, dining sets in the dining room, books in the library, and 'mantiques', such as

beer signs, tools, and vintage pin-up calendars, in the basement. Even the knickknacks throughout the old place were
arranged where one might expect to find them.

During business hours, the wafting aroma of freshly baked
chocolate-chip, peanut butter, or oatmeal cookies (no raisins,
please) would lure patrons to the kitchen, where they were
welcome to sit at the yellow-and-white boomerang-print lami-
nated mid-century table to partake of the free goodies, along
with a cup of hot coffee – no purchase required, tips not
encouraged, fresh gossip appreciated.

Customers often claimed that shopping at Trash 'n' Treasures
gave them the vague sense of visiting an elderly relative – a
grandmother, perhaps, or kindly old aunt. Only here you didn't
have to wait to inherit something that caught your eye; for the
listed price (or maybe a haggled-over lower one), you could
walk out with that treasure immediately.

I must add that whenever a patron mentioned the elderly
relative theory, Mother bristled and stiffened and lifted her
chin. 'We prefer, here at Trash 'n' Treasures, to think of
ourselves as a sort of time machine . . . a time machine with
price tags.'

Right now, however, Mother was asking, '*Where* are the
Christmas items?' In her favorite emerald velour slacks-and
top-set, blue eyes magnified by huge glasses, silver hair in a
tidy bun, she stood in front of an empty glass curio cabinet
in the entryway where we showcased our best seasonal
offerings.

I was seated on a stool behind the nearby checkout counter,
working on an inventory spreadsheet, wearing jeans and a
black cashmere sweater, the latter having shrunk because I
washed it to save money on dry-cleaning (and wore it as a
reminder of my folly). Without taking my eyes off the monitor,
I replied, 'That box on the floor is all we have.'

Mother crossed to it, bent, her knees popping, pulled back
the cardboard flaps, peered in, then asked irritably, 'That's *it*?
Did the elves take a holiday?'

Did you know dogs could sigh? Sushi actually did, and –
sensing an argument was coming and not cookies – retreated
to her leopard-print bed on the floor behind me and curled up.

'This elf,' I said acidly, 'told you *months* ago that we needed to stock up on more Christmas items. But did you listen? No, no, no! That rhymes with "ho, ho, ho," incidentally.'

'So, so, so,' Mother said, rising with some difficulty, 'we're just going to have to bring some things from home, to pick up the slack.'

My eyes narrowed. 'Such as?'

Her response had a lightness to it that couldn't have been heavier. 'Such as *your* collection of Paper Moon Christmas cards.'

She was referring to the greeting cards featuring airbrushed artwork created in the 1970s and '80s by a wonderful but long-out-of-business LA greeting-card company. (Worth a Google.)

'Not on your life!' Those cards were getting harder and harder to find, especially unused. 'What about *your* collection of holiday Annalee dolls?' Which I found creepy, especially the elves. And as an elf myself, I spoke from experience.

Anyway, we had come to the point where we were glaring silently at each other.

Finally Mother spoke, in a spirit not of conciliation but reluctant compromise. 'We will display both your cards and my dolls,' she suggested, 'to attract admirers . . . but put high prices on them so they won't sell.'

That didn't seem like a sound business practice, but at least would keep the peace, and – as she'd indicated – provide a nice display.

'All right,' I said. 'We'll offer both my items and yours at prices that we would be fools not to accept, if some fool was willing to pay it.'

'And of course,' she said, 'we are nobody's fools.'

No fooling, I thought.

Last year, Mother had sent me out on my own to seek yuletide stock. To teach her a lesson I brought back only kitschy items, like a framed Christmas tree fashioned from gaudy buttons glued onto green felt, and a wreath made of real fruitcake lacquered for posterity, and a tall green Styrofoam cone holding dozens of old toothpicks on which to stick little cooked weenies – the perfect centerpiece for a loopy holiday party. Instead of being disgusted, Mother arranged my curious finds in the curio along with a sign MERRY KITSCH-MAS! . . . and it all sold! So I ask you, who was the fool in that one?

The front door opened and in with the inclement weather blew Cora Van Camp, a retired court clerk and fellow member of Mother's Red-Hatted Mystery Book Club, a mystery book club of close gal-pals who had been discussing Rex Stout's *Too Many Cooks* for several years because they mostly gossiped while eating fattening desserts.

Cora, petite in stature, was wrapped to the gills in a heavy wool coat, hat, scarf, and gloves. She clutched to her chest a sack from All Sports Artifacts – a nearby sports memorabilia store – as if the wind might carry the bag away.

'What have you got there, dear?' Mother asked. The sports shop was not in competition with us – she was just that nosy.

Cora's features and movements were bird-like, bringing to mind Elsa Lanchester in *Bride of Frankenstein*. She replied, 'It's a Christmas gift for Raymond. Something my better half has always wanted!'

According to Mother, Cora's 'better half' was a beer-guzzling lout who spent most of his time in a recliner glued to ESPN, where he would watch anything they foisted upon him including toe wrestling, if there was such a sport.

THIS JUST IN: Wait! There is! In England. What will the Brits think up next?

'And what gift is that, Cora dear?' Mother asked.

The twitchy woman reached into the sack and withdrew a baseball encased in a clear plastic container. 'It's signed by Babe Ruth, and I just *know* it's authentic.'

'Oh? And why is that, dear?'

'It came with a certificate of authenticity!'

As little as I knew about sports collectibles, I was nonetheless aware that the Babe had autographed so many balls over his lifetime, collectors joked that the smudged ones were the rarities.

Mother held out a hand. 'Might I see the certificate?'

'Certainly! It's a lovely example.' Cora reached back into the sack.

Joining me behind the counter, Mother set the certificate on the counter, then shooed me off the computer. While I looked on, her fingers danced across the keyboard.

A headline popped onto the screen: 'Two Arrested in Fake Babe Ruth Baseball Scam'.

'Just as I suspected,' Mother pronounced. 'Yours is faux ball.'

'A foul ball?' Cora asked, blinking. 'How can you tell, Vivian?'

'Not "foul", dear – faux.'

I'd thought she said 'foul' ball, too . . . and as it turned out, that would have been apt, as well.

'What do you mean?' Cora asked, frowning.

'A counterfeit, a forgery, a fake,' Mother replied.

'Oh dear, oh dear, oh dear,' Cora lamented, avian movements increasing to such a degree that I feared she might take flight.

'Are you sure?' I asked Mother. 'You didn't even *look* at the ball.'

She turned to me, a put-upon schoolmarm about to instruct her most slow-witted pupil. 'It's not the *ball* that informed me, dear – although I would bet my life the signature *is* forged . . . it's the certificate.'

'Oh. You mean, the certificate is fake.'

She shook her head. 'No, it's real enough, and from a highly respected company that authenticates sports memorabilia.'

I shrugged, held my hands out like a beginning Little Leaguer hoping to make a catch. 'Then I don't get it,' I said.

Mother explained, 'What these criminals did was to take in a *real* autographed Babe Ruth baseball for authentication, then make copies of that certificate to use with balls that *were* forged.' She tapped the screen. 'It's all here in this article.'

I nodded. 'What slipped them up?'

'Someone realized all the certificates had the same certification number,' Mother said, adding, 'But not until fifty or so dealers and pawnshops throughout the country fell for the ruse at a thousand dollars per foul ball.'

Including, apparently, the local owner of All Sports Artifacts.

'What did you pay for it?' Mother asked her distraught friend.

'Two thousand,' Cora replied, teary-eyed, chin quivering.

Ouch.

'Well, dear,' Mother said. 'Let's go get your money back.'

'You mean, you'll come with me?' Cora asked.

'Of course. And I'll print out a copy of the article and we'll take that along.' She turned to me. 'You come with us, dear. It'll be useful schooling for a beginning antiques dealer.'

We'd been dealing antiques together for years now, but I let that pass.

Mother started the printer, saying, 'We'll close up for an hour since it's nearly noon, then all have a lovely lunch at the Merrill Hotel.'

While I didn't particularly want to get in the middle of what could be a dispute between dealers, the food at the hotel was delicious, and what waited for me here in our 1950s Frigidaire was a soggy day-old tuna sandwich brought from home yesterday.

Cora, coming in for a landing with a smile, said, 'And I'll pay!'

Even better.

Pearl City Plaza was just a block from our shop. The row of Victorian buildings had been gentrified and transformed into bistros, boutiques, and specialty stores, with nice apartments on upper floors. The shopping destination was so named because Serenity had once been known as the 'Pearl Button Capital of the Midwest', a half dozen or so factories lining the river, where hundreds of workers toiled on machinery that punched out buttons from harvested mussel shells.

A thriving industry for nearly a century, pearl buttons gave way to the advent of manufacturing of cheaper plastic buttons, along with a growing awareness of the need to protect the now endangered mussel species that were so important to the ecosystem of the river.

Since Mother, Cora, and I would be going to lunch after our visit to All Sports Artifacts, I left Sushi behind. The little pooch wasn't happy about that, so – anticipating the possibility of mischief occurring during our absence – I gave her a cookie deterrent. Peanut butter, not chocolate chip, as chocolate is bad for dogs. Or so everybody says, and who am I to argue with everybody?

All Sports was one of the specialty shops in the Plaza, located between a ladies' boutique and an upscale bar. When Mother, Cora, and I entered the store, our cheeks red from the frigid wind, we found the owner, Mark Wheeler, seated on a high stool behind a long glass counter.

Wheeler, in his mid-forties, casually dressed in a Chicago Bears sweatshirt and jeans, was (as the expression goes) ruggedly handsome, with a thick head of barely graying brown hair and a neatly trimmed beard. He had the reassuring male look of a former collegiate jock. He'd consulted with us now and then on our basement display of 'man cave' collectibles.

'Vivian . . . Brandy, it's been a while,' he said pleasantly. Then, noticing the diminutive Cora behind us, his smile faded a bit.

Every shopkeeper knows that when a recent customer returns, purchase sack in hand, something is up – especially when accompanied by reinforcements. And Cora's expression . . . well, let's just say she shouldn't play poker. Or rummy. Or bridge.

'Hello again, Mrs Van Camp,' Mark said. 'Hope there isn't a problem.'

'I'm afraid there might be,' Cora said, giving him the benefit of the doubt, almost apologetic.

'Oh?' he asked. 'How can I help?'

Cora looked at Mother, who gave the woman a supportive nod and approached the counter.

Mother placed the printout of the fraud article before herself on the glass, then slowly rotated it around, with a nonsensical theatrical flourish, for Wheeler to read.

(*Vivian to Brandy*: That was *not* a nonsensical theatrical flourish! Furthermore, responding to your earlier accusations, I am not nosy, or (as you imply) petty, nor have I ever called Cora's husband a lout. I may have referred to him, upon occasion, as an oaf, and a dullard, and a nincompoop, but those are not the same thing as a lout, and any true wordsmith would know the subtle difference in each appellation.)

(*Brandy to Vivian*: I forgot 'pretentious'.)

(*Editor Olivia to Brandy and Vivian*: Ladies, must you begin squabbling in the very first chapter? These parenthetical outbursts simply have to end. They are tiresome, distasteful, and disrupt the flow of the narrative. Readers might be prone to finding both of you juvenile, annoying, and unpleasant.)

(*Vivian to Olivia*: I am *not* juvenile! And, anyway, Brandy started it. And I have a right to defend my honor.)

(*Olivia to Vivian and Brandy*: Might I offer a suggestion? Any rebuttals either of you have should be addressed at the *beginning* of your chapters, keeping it to one paragraph.)

(*Brandy to Olivia*: I'm OK with that.)

(*Vivian to Olivia*: Fine. But while we're at it, are run-on sentences and the use of ellipses to connect two disparate thoughts acceptable? What about a paragraph within a paragraph? Is that, as our Australian mates would say, fair dinkum? Since Brandy has more chapters than I, and therefore more opportunity to malign me, my paragraphs may tend to run longer. And, this exchange stays in, right? Hello?)

Mark's frown deepened as he read the article. When finished, he asked Cora for the baseball's certificate of authenticity, which she again produced.

Comparing its number to the one listed in the article, his expression aghast, he said, 'Mrs Van Camp, I assure you I was unaware of this scam. I am *so* embarrassed, really mortified, and hope you realize I would *never* sell anything that I knew – or even *suspected* – was a forgery.'

'Of course not,' Cora said graciously.

Mark continued, 'Normally, I keep up with notices of fraudulent items.' He tapped the article. 'But somehow this one didn't get on my radar. I bought that particular signed baseball some time ago, from a third party, who I believed to be reliable.'

'I understand,' Cora replied. 'However, I am disappointed, to say the least. Oh, not in you, Mark – in not having the perfect gift for my better half!'

He raised a palm. 'Not only will I refund your money,' he

said, 'but, please – you may select the item of your choice here in the store, at no charge.'

'Really?' Cora asked, setting her sack on the counter.

Mark nodded. 'This was entirely my mistake, and I want to do more than just make it right.'

The former court secretary's eyes scoured the merchandise under glass, and landed on something.

'My husband has also always wanted a baseball signed by Ty Cobb,' she said. 'But I couldn't *begin* to afford one.'

The obviously vintage ball had a price tag of $5,000, and to his credit, the dealer didn't flinch. He simply unlocked the case, retrieved the item encased in a similar plastic box, and in one swift motion – like ripping a band-aid off so it doesn't hurt so much – exchanged it with the bogus ball in Cora's sack.

'Now I'll credit back your card,' he said.

'Let's just call it even,' Cora responded.

Mark's smile couldn't have been warmer. 'Thank you,' he said. 'That's very generous of you, Mrs Van Camp.'

'No, thank *you*,' she said giddily. 'Raymond will be so surprised come Christmas morning!' Cora turned to Mother. 'Do you mind if I skip lunch? I want to go right home and wrap this up.'

'Not at all,' Mother said, adding, 'As a matter of fact, I have something else to discuss with Mr Wheeler.'

After our free lunch flew out the door, Mark guardedly asked, 'More bad news, Vivian?'

'No,' Mother said with a smile. 'A possible business opportunity for both of us.'

I had a fair idea what she was referring to. Ever since we added mantiques to our basement, men had complained that we didn't carry any sports collectibles, which was true because 1) they could be expensive, 2) the field was fraught with forgeries, and 3) we had no interest in, or knowledge about, the stuff.

Mother batted her eyelashes, which behind the magnified lenses looked like huge wriggling spider legs. 'Would you consider consigning some of your merchandise to us?'

'Well, I have done that in the past, when I helped you with your mantiques section.'

'I mean a *display case* worth! Nothing expensive, mind you – nothing the likes of which would raise our insurance coverage. It would fill a void we need, but would rather not wade into . . . and also give your shop more exposure. You could put a sign right in the case saying, For More Sports Treasures, See All Sports Artifacts at Pearl City Plaza!'

Mark considered the offer, scratching the side of his head. He sure was a hunky son of a gun. 'As a matter of fact, Mrs Borne—'

'Vivian, dear.'

He smiled. 'Vivian. I have quite a few items I'd love to get out of storage – playing cards, pennants, sports buttons, and the like. I can loan you a display case that I've outgrown. Even has a working lock.'

'That would be *wonderful*,' Mother cooed.

Was she flirting with him? Yuck! Of course, I was the one thinking of him as a hunk . . .

While Mother and Mark cemented their new arrangement, I wandered over to gaze at a wall of autographed baseball bats and golf clubs, their handles secured by tamper-proof brackets.

Two female players were represented among the golf clubs: a wood for seven hundred dollars signed by Jin-young Ko, noted as the current number one player on the LPGA circuit; and a short driving iron inscribed by Patty Berg, who must have been diminutive because the club looked like it had belonged to a child; the iron's price tag was a 'firm' two thousand.

Since it sounded like the conversation between Mark and Mother was winding down, I returned to her side.

Mark was saying, 'Vivian, I want to thank you for bringing that Babe Ruth baseball to my attention. One bad social media post can ruin a reputable dealer.'

And bird-like Cora did so love to tweet.

He continued, 'Unfortunately, this wasn't the first time I've had to depend on you to help me out.'

Mother raised her eyebrows. 'Oh? To what are you referring?'

'Those Air Jordan 2 OGs,' Mark said.

In 1986, Nike designers decided to change the design of

the Air Jordan after their legendary basketball player namesake developed a foot injury and needed more support. Made of lizard skin, and lacking the swoosh logo, the unusual sneakers commanded a hefty price because only a few dozen were produced. (I guess Michael didn't like them.)

Mother touched her bosom. 'Why, I'd forgotten all about that.'

No she hadn't. Mother never forgot any favor she'd done someone, particularly another dealer, filing it away for future payback. But what she had forgotten – or chose not to mention, anyway – is that it was my son Jake, her fourteen-year-old grandson, who had gone into All Artifacts when visiting us this summer. He'd spotted the sneakers, knew they were fake, and, not wanting to confront Mark, told Mother, who took her grandson's place as the bearer of bad news.

She was saying, 'Well, I don't envy you, dear. With all the advances in technology, it's more and more difficult to distinguish friend from faux – as in, eff ay you ex. A little literary pun.'

Mark smiled politely.

I was wincing, if you haven't already guessed.

Mother continued, 'That's why we carry only a few autographed movie star photographs, purchased from a reliable source in Hollywood.' She shrugged. 'And, quite frankly, for the relatively small price we charge for a signed movie star 8" by 10" glossy, sometimes the customer isn't terribly concerned about whether the signature is authentic or not.'

Mother should know; she'd forged a few herself.

(*Vivian to Olivia*: Oh, this is just too much! You cannot expect me not to refute this on the spot, double negative or not! Or was that a triple negative? Are you there?)

'It's not only that collectibles are being forged so well these days,' Mark was saying, shaking his head, 'it's the authentication that now comes into question. Because of what just happened to me, in the future I'm only going to buy high-priced items that have been DNA'd at the time of certification. It's come to that!'

My stomach growled. Like a hungry little kid, I tugged on Mother's arm; she got the hint, and said her fare-thee-wells.

She gave the good-looking dealer a smile and nod on the way out, and maybe I did, too. I'm human. Ish.

Outside, the frigid air felt good as we walked the short distance to the Merrill, a five-star hotel whose glassed-in eatery off the lobby offered a magnificent view of River Park, the Mississippi, and our bridge beyond, whose lighted arched beams offered a stunning laser show every evening.

I ordered the bacon cheddar burger with sweet potato fries, and coffee; Mother chose the Caesar salad with shrimp, and hot tea. Glittering silver Christmas trees were spotted around us in the modern lobby restaurant.

While we waited, I commented, 'I don't know how Mark makes much money with the outrageous prices he has on some items.'

'Such as what, dear?'

'How about a golf iron signed by Patty Berg – for *two grand.*'

She shrugged. 'Ms Berg *is* in the golf Hall of Fame, and still holds the most major wins of any female golfer.'

Mother always fancied herself on the LPGA circuit, but I've seen her play and it isn't pretty; she's even terrible at miniature golf.

'And often dealers,' Mother said, 'have trouble parting with an item unless it's for a very high price.'

Like our soon-to-be Christmas cards and elf dolls display in the curio cabinet.

The food arrived, and as Mother yammered away about the time she'd hit a hole in one (after it bounced off a tree), I tuned her out, watching a barge make its way south on the choppy river. Somebody was going somewhere. You had to envy that.

It was one thirty when we returned to Trash 'n' Treasures; we'd been gone longer than expected, and my cookie deterrent had been only partially successful. Predictably, Sushi had misbehaved. No, not a brown cigar . . .

I'd left an unopened package behind the counter delivered to the shop from Zappos containing a pair of Kate Spade yellow flats that looked like taxi cabs. Sushi had chewed through the cardboard, gotten the lid off the shoebox, only to drag the flats by the front door so I would see them upon entry, noting her displeasure. While both cabs were dent-free, her message was clear: I chose not to chew. This time.

Can a dog be naturally vindictive? Or is Sushi's spitefulness something she'd learned from observing me? For example, Sushi had been watching when I set Mother's adjustable mattress to a rock-hard sleep number of one hundred out of annoyance with her snoring. And Sushi was present when I put pine needles in the toes of my favorite Uggs after I'd repeatedly told Mother to stop wearing them. Of the former, Mother said the following morning, 'That was the best night's sleep I'd ever had.' Regarding the latter, I forgot about the needles, and later put the Uggs on myself . . . and it was ugly.

Currently Mother was playing back a message on the answer machine.

'Hello, this is Clare Shields, the producer for Nicole Chatterton, who would like to feature Vivian Borne in an upcoming segment of her podcast, *Killers Caught*. Please call me at your earliest convenience. The number is . . .'

'Finally!' Mother said, jotting the information down. 'Recognition!'

Brandy's Trash 'n' Treasures Tip

Sports memorabilia is considered to be any items closely related to the sports industry and players, such as equipment, trading cards, photos and autographs, clothes, programs, and toys. Mother's cache of torn ticket stubs from Cubs games she had attended are *not* considered sports memorabilia; they're just plain trash.

TWO
Blindsided

Mother and I and Sushi lived on a tree-lined street in a three-story white stucco house with green shutters and wide front porch, its stand-alone garage filled so full with yard-sale finds (mostly Mother's) that the double wooden doors bulged in a valiant effort to keep everything inside.

Have you ever spotted a unique antique somewhere, and thought *I love that but it's not my furniture style*, and left it behind? Mother and I solved that problem by having every room in our home represent a different era. The living room/parlor contained Victorian furnishings; dining room, neoclassical; kitchen, mid-century modern. The library was an eclectic mix of old books (mainly first edition mysteries), salvaged musical instruments (with an emphasis on cornets), and a stand-up piano that nobody in the house could play except mice at midnight. Tucked behind the piano was an antique schoolroom blackboard with wheels on which Mother would compile her list of suspects at the beginning of a case. Yes, I had long since resolved that murder cases were a part of our lives. The air in there reeked of rotting paper, dried spit, and chalk.

Upstairs, my domain was strictly art deco, with a beautiful 1930s maple bedroom set, the vanity having a huge round mirror; Mother's room was art nouveau, where she rode the wings of Morpheus in an elaborately scrolled brass bed. And the guest quarters had a '70s psychedelic vibe to keep visitors from staying too long, not that spending time with us encouraged a long stay out of anyone.

At the moment, Mother and I were having supper at our Duncan Phyfe table, discussing the podcast invitation, which she'd received this afternoon. Or rather, she was talking while I was stuffing my face with meatloaf, gazing at her like Sushi wondering what the gibberish these humans spouted was all about.

Eyebrows lifting above her thick eyeglass frames, Mother was saying, 'To be interviewed by Nicole Chatterton for *Killers Caught* would certainly be a feather in my cap. I watch her video podcast every week.'

Personally, I avoid true crime shows of any kind, which have unfortunately become in recent years a busman's holiday. *My* Guilty Pleasure video podcast is courtesy of a woman who discusses footwear trends from inside her shoe closet.

Mother went on, 'Nicole wants to interview me about all my cases, and visit the sites of murders I've solved.'

Where was I in all this? Not that I cared.

I swallowed and gave my fork a rest. 'So you've already talked with her?'

'No. The producer, Clare Shields, lines up the talent.'

The talent? Did she really just refer to herself as the talent? Why was I surprised?

I asked, 'And you agreed to appear on the podcast?'

'Of course,' Mother replied as if I had cotton for brains.

'When and where?'

'On our turf, at the shop, this coming Monday, when we're closed.'

I frowned. 'So soon? That's just two days from now.'

'They're only coming from Chicago.'

Beneath the table, Sushi pawed my leg for another bite of meatloaf, an order I obeyed.

'Well, count me out,' I announced.

Mother gave me a sympathetic look. 'There was no mention of you, dear.'

Which, I admit, annoyed me a little; after all, I was co-author of our novels chronicling the cases. The primary author, really. I mean, I didn't want to go to the party, but it's nice to be invited.

'Clare did say,' Mother tossed in, 'she'd like to have Sushi in some of the shots.'

Double whammy.

'Fine,' I retorted. 'But I'll be present just to make sure you don't say anything libelous.'

Mother splayed a hand on her chest. 'Dear, you think so little of me. Anyway, it would be slander, not libel.'

I grunted.

She continued, 'I'm sure you can find *some* work to do out of camera range. Some quiet tidying up, upstairs. Some bookkeeping.'

You would think I didn't contribute anything to this enterprise! What about the recipes I include in the books? For example . . .

Easy Meatloaf

<u>Meatloaf ingredients</u>
2 lbs. ground round steak
2 eggs, slightly beaten
1½ cups bread crumbs
¾ cup ketchup
½ cup warm water
1 pkg. onion soup mix

In a large bowl, combine thoroughly the ground round steak, eggs, bread crumbs, ketchup, water, and soup mix. Put into a loaf pan and bake at 350 degrees for one hour.

<u>Meatloaf topping</u>
¾ cup ketchup
1½ tsp. white vinegar
2½ tblsp. brown sugar
1 tsp. garlic powder
½ tsp. onion powder
¼ tsp. ground black pepper
¼ tsp. salt

In a small bowl, mix all ingredients together. Halfway through the meatloaf's baking process, spread the sauce on top of the meatloaf and return the pan to the oven to cook completely.

While I'm on the subject of recipes, Mother and I would like to thank those who read *Antiques Liquidation* and commented on the delicious variety of dishes that could be made using rusks (dried bread discs), after Mother mistakenly ordered six *cases* of them instead of just the six needed for a single recipe.

The above meatloaf is another example of using our overstock by substituting rusks for breadcrumbs. (Bonus: since many of them arrive broken, there's not much crumbling to do.)

Monday morning, after working all Sunday at the shop to get it spruced up, Mother, Sushi, and I returned promptly at eight to wait for producer Clare Shields and podcaster Nicole Chatterton to arrive from the Merrill Hotel where both women were staying.

Since I was not to be on camera, I'd dressed in sweater and jeans, spending little time on hair and makeup. The more in demand Sushi – much to her annoyance – was given a bath, nail trim, and perhaps most insulting of all, a little pink bow to keep the hair out of her eyes. Vivian Borne, on the other hand, went quite the distance in grooming; I hadn't seen such a production since the teenage lead came down with mono and Mother tried to pass herself off as Maria in *West Side Story*.

And, yes, that was worth seeing.

Up since five o'clock, Mother first took a leisurely bubble bath, followed by a self-administered pedicure/manicure. Then came an elaborate process of applying face and neck lift tapes attached to elastic bands that went under her hair and around her head to pull back sagging skin. After that, she applied a liberal amount of makeup, and finally ratted her silver wavy hair to a messy French twist à la Brigitte Bardot.

That was worth seeing, too.

The clothes she selected had been appropriated from my closet: a white silk long-sleeved blouse and black velvet slacks. For shoes, Mother had managed to squeeze her feet into a pair of my pointy-toed blue suede pumps.

'How do I look?' she asked, standing in front of a full-length mirror in her bedroom.

Actually, having endured the entire procedure, I had to admit Mother looked quite attractive, appearing years younger. But, not wanting it to go to her head – or encourage a regular raiding of my closet – I said, 'Not bad.'

But something was missing.

'What about your glasses?' I asked.

'I'm not going to wear them,' she announced.

That meant trouble, because without them, Mother was a female Mr Magoo (younger readers: a politically incorrect cartoon character maligning elderly near-blind males). Also, I notice that when I don't wear my contacts, and fail to replace them with glasses, my I.Q. drops twenty points. Mother might be courting a similar fate.

'Well, put them on now,' I replied. 'You can ditch 'em later for the interview.'

She shook her head. 'They'll leave little marks on my nose.'

I sighed. 'Well, what then? Do you expect me to lead you around by the hand?'

'Oh, would you? You are such a generous girl.'

This was not sarcasm. I had volunteered and now was fully enlisted.

As requested by Clare in an email, Mother and I arranged a 'set' in the shop's front parlor, placing two Queen Anne needlepoint chairs angled toward each other in front of the lit fireplace. A library table was commandeered for the recording equipment, where Clare would sit in her dual capacity of technician/producer.

We had just finished when the doorbell rang (as Rex Stout would say), and Mother and I, with Sushi trotting behind, went to greet our guests at the door, me gently guiding La Diva Borne by the elbow.

Nicole Chatterton entered first, decked out in an expensive red wool coat featuring gold buttons with Chanel logo, knee-high cream-colored Louboutin boots (I had already checked for red soles), and lugging a Louis Vuitton bag. Her jet-black hair was worn shoulder-length and straight, facial features so perfect they might have been designed on a computer (let's see . . . I'll take those eyes, that nose, that mouth . . .), and enhanced by makeup that caused Mother's to recede by comparison into relative restraint.

The podcaster could have been twenty-five, or thirty-five, or even forty-five (with assistance, and I mean scalpels not skin-lift tapes).

Our elegant guest extended a black-leather-gloved hand to Mother. 'This is such an honor to meet you in person, Mrs Borne. I've read *all* of your books.'

The hand offered in friendship was close enough for Mother to see and grasp it. 'No, it's *my* honor,' the woman of the hour gushed. 'And I've watched *all* of your podcasts.'

Since Mother didn't introduce me, I said, 'I'm Brandy, by the way.' Then, somewhat awkwardly, 'Chatterton . . . is that British?'

The podcaster smiled, tilted her head close and said, in mock confidentiality, 'The origin is from the phone book . . . Back when it *was* a book and not a pamphlet. Which dates me I'm afraid.' The leather-gloved hand came my way. 'Tabatha Kerschinske from Wichita, Ms Borne. But don't let it get out.'

That charmed me.

But not Sushi. She emitted a low growl, which wasn't how the little dog usually reacted to strangers, normally granting them time to produce a biscuit.

Nicole bent to the pooch. 'Ohhh . . . and aren't you just adorable?'

No biscuit, and the growl became deeper, so I scooped up the former pup, holding her tight. 'She's a little out of sorts this morning, because I gave her a bath,' I said. And nail-trim, and pink bow.

Mother interjected, 'Sushi will be fine by the time we start.'

I wasn't so sure; if Sushi took an instant dislike to someone, it stuck, and there was a reason. Charmed or not, I filed that away.

A commotion turned our attention to the door, where Clare was coming in, bulging bags hanging from both shoulders, a tripod in each hand, a female bellboy who lost her luggage cart.

Younger than I, late twenties, and shorter, the producer sported a black leather jacket, T-shirt, jeans, and sneakers. Her hair was cropped short, face free of cosmetics.

An arm of one tripod was extended toward Mother, and Mr Magoo reached out and shook its 'hand'.

'You must be Clare,' Mother enthused. 'My, what a firm grip you have!'

'She's joking,' I said, forcing a laugh. 'Let me give you a hand.'

A real one.

I gestured to the white utility van parked at the curb behind Nicole's sleek silver BMW.

'No thanks,' the producer replied curtly, and moved briskly past us.

In the parlor, Nicole placed her coat and designer bag on a chair, then stood accessing the set.

'Very nice,' the podcaster commented. 'But could the fire be higher, and the chairs moved a bit closer together?'

Mother said, 'Might I be so bold as to suggest that two of our standing antique lamps be used in place of hot key lights?'

She was showing off her street cred from having worked on a reality show.

Nicole gave her an appreciative smile. 'Very good, Mrs Borne—'

'Vivian, dear.'

'Vivian. The fire should provide enough extra light to support your lamps, where key lights would heat things up.'

Actually Mother wasn't concerned about heat – I'd never seen her sweat in the hottest of weather – but she knew softer lighting would be better for her face.

Since Clare was busy setting up the equipment, I put Sushi down – with a whispered warning to behave – and tended to Nicole's requests, adding more logs to the fire, adjusting the chairs, and commandeering two lamps (one with a Tiffany-style glass shade, the other a beige satin shade with hanging tassels), which I placed behind each chair.

Pooped, I retired to the horsehair couch that Mother and I couldn't sell in today's understandably animal-cruelty conscious climate. (Before the turn of last century, tufts of hair were taken from a horse's tail and neck, then woven into upholstery for durability and quality. The furniture is *not* covered in the animal's skin. Still, the couch usually elicited an *Ick!* from customers who inquired about the material.)

A pouting Sushi joined me (she liked the couch just fine) while I watched Clare quickly and efficiently set up a laptop and monitor, along with other equipment I didn't understand, then attach cameras to the two tripods to simultaneously capture separate shots of Nicole and Mother. The two women were positioned in the needlepoint chairs, fitted with wireless microphones, checked for sound, and finally, a release form was presented to Mother to sign for the use of her image and speech.

I brought Sushi over, placing her in Mother's lap, but she wouldn't stay put more than a few seconds, probably due to the warmth of the fire, so the presence of a cute little dog was abandoned in favor of getting the show going.

'Ready?' Clare asked her boss from her station, adjusting her headset.

Nicole nodded, looking into her camera. 'Five . . . four . . . three . . .'

'Welcome to another episode of *Killers Caught*,' the podcaster said with grave conviction. 'I'm your host, Nicole Chatterton, and today I will be interviewing true crime's infamous amateur detective Vivian Borne in her antiques shop in Serenity, Iowa.'

Mother didn't react but I didn't miss it: 'infamous' was not *a good sign . . .*

Nicole swiveled to Mother. 'Vivian, it's such a pleasure to have you on my podcast today . . . no, I'm going to amend that statement. It's an honor. I've read every one of your seventeen true-crime accounts detailing the various murders you've solved over the past few years.'

'How very kind of you,' Mother replied.

'In fact,' Nicole went on, 'I'll be visiting many of the sites where these brutal killings took place.' She paused. 'What would you say was your most challenging case?'

'Well, dear,' Mother replied, 'the case recounted in *Antiques Wanted* was a real humdinger, racking up quite the body-count.'

Ooooh . . . Mother's insensitivity to such things was already on display . . .

Nicole thought about that for a troubled second, then said, 'It's hard to believe a quaint little Midwestern town would become such a killing ground.'

I had a good view of Clare's monitor with its split-screen shot of each woman, and saw the way the podcaster's eyes suddenly went dead – like a shark in attack mode.

'In fact,' Nicole continued, 'Serenity is listed in the *Guinness Book of World Records* as – and I'm quoting here – "the town with the most murders per capita of any city in America."'

'Quite the distinction,' Mother responded cheerfully, obviously having no clue where the interview was heading.

'Is it?' Nicole asked flatly. 'I found the statistic so disturbing that I consulted Lloyd's of London, who said the odds of so many murders in a town of this size were, roughly . . . one in one million.'

'Well, someone has to win the lottery,' Mother burbled, adding, 'Besides, the murders didn't *all* take place in Serenity. Some occurred in nearby towns.'

'Cases in which you were *also* directly involved.'

Her smile weakened as she shrugged. 'Well, naturally.'

Something was happening to Mother's face. It was beginning to sag, the heat from the fire affecting the glue of the facelift tapes.

The podcaster said, 'According to your books, your daughter Brandy was also involved in these murders.'

'She *assisted* me, yes,' Mother allowed.

Mother, I thought, *we weren't* involved *in the murders – we were* investigating *them.*

Nicole said, 'As was, in several of the murders, your grandson Jake.'

At the mention of my son's name, I jumped to my feet. 'Agree to edit that out, or this interview ends now.'

Nicole looked my way, blandly indifferent to my existence. 'Why? You write about him in the books.'

'He's a minor,' I said, 'and I don't want him mentioned. *At* all.'

'Nor do I,' Mother said firmly.

Nicole shrugged. 'All right.' She nodded to Clare, and I watched the monitor as the producer backed the footage up and deleted it.

'Mrs Borne,' the podcaster proceeded in a friendlier tone, 'I understand you've performed in many plays in a variety of roles over the years. Am I right?'

'Yes, mostly through our community theater, although I've also directed and appeared off-Broad—'

Nicole interrupted. 'Some of these roles were young women, older women, and . . .' She flipped a hand. '. . . even the occasional man.'

The podcaster's destination had become clear. I gave Mother a 'cut' sign, running a finger across my throat, but she either didn't – or couldn't – see me.

Mother had, however, intuited the danger. 'Miss Chatterton, what are you trying to say?'

'Only that *you* may have committed all these murders yourself, possibly with the help of your daughter and . . . perhaps others.'

Mother stood faster than her knees could rightfully manage. 'How *dare* you insinuate that!' she said, shaking a finger.

It wasn't an insinuation – it was an accusation. And slander. Or libel. Or . . . well, something!

Mother was roaring. 'You . . . you, charlatan! Snake in the grass!' Other fingers joined together to make a fist. 'How would you like to have a knuckle sandwich, Miss Kerschinske!'

Mother's outburst was punctuated by rubber-banded tapes flying off her head, little rocket ships leaving the Death Star.

With Sushi barking protectively, I crossed to the wall and yanked the plugs on the equipment.

'We're done here,' I said.

With a smug smile, Nicole stood regally, gathered her coat and bag from a chair, and strode from the parlor, leaving Clare to handle any further wrath.

Sometimes, I've learned, being understated can make a better point.

'That wasn't very nice,' I said to the producer.

'Well, *she* isn't very nice,' Clare responded, matter-of-factly, which spoke volumes about their working relationship.

Mother stormed over. 'And what's *your* excuse, young lady?' she asked.

Why *did* Clare put up with her boss?

Could she be in love with Nicole?

That evening, Mother sat glumly at the table while we shared a pasta casserole I'd made earlier with leftover meatloaf, busying myself in the kitchen to give Mother time to process the podcast debacle.

I wasn't about to bring up the subject – why pour salt on her wounded ego?

Finally she spoke. 'I didn't see that coming until it was too late. Call me Miss Bungle. Still, I can take solace knowing that prematurely ended podcast will have to be scrapped.'

I set my fork down. 'Will it?'

Mother frowned. 'What do you mean?'

'You signed a release form. Nicole can use everything that was recorded, including your outburst. And she can leave in your rubber bands flying off, and edit out "Kerschinske".'

Mother sat back in her chair. 'Oh, my word. I never thought of that. She'll take the footage and wrap it up in every hare-brained theory she has about me . . . about *us* . . . being some kind of demented small-town serial killers!'

Now I was included.

She tossed her napkin on the table, pushed back her chair, and stood with purpose.

'Where do you think you're going?' I asked.

'To see Nicole, and get that release back.'

'Oh, really? And what if she refuses?'

'I'll appeal to her better nature.'

'Do we think she has one?'

A forefinger rose high. 'I'll point out that she libeled us!'

'That might work at that. But isn't it slander?'

'It's defamation by any name.'

I followed Mother into the living room, where she'd left her cellphone. Soon she was calling the Merrill Hotel.

'Connect me to Nicole Chatterton's suite,' Mother said, business like.

Moments later I heard the podcaster's voice answer rather coldly: 'What is it you want, Mrs Borne?'

Mother, in a syrupy-sweet voice, said, 'I must apologize for my atrocious behavior this morning, but I'd like a re-do . . . a second chance to complete your podcast with me in person . . . Fine . . . Excellent . . . I'll see you at seven thirty, then.'

After the call ended, I asked, 'How is a re-do going to help anything?'

'I'll know what this is about, this go-round.'

'And then what?'

Mother shrugged. 'All I need do is get my foot in the door, then I'll wing it.'

Riiiiiiiight.

Here are some examples of Mother winging it: starting a fire at the fairground to attract help, the blaze getting out of hand and burning down the outdoor stadium; breaking a window to gain entry into a suspect's home, only to find out it wasn't the suspect's house; stealing a golf cart to chase a killer after confronting him on the back nine, causing thousands of dollars of damage to the newly sodded fairway. (More examples, upon request.)

'I'm going with you,' I said.

She raised two palms in a grand gesture. 'No, dear. Your presence would only put the woman on her guard.'

'Well, at least I have to drive you there,' I argued. 'It's too cold for you to use your Vespa.'

Due to vehicular infractions (too numerous to mention) Mother's driver's license had been revoked. She was, however, authorized to operate a scooter.

'Besides,' I went on, hearing crackling against the window-panes, 'it's starting to sleet outside.'

'Very well,' Mother replied. 'But you'll wait in the car.'

At least I'd be close by if there was trouble.

Leftover Meatloaf Pasta Casserole

Ingredients

1 16 ounce package of penne pasta (or substitute your
    favorite noodle)
leftover meatloaf crumbled (amount to your taste)
1 cup frozen corn
1 15 ounce can tomato sauce
⅛ tsp. dried basil
⅛ tsp. dried oregano
⅛ tsp. onion powder
⅛ tsp. garlic powder
⅛ tsp. salt
⅛ tsp. black pepper
1 tblsp. white sugar
¼ cup Parmesan cheese
½ cup shredded Cheddar cheese

Directions
Preheat oven to 350 degrees. Cook pasta according to
package directions. In a small bowl combine all ingredients except the two cheeses. Drain pasta and put into
casserole dish. Add crumbled meatloaf, and stir in tomato
mixture. Sprinkle the Parmesan and Cheddar cheeses on
top. Bake for 30 to 40 minutes. Serves 6.

Mother always arrives early for any appointment, and her
meeting with Nicole was no exception. We left the house at
a quarter to seven for a seven thirty meeting.

Outside, it was pitch black, cold, and indeed was
sleeting as we hurried to our SUV. We were silent on the ride
– mother was most likely formulating a plan, and since I hoped
she came up with one, I didn't want to interrupt her thoughts.

Sometimes you simply do have to burn down an outdoor
stadium.

A few minutes before seven, I pulled into the lot of the
hotel, parking in a handicapped spot using a hanging tag
Mother had gotten after bunion surgery last year. She exited

and I watched her walk in her unique post-hammertoe surgery way to a side entrance, and disappear.

Mother wasn't gone long, perhaps fifteen minutes, and I concluded that her talk with the podcaster hadn't gone well; plus, she was moving too quickly, I thought, for these slippery conditions. And her post-surgery feet.

Inside the car, Mother said, 'Take me home.'

'What happened?' I asked.

'Home, dear. I'll tell you there.'

I drove out of the lot.

Though I tried to wheedle information from her, she refused to say more. What had happened back there? She certainly hadn't been gone long enough for a re-do of the podcast!

After entering the house, Mother kept her coat on while I trailed her from room to room as she collected items in a tote bag: reading glasses left in the living room; medicine from the kitchen cabinet; a pepper shaker off the dining-room table; and an Agatha Christie novel from the library.

Was she going somewhere?

We had circled back to the living room, where finally I raised my voice in frustration. 'OK – did you get that release back or not?'

'No, dear, I did not.'

Flashing lights drew my attention to the picture window, where a police car was pulling up in our driveway.

'What do *they* want?' I wondered.

'That would be me,' Mother replied. 'I didn't tell you anything because I didn't want you to be charged as an accomplice after the fact.'

'After the fact of *what*?'

A banging commenced on the front door.

'*Entrez!*' Mother called out.

Shawntea Monroe, a navy parka covering her police uniform, stood in the doorway, bad news in a frame. 'Vivian Borne—' the Black officer began.

'I know, dear,' Mother interjected. 'You're arresting me for the murder of Nicole Chatterton. I have the right to remain silent. Anything I say can and will be used against me in a court of law . . .'

Brandy's Trash 'n' Treasures Tip

As a sports fan, decide what you want to collect. Do you
have a particular interest in a sport, athlete, team, or item?
Sometimes a collection that had once belonged to a family
member can be built upon, or enjoyed. But express your interest
early. As a kid, I found some old baseball cards of Mother's
stored in the attic, and attached them with clothes pins to my
bicycle spokes to sound like a motorcycle when pedaled. Later
I learned the now-creased, muddied cards could have bought
an actual Harley-Davidson.

THREE
Full Court Press

Dearest ones! This is Vivian Borne coming to you live from the Serenity County Jail, where I am a guest pending my arraignment for the murder of Nicole Chatterton.

But first I must address an issue I've been campaigning against for some time (unfortunately to little or no avail), and that is the continued usage by the media and others of the term 'bad actor' when describing nefarious or dubious persons. While there *are* bad actors who appear on stage and in movies, there is no reason to degrade them – they are trying their best! Sadly, I am now hearing the more specific 'crisis actor', 'bad-faith actor', and 'fringe actor'.

For your information, *most* actors (the ones I know at any rate) *are* in crisis mode – it's the nature of the profession and the unique personalities drawn to it. Furthermore, to accuse actors of not having faith, well, it's difficult to make it to church on Sunday – or synagogue on Saturday, or mosque on Friday – after evening performances, or long days of filming. Did you know that Raymond Burr slept every night on the set of his *Perry Mason* TV show because he was too exhausted to drive home?

And picking on a fringe actor – those who are trying to gain a foothold in the profession – is the most egregious of all. There's nothing wrong with actors taking on fringe parts – even a walk-on without dialogue. They have to start some-where! What if John Wayne, who'd been employed as a young prop man, hadn't been noticed by director John Ford, who subsequently first used The Duke as a background extra? Where would we be today without *Stagecoach* or *The Searchers*? Let's all work together in putting an end to the malignment of this noble craft of acting!

But getting back to our story (and my life!) . . .

A few years ago, Serenity built a state-of-the-art county jail after I'd spent several nights in the old crumbling bug-infested one after chaining myself to the front door of an historic building destined for the wrecking ball. As a result of that incommodious stay – as any stay lacking a commode might be so described – I vowed to do something about the old hoosegow, as there existed a possibility that I might be in trouble with the law at some point in the future, which turned out to be an astute precaution.

After my release, I spearheaded a committee to raise money for a new facility, along with public awareness that criminals were people, too, and deserved better than cockroach cellmates.

The modern three-floor red-brick building has no fence or guard tower; in fact, if it weren't for a signifying sign, one might mistake it for a large clinic or perhaps educational facility. It's conveniently located next to the police department and across the street from the courthouse, the wheels of justice in Serenity well-greased and moving efficiently. A perp could be booked at the police station, moved to the county jail, then taken to the courthouse for arraignment with ample efficiency and scant opportunity for escape.

Upon my arrival from a holding cell at the police station the night previous, I was first placed in what they call a pod: a separate area to determine whether or not I was mentally capable of joining the rest of the inmate population. Once it had been ascertained that I was not deranged, merely 'eccentric', I was given my very own cell on the third floor, which is restricted to female prisoners.

The processor was kind enough to grant my request of boarding in the same cell as my previous stay a year ago, where I had scratched a cheery message on the wall, HANG IN THERE! to keep my spirits (and those of later occupants) up.

From my tote bag, I'd been allowed to keep my reading glasses and my current Agatha Christie book; my bipolar medication was turned over to the jail nurse to dispense, but unfortunately the black pepper (to counteract the bland jail food) got confiscated.

My room was small but clean, containing a single bed (not too hard), a stainless-steel stool (no lid), and a sink with mirror (not glass). Several shelves for storage were provided, and a high window (too small for even the town's little person, Billy Buckly, to climb out), which brought in a nice morning stream of sunshine (vitamin D is so important!).

So, dear reader, do not agonize over me as I was quite comfortable – to put it in jail parlance: three hots and a cot. And it seemed rather like old home week for me (or months, or years, depending on the outcome of my trial), if any current inmates turned out to be cast members from the Jailbird Players.

You may not realize this, but a great deal of thought goes into the sparse furnishings of a cell, due to various security issues. I imagine there is some kind of inspector – let's call him or her a Prison Cell Checker-Outer – who goes around visiting cells, trying to find anything a prisoner might use to harm him/herself (or perhaps a guard). For example, hooks and shelves will only hold a weight of ten pounds, and if anything is deemed to be a risk, that feature is changed or removed.

Wouldn't a Prison Cell Checker-Outer be a marvelous line of work? Think of the job satisfaction he/she might feel, in trying to keep everyone safe. Unless in the course of his/her inspection, he/she managed to accidentally hang him/herself.

But I digress.

Since my arraignment was scheduled for eight o'clock this morning, I had retained the clothes I'd worn last night when apprehended.

Oh! Before I continue, a few words about point-of-view when writing a novel (I have heard from so many aspiring fiction writers that they have learned what not to do, reading my chapters!). When you read chapters written by Brandy, you are inside her head, that is to say you are only privy to her thoughts or what she knows or thinks she knows. When you're with me, you're in my head – an infinitely more inter-esting place to be, I grant you – and I only know what I know. Unless I know someone else knows it, or unless I know that they know that I know it.

Clear?

What I'm getting at is, since I'm obviously aware whether or not I killed Nicole, *you* also would be likely to be in the know, because you're privy to my thoughts. Once in a while, in my Point of View (POV), I keep something from the reader by *not thinking about it*; but to be fair, let's get this out of the way: I freely and fully admit to *not* having killed that terrible woman.

At seven forty-five, my cell door clicked open, and guard Patty – attired in the jail's standard tan uniform, my coat hanging over one arm – stepped in to escort me on my walk of shame to the courthouse. (But I had nothing to be ashamed of, remember!) In her forties, rather plain with dishwater blonde hair, Patty made it obvious that any enthusiasm she might ever have had for her job had long since escaped. (I thought that an apt verb!)

She smirked. '*Why* am I not surprised you're back.' No question mark, but that wasn't really a question.

'It's nice to see you, too, dear,' I replied. 'Any word from my attorney?' Brandy would certainly have roused Mr Ekhardt from his slumber last night.

'He'll be at the arraignment.' She held out my coat. 'Let's go.'

Patty escorted me in handcuffs (*moi* in cuffs, not Patty!) through two security checkpoints, then toward a back door leading to the officers' parking lot. Usually perps heading to arraignment exit a side door facing the courthouse and proceed on foot. Perhaps it was too icy and I was being taken by car. But when we stepped through the back exit it became clear the concern was not icy sidewalks.

The air filled with shouts from reporters, their cellphones thrust toward me, as Patty tugged on my arm, pulling me toward a prisoner transport van parked near the door.

I shouldn't have been surprised by the appearance of the Fourth Estate; after all, I was a public figure, a well-known amateur sleuth, regional renowned thespian, and former reality show star.

'Did you kill Nicole Chatterton?' one yelled.

'Do you have anything to say?' another hollered, as Patty

not too gently pushed me into the back of the van, then slammed its door.

Slowly, the vehicle made the short distance to the courthouse – reporters surrounding the vehicle, jogging along, shouting further questions, police officers doing their best to shoo them away as the van arrived at a special entrance for prisoners.

I thought it all quite thrilling; that is, until one female reporter blurted as I exited the van, 'If *you're* not the bad actor in this, who *is*?'

Imagine me, who has never given a bad performance in her life, being confronted thusly? I did not dignify that with a response.

The courthouse was a late-nineteenth-century white limestone edifice of Grecian grandeur that looked like a giant wedding cake, with a clock in the belfry that hadn't worked since Rutherford B. Hayes was president. Every so often – mostly in the dog days of summer – folks working at, and affiliated with, the un-air-conditioned building would start a campaign to replace the old gal for an institutional-looking younger one. That's when I'd rally the troops, bringing to bear the full force of the Serenity Historical Preservation Society, along with the threat of my vast knowledge of skeletons in the closet of prominent individuals in the community, who wouldn't want dem bones dem bones to come rattling out. Suffice to say, uprising squelched.

As it was winter now, however, the old boiler system with its myriad of radiators chugged along keeping the courthouse toasty – perhaps too much so – and all was quiet on the Western Front.

When no trials were in progress, arraignments were often held in the main courtroom, which would be the case (pun intended) this morning. I almost looked forward to revisiting the vast room with its high molded ceiling, hanging globe light fixtures, long graceful windows, walnut wainscoting, and pews worn so smooth from backsides that the wood looked fairly polished. One could easily imagine Clarence Darrow here, making a monkey out of William Jennings Bryan opposing the teaching of Darwin's Theory of Evolution. (Do you recall that familiar chart chronicling the progress of man that begins with a monkey on all fours and gradually ends upright? I make that journey every morning when I get out of bed!)

Why in that very room awaiting me, my attorney, Wayne Ekhardt, had made his claim to regional fame in the 1950s as a young public defender who got a woman off for murder after she'd shot her abusive husband in the back five times, claiming self-defense. Husbands remain on alert to this day!

Since arraignments were over quickly, the procedure was usually lightly attended for Felony Murder – a concerned parent or two, sobbing spouse, one bored newspaper reporter, and inevitably Mrs Mackelrath, an elderly widow who never missed an arraignment because she had nothing better to do. (Remember the little old lady in the hat who's seated in the back of the courtroom in nearly every *Perry Mason* episode?) In my case the procedure would be different, not only due to the notoriety of the people involved, but to what Patty told me as we stood in the wings, behind a closed door, waiting for the bailiff to collect me . . .

'You should know she leaked it,' Patty said, in a surprising show of sympathy.

'Who leaked what, dear?' I asked.

'That producer – Clare Whatever. Uploaded a clip of your interview to YouTube.'

Sobering news. 'Which portion?'

'Where you threatened Nicole.'

As if I'd had to ask!

The door opened to reveal the bailiff, a tall burly uniformed man whose appearance would discourage the most hardened criminal from continuing down an illegal path.

The bailiff led me by the arm into the clamoring courtroom where every pew was filled, then over to the defendant's table in front of the judge's bench. I'd only been able to glimpse Brandy seated behind Mrs Mackelrath, my darling daughter looking sad and wrung out. Still, an encouraging wave or reassuring thumbs up from the girl would have been welcome.

Mr Ekhardt had yet to arrive, not surprisingly, as the man usually made an entrance (some people are such hams!).

Although retired, Wayne maintained a small office and kept a few special clients, like myself.

Seated across from me at the prosecutor's table was the county attorney, middle-aged, bespectacled, with salt-and-pepper hair, his presence today only a formality.

A door next to the bench opened and His Honor swept in, long black robe flapping like Batman's cape. Judge Morales was newly appointed to the bench, so I'd yet to develop a history with him . . . which was a plus, should he preside over my trial. These judges can be vindictive, you know.

He settled into his leather chair, gazed out over the crowd, which had quieted, checked his wristwatch, frowned, then stared at me. 'Mrs Borne, do you need court-appointed counsel?'

'No, Your Eminence . . . that is, Your Honor. Mr Ekhardt should be zipping along shortly.'

The judge sighed. 'Very well, the court will wait another minute, but then will have to proceed without him.'

'That's fine with me,' I said, chipper. 'Not my first time at the rodeo.'

I hadn't meant that to be amusing, but the gallery giggled anyway. Nerves, probably.

The judge banged his gavel several times, announcing forcefully, 'Any further such outbursts and I'll clear the courtroom!'

The silence was immediate. Pigeons could be heard outside cooing on the windowsills. I was pleased that the first admonition of the day had not been directed to me.

Then a murmur began toward the rear, causing all and sundry to twist toward the courtroom doors, where Wayne Ekhardt was emerging like a zombie from a crypt. Ninety-eight and counting, the nonagenarian took so long in entering that the door had time to close, hitting him in the backside, sending the man lurching forward and nearly falling.

Wayne did know how to make an entrance.

Bespectacled, with a white-fringed liver-spotted head, the frail attorney had lost even more weight since last I'd seen him, all but disappearing into his dapper pinstriped suit, a small boy trying on his father's clothing.

Everyone watched silently as the once formidable and robust

attorney moved slowly down the center aisle, rivaling Tim
Conway enacting an old man on *The Carol Burnett Show* (or
for you Brits, the shuffling elderly gent in *Little Britain* who
endlessly approaches bank worker Carol).

At last, Wayne reached our table, easing unsteadily down
into his designated chair, collapsing further into his suit, like
Dracula meeting sunshine.

All eyes returned to the bench, where the put-upon judge
banged his gavel, and the bailiff, positioned before the
American flag, proclaimed loudly, 'Hear ye, hear ye, court is
in session, the honorable Judge Morales presiding.'

Morales cleared his throat. '*The State versus Vivian Borne.*
Does the defendant have representation?'

Since Wayne was already asleep, I said, 'Yes, Your Honor.'

'Let the record reflect that Wayne Ekhardt is counsel for
the accused.'

'The record' was now a computer system called DART that
had replaced human court reporters who had previously sat
diligently at their little machines. (My favorite *Perry Mason*
episodes are the ones in which the judge asks the court reporter
– often played by milquetoast actor George Stone – to read
back testimony from his scrolling tape.)

Morales was asking, 'Mrs Borne, do you understand the
process of the arraignment?'

'Only too well.'

Titters from the audience.

Morales let that pass. 'You are charged with Felony Murder.
How do you plead?'

In past arraignments I have preferred pleading 'no contest
or nolo contendere', the seldom-used third alternative response;
but considering the severity of the charge, I replied, 'Not
guilty.'

Morales banged his gavel, startling Wayne awake, who
clutched his chest. Well, if the poor man had to go, dying in
the saddle, as they say, was how he would have wanted it.

'Mr Ekhardt are you all right?' the judge asked, concerned.

The lawyer's speckled head moved up and down.

Morales proceeded, 'Vivian Borne, you will be remanded
to the county jail awaiting trial. Bail is denied.'

As the gavel banged one last time, the courtroom came alive – as if teacher had left the classroom – everyone talking at once, some reporters shouting, 'Vivian, did you do it?', while others rushed for the exit to get a photo outside of me leaving.

The bailiff removed me from my chair and whisked me away, allowing for a mere glance back at Brandy, who remained seated, looking glum.

Back in stir before nine o'clock, I was given my prison uniform – orange short-sleeved top and slacks with elastic waistband and orange slip-on tennis shoes. A while back I had my skin and hair coloring evaluated, and it turned out that I was a 'fall', designating the autumn color palette as the most complimentary. And nothing says 'fall' better than bright orange!

I'd just finished dressing in my cell when Patty came in to inform me that Brandy was here, and I could have ten minutes with her. The guard then escorted me through an electronic door to one of several small cubicles serving as visitor's stations. Inside, I sat in a bolted-down chair across from Brandy who was in her own cubbyhole, a Plexiglas window between us. No phone – just small holes in the plastic.

Brandy had on the most unflattering shade of mauve, which made her face look even more pale and sickly. She really should have her colors done!

'How are you, dear?' I asked.

'Mother . . . what happened?'

'What happened where? What happened when? Please be specific, dear.'

'At the hotel last night! In that woman's suite!'

'Oh, that.'

'Yes, *that.*'

The following is what I told Brandy.

After entering the lavish lobby of the Merrill Hotel, I stopped at the front desk to confirm Nicole's room number, also inquiring about the time, then proceeded to the elevators and ascended to the fifth floor. After leaving the elevator, I encountered our esteemed mayor, Robert Goodall, and his lovely secretary Gwen, exiting a room, and proceeded to inform the embarrassed couple not to worry about their tryst, as my lips were sealed. No business of mine, and anyway His Honor's wife Martha was an unpleasant woman who consistently passed along the most scurrilous gossip (and rumor had it she'd had many affairs herself, so who was she to talk?).

Approaching Nicole's suite, I noticed the door ajar, the dead bolt lock having been turned to keep it open. Classical music played from within, so perhaps the podcaster anticipated she might not hear my knock.

After entering, I called Nicole's name and identified myself, receiving no answer.

The entryway emptied into a nicely appointed living-room area – couch, several chairs, coffee table, flat-screen TV, a few lamps, heavy curtains shut.

I followed the music into the bedroom, where the source was coming from a clock/radio. I then saw Nicole sprawled on the floor by the bed, her dark hair matted with blood. Finding no pulse, I picked up the portable phone on the night-stand to alert the front desk, but noticed a briefcase on the bed. Replacing the phone – a few more minutes wouldn't matter to the already deceased woman – I began rifling through the case, hoping to find my release form. That's when Clare entered the bedroom. As the producer screamed, I took the opportunity to flee, knowing had I stayed, there might be no chance to return home.

Across the Plexiglas, Brandy asked incredulously, 'Just so you could get some stuff for your jailhouse stay?'

'Dear, you know I can't read without my other glasses. And you know what happens if I miss a single pill! Plus, have you forgotten how dreadfully bland the food is in this place?'

Perhaps not; she'd gained five pounds during the month we'd spent inside for breaking and entering, chowing down happily on the carby fare.

'Mother!' Brandy wailed. 'Leaving the scene is practically an admission of guilt! And this time the evidence *really* looks bad. The police think the phone is the murder weapon Nicole was bludgeoned with because it had blood on it, along with your fingerprints. And further evidence was the release form, because you were caught going through her briefcase.'

'Dear . . . do buck up and dry your eyes. Mother has an ace up her orange sleeve.'

Brandy sniffled. 'She does?'

'I was wearing my spy necklace camera recorder that will show my every movement since I left you in the car.' (Sorry readers, this *is* something I'd kept from you by not thinking about it until now.) I continued, 'I didn't want Nicole to misrepresent our meeting.'

'Where's that spy necklace?' Brandy asked. Color had returned to her cheeks; perhaps mauve wasn't such a bad shade for her after all.

'In the Roseville vase on the buffet,' I said. 'I needed the necklace to reside in a safe place, and didn't care to be caught with it on my person.'

'Why not? It could clear you right now!'

'I have a reason.'

'So I can't tell Tony?'

Tony was one Anthony Cassato, Brandy's fiancé and Serenity's chief of police, having arrived several years ago from New Jersey to take up the spot of top cop.

I held up a palm. 'Not yet, dear.'

'Why?'

'Because first I have a task to complete in here. Then you can deliver the necklace to the chief.'

Brandy must have known it was fruitless to ask what that task was. 'You're not going to get yourself into more trouble?'

'No, dear.' At least I wasn't planning on that.

My cubbyhole door opened and Patty stepped in. 'Time.'

Dear reader, I'm in quite a quandary here, which has nothing to do with the murder. No. Rather, the problem lies in the length of my chapters, which has been contractually imposed on me due to my supposed tendency to run long. Specifically, I cannot exceed five thousand words per chapter.

In *Antiques Liquidation*, I went over my word count in one chapter, which was then edited, resulting in a limp conclusion – lacking the usual Vivian Borne flair, a cliffhanger propelling the reader forward into the next chapter even though they are bleary-eyed and it's late into the night and they have to get up early the next morning. Therefore, I will sacrifice any word count due me here, to end this chapter properly.

As some of you may know, I have been receiving anonymous letters via the mail that have become ever more threatening in nature. While I know it's hard to fathom, a few people out there dislike me – particularly those I was directly responsible for putting behind bars.

One of these people, I discovered, had been remanded to the Serenity County Jail from the state penitentiary, due to overcrowding, and was at the top of my list as the poison-pen writer.

In order to disguise her identity from those who haven't read about that case, I will give her a nickname – Three Fingers Frieda.

She was a hardened criminal, multi-murderer, and mentally unstable, to boot.

And I intended to confront her.

Vivian's Trash 'n' Treasures Tip

If buying sports cards is your passion, make sure to protect your investment by using the correct holders and folders, and storing them in a secure place. I used to have a collection that included Mickey Mantle and Roger Maris baseball cards, which would be quite valuable today. I wonder what happened to them? (The cards, not Mr Mantle and Mr Maris, RIP.)

FOUR
Long Shot

Take a deep breath – after spending time in Mother's mind you may need to reorientate yourself to the relative normality of her daughter, who I happen to be.

After Mother's arraignment and my visit with her in jail – where I'd learned she'd been wearing her spy necklace when Nicole's body was discovered – I went directly home to retrieve it.

Though immensely relieved a get-out-of-jail-free card existed for Mother by way of the cam-voice recorder, I wasn't going to wait to show it to Tony – and I think she knew that, or else why tell me about the necklace?

Also, I knew why she wanted to remain temporarily in custody, because Patty told me on the way to the visiting station that Three Finger Frieda was currently incarcerated at the jail, which greatly disturbed me. It was just like Mother to keep that juicy (dangerous) tidbit to herself.

Since Tony was away from HQ, and wouldn't be back until eleven this morning, I left home shortly before then, taking Sushi along because if the little darling got a whiff of the chief on me later, particularly if the scent of Tony's dog Rocky – the love of her life – had been transferred onto him, no shoe of mine would be safe from those sharp little teeth.

Arriving at the police department's modern red-brick building adjacent to the jail, Sushi and I entered the glass door into the small, depressing waiting room, past a row of mismatched chairs and a humming vending machine, then proceeded to the Plexiglas window behind which a female receptionist/clerk named Sarah sat in civilian attire, toiling away at a computer.

A uniformed dispatcher used to inhabit that spot, until the new communications center was installed in the basement, combining the police, fire, and sheriff's dispatchers into one unit, something Mother had campaigned on prior to her short tenure as sheriff. But she outsmarted herself.

As a private citizen, Mother had found the lone female dispatcher easy prey from whom to wheedle confidential information (for a part in a play, Godiva chocolates, or a questionably signed 8" by 10" movie-star glossy) and – after becoming sheriff and installing the new system – Mother figured she'd always have access to up-to-date intel. Now, Citizen Vivian once again, she'd been barred from the basement.

'Brandy Borne to see Chief Cassato,' I said through the circular holes in the Plexiglas.

(Personally, I prefer using 'said', and 'asked', because it's exhausting thinking up other dialogue tags.)

'I'll inform him you're here,' Sarah said, business like, her eyes barely leaving the monitor. (Mother had yet to determine the woman's weak spot.)

Assuming my wait might take a while, I set Sushi down, crossed to the vending machine (why was it humming? It didn't know the words) for a bottled water, then took a chair next to a large potted floor plant positioned in front of a window.

The banana tree owed its continued existence to Mother and me, the two of us spending so much time here cooling our heels that the custodian no longer bothered with tending to the plant. Mother would get out her cuticle scissors and trim the large leaves, while I gave the base water, searching futilely for signs of bananas.

OMG there were some! On the side facing the light dangled a grouping of tiny fruit. Our care and patience had finally paid off!

Suddenly Sushi, who'd been watching me, leapt in the air, and pulled the entire mini-bunch off, perhaps envious of the attention I'd been granting the plant, or maybe curious about its new addition. My money was on the former.

I was about to scold the banana-snaring canine when the receptionist announced Tony's availability, so I scooped Soosh up, along with the baby bunch.

Sarah buzzed me through a steel door and into the inner-station sanctum, where I walked down a long beige-tiled corridor whose tedium was broken by framed photos on the walls depicting police chiefs of bygone days, who looked back at me suspiciously. Wouldn't you?

One of the frames always hung crooked no matter how often Mother would straighten it. On our last visit she'd been uncustomarily chewing gum and, when she reached the offensive photo, Mother stuck the wad behind the frame so it would stay put. She'd be pleased to hear the Wrigley Company's star performer was still holding strong.

I proceeded past several detectives' offices, a tech lab, and a lunch/break room that could use better ventilation. The chief's domain was at the end of the hallway on the left, the door open.

Tony's office was small by executive standards, the furniture perfunctory – desk with computer, two visitor's chairs, file cabinet, coffee station, vertical blinds (closed). His predecessor had left behind a framed series of ducks-in-flight prints on the walls, which Tony had never bothered to replace (he did like to hunt, though). Nor had he added any personal touches, such as a photo of his grown daughter . . . or me, for that matter.

He had arrived in Serenity five years ago from New Jersey to replace the then-current chief who was ailing, and no one – not even Mother – had known much about the new mystery man.

And with good reason, as it turned out. Tony was in WITSEC (Witness Protection Program) after testifying against the New Jersey Mob, who eventually dispatched an assassin to Serenity, putting my life in peril as well (*Antiques Knock-off*). But, after Mother and I made a trip to New York for a comics convention (*Antiques Con*) to sell an original Superman drawing discovered among the contents of a storage unit we'd bought in an auction (*Antiques Disposal*), Mother performed a huge favor for the New Jersey Godfather, resulting in the hit on Tony being called off. The collateral damage that might have been Mother and myself was also spared.

As I entered his office, Tony – in his standard uniform of

light-blue long-sleeved shirt, navy tie, gray slacks and (I assumed) brown Florsheim shoes – rose from behind his desk.

Sushi wriggled from my arms, dropped to the floor, and disappeared behind where she could bask in the scent of Tony's pantlegs to her heart's content.

'Brought you lunch,' I said, placing the bananas on his desk.

He frowned. 'What's that?'

'The first crop from the banana tree – compliments of Sushi who tugged them off.'

He glanced down. 'I'd thank her, but she's occupied.' His gaze rose and it was apologetic. 'Sorry I didn't make the arraignment.'

I shrugged. 'Seen one Vivian Borne arraignment, you've seen them all.' I corrected myself. 'Although she did plead "not guilty" this time instead of "nolo contendere".'

'Well, that's a change, anyway.' He studied me. 'You seem to be coping.'

'I am . . . considering.' I settled into a visitor's chair, and he returned to his.

Sushi reappeared to sprawl at my feet, spent, the aroma of Rocky on Tony's slacks an overwhelming aphrodisiac.

From my bag I withdrew the spy necklace and placed it on the desk.

Tony picked up the large black pendant, examined it, and asked, 'What's this? Oh . . . a hidden camera?'

'Yes . . . with a built-in DVR. Mother was wearing it when she found Nicole.'

Tony smiled. 'Guess we should never underestimate Vivian Borne. Well, let's see what's on it. Do you have the USB cord?'

I did.

I came around the desk as he connected one end of the cord to a computer port, the other to the back of the pendant, then downloaded its stored memory.

But the monitor showed nothing.

Tony repeated the process to the same result.

Brow furrowed, he asked, 'When was the last time this was charged?'

Looking over his shoulder, I shrugged. 'I don't know. It's been a while since Mother used it. Quite a while, in fact.'

Tony frowned. 'I'm afraid the lithium battery is dead.'

'Oh, no . . . what now?'

He drew a breath in deep, let it out. 'I'll have Tech take a look at it . . . maybe they can find something. But I have my doubts.'

As did I.

Tony stood, faced me, and placed his hands on my shoulders. 'Brandy, you know I'll do everything I can to clear Vivian. We'll go over every frame of the hotel's security camera footage, along with interviewing hotel staff working that night. Plus, I'll be re-interviewing Nicole's producer, Clare Shields.'

'My take is Clare was in love with Nicole,' I said. 'And that it may not have been reciprocated, which could provide a motive for Clare.'

'And she had opportunity,' Tony reminded me. 'There's a connecting door between her room and the suite, you know.'

My eyebrows took a hike. 'Which made it very convenient for Clare to suddenly arrive after Mother found Nicole's body.'

'But, right now,' Tony continued, squeezing my shoulders then releasing his gentle grip, 'I need to give Vivian the bad news about the necklace.'

Dismissed, I gathered Sushi, and Tony walked me to the rear exit.

At the door, he put a hand under my chin, lifting my face closer to his. 'Before I let you out of my sight,' he said, 'I have to know you'll be OK.'

I summoned a weak smile. 'I'm all right.'

A quick kiss would have been appreciated, but that wasn't Tony's way at work.

I stepped out into a cold, gloomy day.

What I wanted to do was go home and crawl under the bedcovers. Staying busy at the shop for the afternoon, however, might be more productive than moping around . . . plus, if Mother's case went to trial, we'd be needing extra money, and – like almost every retailer – our most lucrative time was the holiday season.

After arriving at the shop with Sushi, my first task was to hoist two flags on the porch pole – one with my name, the other Sushi's – to inform customers that 1) we were open, and 2) just who was there. Mother had such a flag, as well, though hers was twice as large as ours. Like her personality.

Next I got the coffee brewing, but no cookies baking, as I wasn't in the mood to feed customers who'd mostly be coming in just to hear about Mother. Yes, I was that petty – *no cookies for you!*

I'd just settled behind the counter – Sushi was in her leopard-print bed pouting over the oven staying cold – when the mayor entered, bringing along a blast of winter air with him.

Robert Goodall had been elected long before my return to Serenity from my Chicago marital debacle. Our mayor was so popular that in recent years no one bothered opposing him for reelection. In his early sixties, with a jovial face, ruddy cheeks, white hair, and neatly trimmed beard, the mayor made the perfect Sundblom/Coca Cola Santa Claus in the annual Christmas parade; as a character in the original *Miracle on 34th Street* remarked of Kris Kringle, he didn't even need extra padding.

But Goodall didn't look all that jolly at the moment.

'I'm so sorry about Vivian,' he said, approaching the counter.

'Thank you.'

'Please tell her I believe she's innocent.'

'I will.'

Surely our married mayor must have suspected that Mother told me about running into him – and his secretary – at the Merrill. Was he here to make sure I wouldn't tattle?

But His Honor surprised me, saying, 'My secretary, Gwen, and I talked it over and decided we'd like to come forward about seeing Vivian that night on the fifth floor of the hotel, if you think it could help.'

I had to give the man credit; Serenity was conservative enough that even an implied confession of infidelity might cost him the next election. Or maybe he figured their stay at the Merrill would come out in the investigation and he best get out in front of that. And I wondered if the pair's testimony could more likely hurt Mother's case.

'What time did you see her?' I asked.

'I can't be precise,' he said, 'but we came out of our room a little after seven.'

'And how long was your conversation with Mother?'

'A matter of seconds. Then Gwen and I walked down the hallway toward the rear stairs, so we didn't actually see Vivian enter Nicole's suite.' He paused. 'But she didn't *look* like a person who was about to kill someone.'

I smiled wryly. 'I don't think that will hold much weight in court.'

The mayor shook his head. 'Sorry. It's just that I know how devious interviewers like Nicole can be. They assure you it will be friendly, and then out come the fangs once the cameras are turned on. It's happened to me plenty of times . . . but so far my friends have always come to my defense. So please tell Vivian she can count on me.'

'I will,' I said. 'And I appreciate it, and so will Mother. She'll understand what this could cost you. I certainly do.'

He shrugged a shoulder. 'It's the right thing.'

Then, now that he'd proven himself cookie-worthy, I offered to bake some.

'No time for cookies, I'm afraid,' the mayor said. 'I have to get back to city hall . . . But if you have coffee, I'll help myself to some to go.'

He disappeared into the kitchen, returned a moment later with a Styrofoam cup, thanked me for the java, and let some more chill air in, leaving.

From her leopard-print bed, Sushi stared up at me with accusing eyes. She clearly conveyed to me that she had heard the word 'cookies'. More than once!

'All right,' I grumbled. 'I'll make some.'

From the 1950s Frigidaire, I selected prepared chunky peanut-butter dough, dropped spoonfuls onto a cookie sheet, and had just put them into the preheated oven and set the timer when the little bell over the front door announced more customers.

In the entryway I found the members of Mother's Red-Hatted Mystery Book Club, shivering in unison, like carolers who'd forgotten the words. In addition to Cora Van Camp were retired nurse Frannie Phillips, former math teacher Alice Hetzler, and country club social director Norma Crumley. Adding in Mother, the group of five women had legalities, health, statistics, social drama, and murder/mayhem well covered.

Cora, her head jerking, said, 'We're all so terribly distressed by Vivian's arrest.'

I wasn't anxious to have this conversation, but these women were Mother's dearest friends – except for Norma, tolerated only because of the woman's access to the juiciest gossip among the hoity-toity.

'Yes,' Frannie said, 'we *know* Vivian's innocent.' Tall and slender with wiry gray hair, in all her years at the hospital she never learned to give a painless injection.

'Please let Viv know we're thinking of her,' said Alice, whose dyed brown hair always had a growth of white at the scalp – and it was not a fashion statement. She flunked me in Algebra and I still hold a grudge. I should have at least made a D-.

Norma, thrice divorced, addicted to plastic surgery, said, 'And if there's anything we can do, please let us know.'

(Hold on . . . using 'said' and 'asked' does get monotonous, doesn't it? Stand by!) (And our books would be lost without exclamation points.)

'I'll tell Mother you dropped by,' I replied, with a friendly finality that signaled I was done talking.

But they weren't.

Frannie, shaking her head, commented, 'First those dreadful letters . . . and now a murder charge.'

I goggled at her. 'You *know* about the letters?'

'We all do,' responded Alice.

Cora and Norma nodded.

I could feel my face reddening. I'd only learned about the nasty missives by snooping in Mother's bedside drawer. I'd been waiting for her to tell me, knowing it would be hard for her . . . yet she'd confided in them, not her own daughter? I was livid!

Frannie, somehow not sensing anger shimmering off me like heat over asphalt, quipped, 'Vivian *always* confided in us girls.'

None of them had been 'girls' in this century!

The oven timer dinged.

'How special,' I said. 'If you'll excuse me.'

Fuming, I went into the kitchen, slipped on a mitt, and took the cookie sheet out of the oven, placing it on the stove to cool. Then I returned to the 'girls'.

The former nurse picked up where she'd left off. 'Anyway, we've been putting our heads together regarding those letters, and have come to the conclusion that the sender must be someone who feels Vivian did them some injustice – that is, in *their* eyes.'

Which was no more than half the population of Serenity.

Alice was saying, 'We don't think the sender is one of the murderers your mother caught, who is still in jail – due to the postmark, you see, which is local. And I believe both outgoing and incoming mail at the jail is pre-read.'

'Well, thank you,' I replied, nearing the end of my ability to pretend being civil, 'I'll pass your thoughts along to Mother.'

Faces fell, so – feeling they may have sensed my irritation – I interjected, 'But, please, keep working on who might be responsible. And, while you're here, do have some cookies and coffee.'

'How nice, but we're all watching our waistlines,' Norma replied, having appointed herself spokeswoman for the group, several of whom looked bereft at the notion of no coffee and cookies.

Here's a waist-watching recipe Mother took to their last meeting, returning home with an empty pie plate.

German Chocolate Pie

Meringue shell

2 egg whites, room temperature
⅛ tsp. salt
⅛ tsp. cream of tartar
½ tsp. vanilla
½ cup sugar
½ cup finely chopped walnuts or pecans

Beat egg whites with salt, cream of tartar and vanilla until foamy, then add sugar slowly (2 tblsp. at a time) beating well after each addition. Continue beating until very stiff peaks form. *Carefully* fold in the nuts. Spoon into lightly greased 8 inch pie pan to form nest-like shell, building up sides ½ inch above edge of pan. Bake in slow oven 300 degrees for 45 to 55 minutes. Cool. (Crust will fall and crack.)

Pie filling
4 oz package Baker's German sweet chocolate
3 tblsp. water
1 tsp. vanilla
1 cup heavy cream, whipped

Melt the chocolate and water in a saucepan over low heat until creamy. Cool completely. Fold the vanilla and whipped cream into the cooled sauce. Pour mixture into the meringue shell and refrigerate 2 hours. Serves 6 (or 8 who are watching their calories).

Norma did, however, excuse herself to partake of some coffee to go. After the women departed, I went out to the kitchen to put the cooled cookies on a plate and discovered two were missing from the sheet. So much for the socialite's waistline.

Behind the counter again, I was wondering if Tony had told Mother yet about the uncharged spy necklace when the back doorbell buzzed, which only happens for a delivery. Since I couldn't recall anything I'd ordered, I figured it must have been something Mother had purchased and failed to mention (not a rare event).

Sushi beat me to the door where I found Mark Wheeler of All Sports Artifacts standing on the stoop, his heavy parka zipped to the neck, jeans and construction boots lending him his usual appealingly macho flair. Behind him, parked in the alley, was a late-model silver truck, its back end loaded with boxes, along with a display case.

Sushi growled, and I shushed her with a hand.

'This may not be the best time,' the sport store owner said, apparently aware of Mother's predicament, 'but I'm heading to a trade show in a few days, and thought I could set up my merchandise.'

'No, that's fine,' I said. 'Come in out of the cold.'

He stepped into the mudroom, stomping snow from his boots. 'I thought I should see where you want the cabinet to go in the basement.'

'Actually,' I replied, 'I don't have a place picked out.' That would have been Mother's job. 'So put it anywhere, just move things around as necessary.'

'Great.'

'Do you need help?' I asked.

He had a nice smile and he showed me half of one. 'Nope. The cabinet comes apart, and the boxes aren't heavy. I'll set everything up myself. You won't have to do a thing.'

Exactly what I wanted to hear.

'You know the way to the basement?' I asked.

Mark gestured to a door just off the kitchen. 'Through there, isn't it?'

I nodded.

While he returned to his truck, I went back to the computer. Sushi, having lost interest in Mark, curled up in her bed.

About thirty minutes later, Mark clomped up from the basement.

'All set up,' he said, a trifle winded. 'Everything's locked inside the case.' He put a key on the counter. 'I also marked the items with my white tags – unless you'd like me to use your red ones.'

I waved that off. 'No, that will help us identify your merchandise from ours.'

'Let me know,' Mark said, 'if you want anything changed.'

'I'm sure everything's fine.' I gave him a complete smile. 'How about some coffee and freshly baked cookies?'

His laugh was a weary reflection of the hauling he'd just done. 'I could use some caffeine and sugar about now.'

In the kitchen, Mark removed his parka – it was cold in that basement – revealing a gray sweatshirt with his store's logo, then sat at the boomerang-print table while I poured two mugs of hot joe.

'Peanut butter!' he said, reaching for a cookie on the jadeite Fire King platter placed at the center of the table. 'How did you know that was my favorite?'

'Lucky guess.'

Sushi, who had followed us into the kitchen, suddenly warmed to Mark for some reason. Could it have been the cookie in his hand?

'You want a friend for life,' I said, 'just give her a bite.'

He did, then spoke. 'I know you probably don't want to talk about the murder . . .'

Not surprising that he knew. It had been all over the area media.

'. . . but maybe you might like to know I must have been the last person to speak to the Chatterton woman before she died.'

I sat forward. 'Is that right?'

He nodded. 'She wanted to film at my store because of a murder that happened there before I bought the building and moved my business in.'

'I remember,' I said. It was the first case Mother solved in Serenity, a particularly brutal killing not chronicled in our books because I was living in Chicago with my ex at the time.

Mark went on, 'Anyway, Nicole called my cell that night to set up a time to come by the shop.'

'When was this?' I asked.

He reached for his phone in a back pocket. 'I can tell you exactly – it's in my call history.'

Mark accessed the data, turned the cell toward me, then pointed on the screen. 'That's Nicole's cell number, and as you can see she called at 19:05 – or 7:05 pm – and we spoke for thirty-five seconds.' He went on, 'We never got to setting up a time because someone was knocking on her door, and she said she'd call me back . . . but of course she never did. Then, when I heard Vivian had been arrested, I assumed the person knocking was her.'

Except when Mother arrived at the suite, the door had been propped open by the dead bolt.

'Did you hear the knocking?' I asked.

He nodded emphatically. 'Yes, so Nicole must have been standing in the living-room area.'

'It could've been someone from housekeeping.'

He shook his head. 'I'd have heard them call out. But it was insistent. And I think Nicole would've just answered the door in that case, instead of getting rid of me.'

So who'd had a meeting set with the podcaster before Mother's?

I leaned in even more. 'Would you be willing to go to the police station and see Chief Cassato about this?'

'Well, of course.'

I texted Tony, who immediately called my cell.

'What's up?' he asked.

I shared what Mark had just told me.

'Come see me now,' Tony replied crisply. 'Back door.'

I sent Mark outside to bring in the flags while I turned off the percolator, bagged the cookies, and shut down the computer. After locking the front door and setting the alarm, we went out through the back to our vehicles.

At the station, a few raps on the steel door brought Tony, who ushered us in and then down the hallway to the tech room, where Officer Munson – who I knew from previous investigations – sat at the monitor. The screen was frozen, with Mother in the Merrill lobby in front of the elevator with its door open, about to enter. A time stamp in the corner said 19:06 – or 7:06 pm.

Mark showed the chief his phone log with Nicole's call recorded as one minute earlier.

'Tony,' I said excitedly, 'Mother *couldn't* have been the person Mark heard knocking on Nicole's door, because she was still in the lobby!'

'Let's talk in my office,' he said.

We followed the chief back down the corridor, where moments later Serenity's chief of police was settled in at his chair, with us seated opposite.

The chief looked solemnly at Mark. 'I have to ask this, Mr Wheeler . . . is your recollection accurate?'

'It is.'

Tony went on, 'Because, while we can verify Nicole's cell number, the time she called you, and the duration you spoke – we don't have the conversation itself, or the knocking, recorded. Only your word.'

Mark raised his right hand. 'I'll sign a sworn statement . . . even take a lie-detector test.'

'The statement will be necessary, but a lie-detector test . . . however helpful . . . wouldn't be admissible in court.' Tony paused. 'Where were you when you received her call?'

'At home.'

'Alone?'

'Yes. I've been divorced for several years.'

I asked Tony, hopefully, 'Do you think Mark's testimony of someone visiting Nicole *before* Mother arrived would be enough to get the charges against her dropped?'

'Possibly,' he said. 'Still, there's considerable evidence against Vivian.' A pause. 'But it might be enough for her to make bail.'

The desk phone rang.

Tony answered it. 'Yes?'

As he listened, his eyes went to me, and he covered the mouthpiece and whispered, 'It's about your mother.'

My heart sank.

'I'll be right there,' Tony said, and replaced the receiver.

The steely eyes stayed on me. 'A disturbance at the jail.'

I sucked in air.

'Vivian's all right,' he said quickly.

'Oh my God,' I said. 'Three Fingers Frieda attacked her!'

Brandy's Trash 'n' Treasures Tip

With so much counterfeit sports memorabilia on the market, it goes without saying – but bears repeating – that a collector should buy only from a reputable dealer or seller, who guarantees the authenticity of the item, or your money back. That is, unless you can live with a possible faux or fake, like that inexpensive Gucci bag I snagged online.

FIVE
Front Runner

Vivian picking up where she (I) left off.

I have just been informed that my unused word count in my previous chapter does not carry over into this chapter, which I think is highly unfair. Had I known, I would have shared more insights . . . such as the following:

I recently read an article in *Roundup Magazine* where a well-known author expressed his opinion that in composing dialogue there was no reason to use any verbs as speech designations other than 'said' and 'asked'. I strongly disagree! I believe in putting some *zip* into the writing by incorporating other verbs such as remarked, replied, responded, commented, suggested, interjected, and interrupted (intoned might be going a bit too far, and absolutely avoid using 'he ejaculated'). These alternatives show more action and intent than the boring 'said' and 'asked'.

'So spice things up!' she/I articulated.

(Also, ignore advice about not using exclamation points.)

Here's something else I could have broached in my last chapter, had I taken advantage of my remaining wordage (albeit at some risk): I simply can't keep up with all the labels being bandied about by groups of every political persuasion, which really are nothing new and have been around for a very long time.

For example, back in my days of early dating, 'virtue signaling' was when, after an evening of dinner and dancing, I would *not* invite a young man inside my house if my parents weren't home, thus signaling I wasn't *that* kind of girl.

Similarly, 'replacement theory' applies when I buy an expensive kitchen countertop convection oven and the darn thing doesn't work. In that event, I expect it to be replaced by the company *immediatamente*! Nothing theoretical about it!

And 'cultural appropriation' describes exactly the time I had been invited to a dinner party by a grande dame who served the most delicious Greek dessert, and when I inquired about obtaining the recipe was told, no, it was an old family secret, necessitating that I sneak into her kitchen while she was saying goodbye to the other guests, allowing me to snap a cell-pic of the recipe card that had been left on the counter. Cultural appropriation at its most scrumptious!

By the way, do you see how those exclamation points liven things up? You're welcome!

One final comment: I just love the simplicity of the way our new British publishers prefer using single quotes in dialogue instead of the double quotes we Americans utilize. But I do wonder if when the Brits use 'air quotes', is it with one finger on each hand, rather than two? These are the things that keep me up at night.

Oops! I do believe the nurse may have forgotten to give me my bipolar medication this morning.

Returning to my cell after Brandy's visit, I was in lockdown until lunchtime, which allowed me to consider how to deal with Three Fingers Frieda – hereafter TFF – who I assumed was 'top dog' here, that position usually bestowed by the other inmates upon the prisoner who had committed the most egregious felony. Sometimes, the top spot is not voluntarily conferred, rather taken forcibly by the toughest woman through acts of violence. Other times an inmate might knock their leader off her doghouse perch, subsequent to the latter having lost the respect of the others. The worst situation is when two women vie for the title, often resulting in the demise of one, a sobering thought to a two-time former top dog such as myself.

I don't mean to cause you alarm, dear reader, but under the right circumstances, a person is capable of anything (isn't *Chinatown* a wonderful film?), especially a lifer like TFF who has nothing more to lose.

But I wasn't worried, not really – after all, I am well-acquainted with criminal prison protocol and jailhouse lingo, having seen all 692 episodes of the Aussie soap *Prisoner: Cell Block H* (which arrived from Down Under packaged in a heavy

aluminum suitcase containing 40 DVDs). I've also watched
the British prison drama *Bad Girls*, and continue to stay up
to date with jailhouse trends and mores by following the
Australian series *Wentworth*, which has concluded its ninth
season as of this writing – what a humdinger! Whether or not
there'll be a season ten is up in the air, so pins and needles!
(Spoiler alert: Joan Ferguson may have walked off into the
mist at the end, only to return once again like Michael Myers
– you can't kill the boogeywoman!)

Where was I?

Precisely at noon, lockdown was over for lunch, and my
door automatically clicked open. I took a moment to gather
myself – much as when I stand in the wings waiting for my
cue, reminding myself what play I'm in – then stepped out
into the brightly illuminated common room, a ring-shaped
area surrounded by the cells, reminiscent of circled covered
wagons in the Wild West about to be attacked. (Not necessarily by Native American Indians; outlaws were a threat, too,
sometimes *dressed* as Indians.)

Since the county jail was designed for prisoners sentenced
to a maximum of one year, no laundry room existed as at the
state prison, where an out-of-favor inmate might 'accidentally'
get her hands caught in the steaming ironing press usually
operated by the top dog. Nor was there a cafeteria where a
fight might break out between inmates, drawing the guards'
attention away from the top dog shoving a sharp kitchen knife
into a rival's back (referred to as 'dinner and a show'); and
no communal shower room (we had one stall with a queue)
where a victim, marked to be X'd out, could be suffocated
with a plastic curtain.

By way of comparison, things can get pretty dull in the
county jail. Still, with TFF around, I'd need to stay on my
hammertoes.

Several banquet-style tables with attached benches were
scattered around the circle, only one being used by four women
– none TFF. I strolled over with the confidence of a former
top dog.

'Hello,' I remarked pleasantly. 'I'm Vivian Borne – mind
if I join you?'

Shoulders and faces shrugged, and I took a spot at one end. To get the ball (and chain) rolling so to speak, I inquired innocently (everyone's innocent at the county jail!), 'What are you ladies in for?'

For the sake of simplicity, my fellow female prisoners will be referred to by their *court charges* and not their real names, and also because they are NPCs (non-player characters, a video-game term my grandson Jake passed along to me) in this story and will not be seen/heard/used again. So why burden the reader?

When no one answered, I spoke in my director's voice usually reserved for a table reading, 'Let's go around in a clockwise manner.' I fixed my piercing gaze on the woman across from me. 'Beginning with you, my dear.'

'Assault,' the woman replied. She was built like a fireplug, her eyes hooded, her hair in an indifferent crew-cut.

Well-versed as I am in various types of misdemeanors thanks to my own past indiscretions, I requested a clarification. 'Aggravated, serious, or simple?'

'Aggravated,' she answered. 'But since it was my first offense, and the woman recovered, I got a lighter sentence.' Actually, the word she used wasn't 'woman'. Here's a hint: it rhymes with witch.

My eyes went to the inmate seated next to Assault.

'Embezzlement,' she responded, a shapely redhead with green eyes.

So as not to get bogged down, I didn't inquire whether the redhead's charge was related to wire transfer, credit card, cash, property, internet, or NFTs; or if the offense rated class C or D. (Class A would have landed her smack dab in the big house.)

But Embezzlement offered her own clarification: 'I was a bank teller and figured they wouldn't miss the money.'

That's what surprise audits are for, dearie.

Seated across from Embezzlement was a rail-thin blue-eyed blonde, who needed no prompting.

'Controlled Substance,' she stated, adding, 'Using, *not* selling,' which seemed a point of pride.

Since Controlled Substance was also here and not residing in the state penitentiary, I deduced that the drug was marijuana, not yet legal in this state, except for medicinal purposes.

Which left one inmate remaining, seated next to me, a young dark-haired girl wearing a barbed-wire tattooed necklace. When she remained silent, I twisted toward her.

'Oh, come now,' I cajoled. 'It can't be as bad as mine.'

Their faces all asked me, *What's yours?*

'Felony Murder,' I said cheerfully.

The young woman's brown eyes grew big and round, as did those of the others; so they hadn't yet heard about me through the prison grapevine.

'Auto Theft,' she admitted. 'Me and my boyfriend, we boosted a car, an' crashed it.'

'Bad luck,' I said, sympathetic.

'Oh, we crashed it on purpose.'

I'd heard about this strange phenomenon mostly embraced by teenagers, who perhaps spent too much time playing a certain video game. (Full disclosure: I often enjoyed Grand Theft Auto with my grandson, but never once was tempted to make it a reality.)

'Are you girls the full contingent?' I asked lightly.

They all looked at me as if they didn't know what 'contingent' meant. Well, they probably didn't.

'Is anybody else,' I clarified, 'doing time here in the women's wing?'

My new friends exchanged glances.

Finally Auto Theft commented, 'Yeah . . . there's this other gal who's stayin' here 'cause they run out of room at the state pen.'

Just as I'd heard.

Embezzlement interjected, 'She doesn't come out of her cell much, 'ceptin' to eat.'

Such an inmate was a 'slug' in jailhouse parlance.

'We all steer clear of her,' Assault remarked. 'And I suggest you do the same.' Even the fireplug seemed wary of TFF. Clearly these women were 'sucker duckers', inmates who stayed away from troublemakers.

'Sound advice,' I replied. 'I certainly have no desire to challenge her as top dog.'

Auto Theft frowned. 'She ain't *got* no dog. They don't allow no dogs in here.'

'Boy, I wish they did,' Controlled Substance sighed. 'I miss my little Buttercup – she's a Pomeranian.'

Were these women toying with me? Or could they really be so prison un-savvy?

My stomach growled. Having not eaten since my arrest, I was feeling a little lightheaded.

I inquired, 'When are the screws bringing the nosh?'

'The who bringing the what?' Assault asked.

'The guards bringing the meals on wheels,' I clarified. Good grief, didn't these women know *any* prison lingo? Was Australian television forbidden here in stir?

Auto Theft commented, 'I found a fingernail in my soup one time, yuck! . . . but never a screw.'

Embezzlement said, 'I don't think our food actually *comes* from Meals on Wheels, because that's a senior service my grandmother uses.'

Exasperated, I said, 'No, dear, I was stating a prison term for food being brought in on a cart.'

(See how much more interesting that entire scene played by limiting – but not eliminating entirely – 'said' and 'asked'? Full credit goes to a creative writing Master Class I'd taken on-line. Thank you, Neil Gaiman!)

The security door buzzed open, and Patty wheeled through with lunch – by the smell of it, 'slop', a bland tomato-based casserole that I'd come to know all too well on previous visits. If only my pepper had not been confiscated! But slop did come with the most wonderful fresh-baked rolls, so silver lining!

The cart circled our table, wheels wobbling as if they might fall off, while Patty placed our plastic trays in front of us, a frowning waitress resolved to not receiving a tip.

When finished, the slop-dispensing guard glanced over at the nearby empty table and asked, 'Where's TFF?' (She didn't actually say 'TFF', of course, but the woman's real last name.)

Assault said, 'Just leave hers over there,' head-gesturing to another table. 'She'll probably get around to it.'

Patty shrugged, and deposited the tray on her way out.

We began to dig in – well, the other women did while I nibbled at the warm roll – then a cell door opened and TFF made her appearance, causing plastic sporks to freeze midair.

I don't think I'd be spoiling anything for readers who have not yet read *Antiques Fate* by reporting that TFF was now in her mid-forties, having aged every one of the five years since I'd brought about her downfall. She had cow eyes, a weak chin, and her dark-blonde hair showed signs of gray. The woman had also put on weight, which was understandable considering the starchy prison dinner fare.

Expressionless, TFF glanced our way with quiet contempt, then sat alone at the table with her tray.

While the other women returned to their meals, I instigated a conversation to fill the silence, inquiring, 'How many of you ladies have ever trod the boards?'

Blank eyes stared at me.

'Performed in a play?' I clarified.

Negative headshakes.

'My. Not even a school production?'

No answer. Looked like I'd have to start from scratch. Well, perhaps these were diamonds in the rough. Shoplifted diamonds, most likely.

'Well,' I continued, 'often it's the novice who rises to the greatest achievements – a fresh lump of clay to be molded and defined . . . a baby's mind ready to absorb information.'

'Why,' Embezzlement asked, 'is that woman staring at you?'

'What woman, dear?' I asked innocently.

Auto Theft nodded toward the nearby table. 'She does seem to be watching you.'

'Yeah,' Controlled Substance commented. 'What's that about?'

I shrugged. 'Well . . . she and I have something of a history.'

Assault's eyes narrowed. 'What *kind* of history?'

'The kind I would prefer would stay in the past,' I said, and shifted on the hard bench. 'You might say I was responsible for her incarceration.'

'Look,' Embezzlement said sharply, raising a palm like she

was swearing in at court. 'I have a parole review coming up and don't want to get mixed up in *any* trouble.'

'An' my sentence is done in a few months,' Controlled Substance added. 'I don't want *that* messed up.'

'Me, too,' interjected Auto Theft.

Assault shrugged. 'Got nothin' waitin' for me on the outside, so, uh . . . Vivian is it? I'm here if you need me. I got nothin' better to do.'

'How gracious of you, dear,' I told her, 'but, really, I can handle myself.'

I hoped.

With lunchtime over, we had an hour to ourselves before the enforced afternoon lockdown at two, which happily coincided with my usual nap time.

Not a fan of afternoon TV game shows, such as giving answers in the form of questions or putting together puzzles without all their pieces, I opted to return to my quarters to read (or rather, re-read) my Agatha Christie book. I'd just entered the cell, when TFF suddenly materialized, stepped inside, and closed the door behind her.

It was no more ominous than a thunderclap.

Backing up a few steps, I picked up Agatha to use as a shield against the lethal point of a possible homemade shiv.

'Before you do anything foolish,' I said, summoning my acting ability to appear calm, 'might I remind you it was your *own fault* you lost those fingers by trying to shoot me with an antique pistol that backfired.'

When my statement garnered no reaction, I continued. 'Law enforcement was already closing in, so it was only a matter of time before you were caught.'

This was a lie: the officers hadn't a clue that she was the killer. Which was nothing new, of course.

No response from the woman.

'Well, then, do as you must,' I said, and raised one of the fingers her own hand no longer possessed. 'But I must warn you . . . I'm well-trained in judo, karate, and tae kwon do.'

Another fib. I could barely put my socks on in the morning.

'Vivian,' TFF said, 'if you think I'm here to harm you, you're mistaken.'

Was this a trap? A ploy to catch me off-guard?

She gestured to the bed. 'May I sit?'

I nodded, but remained standing myself, Agatha at the ready, with which to block or hurl.

She looked up at me. 'I'm on medication now, and can see so much clearer. What I did was terrible, inexcusable, and I suffer every day with that knowledge. I really do deserve to spend the rest of my life in prison.'

She sounded so sincere. But was this a devious deception by a dangerous person? And why do I keep asking you?

TFF continued, 'Recently, I've written to the families of my victims, letters of apology and contrition that I've sent to their attorneys . . . and you were the last on my list. Then I heard you were here, and was relieved to learn I would be able to apologize in person. So, Vivian, please find it in your heart to forgive me, and know that I am truly sorry for the pain I caused you.'

Oh, she was good. There were even tears in her eyes! I almost believed her.

'My dear,' I said soothingly, playing along, 'I'm so happy you've faced the inner demons that turned you into an outer one, and want to assure you that I do forgive you for your actions against my daughter and myself.'

'Thank you. This is the closure I've sought. I feel genuinely at peace.'

TFF stood.

I stepped back, the book at my bosom.

And she departed.

Could my intuition about her have been wrong?

A folded-up piece of paper had been left behind on the bed. I opened it and read the apology meant for me, written in block letters.

Which did not match the printing on the threatening notes I'd received.

'Are you all right?' Patty asked from the doorway, with surprising concern.

'Tickety boo,' I replied, tucking the letter into my book.

'Your new friends were worried.'

I could see the women grouped together a few steps behind her.

I replied, 'There's not going to be any trouble.'

'Good,' Patty said. 'The chief is here, and wants to see you.'

I had suspected Brandy might turn over the spy necklace to Tony before I gave her the go-ahead. But that was all right, since I'd just eliminated TFF from the top of my poison-pen suspect list.

Patty escorted me to a room generally used by lawyers consulting their clients. Chief Cassato was seated at a table, hands folded as if about to say grace.

The chief, late forties, with a bullet head, graying temples, steely gray eyes, bulbous nose, square jaw, and a barrel chest, wasn't exactly my idea of handsome . . . but his confidence and stature more than made up for it. I could see what my daughter saw in him.

I took the chair opposite. 'Before you scold me for withholding the information from you that I'd recorded my movements at the Merrill Hotel, allow me to explain. For some time, I have been receiving threatening letters – a fact I've kept from Brandy so as not to upset her – and strongly believed that a certain inmate here, who I'd been instrumental in bringing to justice, was responsible for those threats. And therefore I wanted to confront her.' I paused for a breath after that soliloquy. 'However, my assumption turned out to be uncharacteristically inaccurate. In light of that, I'd like to be released, toot sweet.'

Receiving no immediate response, I said, 'How long will that take? The food in here is even more dreadful than during my last stay, and the current talent pool for plays appears rather shallow.'

When the chief remained stone-faced and silent, I asked, 'Proverbial cat got your tongue?'

'Nothing,' he said flatly, 'was recorded on the necklace.'

I leaned forward. 'Forgive me, but it must be the wax build-up in my ears, because I thought you said nothing was recorded on the necklace.'

'I said precisely that.'

'No visual at all?' I asked.

The bullet head moved slowly side to side, like the tail of a jeweled cat clock.

'No sound?'

Another shake of his head.

Oh, dear. That's what you get when you fail to make sure such gizmos are recharged!

'This *is* quite a pickle,' I replied. 'What about the hotel security cameras with time stamps?'

'You're recorded in the parking lot, and entering the lobby, and talking to the registration clerk . . . but once you get into the elevator, that's it.' He shrugged. 'To protect the privacy of their guests, the hallways have no cameras.'

Which would have captured clandestine rendezvous like the mayor and his secretary. And a murderer who apparently knew how to avoid hotel cameras.

The chief continued, 'I'm sorry, Vivian, but your visit coincides with Nicole Chatterton's time of death. And without someone actually witnessing you discovering her body, I don't know how to prove you didn't kill her, especially since your prints are on the suspected murder weapon.'

'But you'll try.' It wasn't a question.

His features softened. 'Of course.' In a rare display of warmth (toward me, anyway), he reached out and patted my hand where it rested on the table. 'We can't have my future mother-in-law behind bars, can we?'

I managed a smile.

'Look,' he said, 'something's come up out of a conversation Brandy had with Mark Wheeler that may . . .'

'Clear me?'

He shook his head. 'Be enough to get you out on bail. No promises.'

Slightly encouraged, I returned to the common area, where the girls, full of questions, ascended upon me.

Auto Theft asked, 'What did the chief of police want?'

'Did he charge you with something else?' inquired Controlled Substance.

'What happened in your cell?' questioned Assault. 'Did you punch your old enemy in the face? I would've.'

'Why won't you answer us?' demanded Embezzlement.

(See how skillfully I avoided using 'asked' four times in a row?)

'Later, girls,' I said, passing them by, appreciating their concern but bound for TFF's cell.

'Hey, it's almost lockdown!' Assault called after me.

Though it was something of a long shot, I thought perhaps my former enemy might have heard – or overheard – who was out to get me through the criminal grapevine.

As usual TFF's door was closed, and I politely knocked. When no answer was forthcoming, I peered through the small window and saw her legs stretched out on the floor indicating she was seated with her back to the door. A peek through the bean slot (through which food is delivered to an inmate on remand) told me more.

Most prisons have a panic button for inmates and guards alike to push in the event of an emergency such as a fight or insurrection, and ours was on the wall a few cells away. I ran to the red button and slapped it, the air immediately filling with a screeching siren. Then I hurried back to TFF's cell.

With some effort – because her body was blocking the door – I managed to squeeze inside.

TFF had set about to hang herself after tying a strip of bedsheet to the doorknob, then twisting the other end around her neck, in noose fashion.

Quickly I loosened the noose and, stretching the woman out on her back, began to apply CPR. (I always perform the life-saving technique while singing the Bee Gees' disco song 'Stayin' Alive', while compressing the chest, because the tune has the correct beat, and added meaning as well.)

Still, I held little hope for revival because TFF had already turned blue, but I kept singing until the paramedics arrived, which was rather quickly, the fire department being a mere block away.

Winded, I retired to a table in the common area to sit and catch my breath. The other women had been locked in their cells.

All I can say is, there went my best lead.

And the Cell Checker-Outer had more work to do.

Vivian's Trash 'n' Treasures Tip

When determining a budget for your sports collection, be sure to include the cost of frames or display cases, expenses not usually recouped if the items are sold. The problem with most collectors – and this extends to areas other than sports memorabilia – is that they tend to spend more than they should.

SIX

Raising the Bar

The following morning, Mother's nonagenarian lawyer Wayne Ekhardt was alert enough to convince the judge and county attorney that, in lieu of Mark's new information, his client should be released on her own recognizance, pending further investigation of Nicole Chatterton's murder.

Mid-afternoon, Mother finally exited a side door of the jail into the parking lot, looking a little forlorn, wearing the clothes she'd been arrested in, coat flapping open in the cold wind like laundry on a line.

'What's with you?' I asked after she'd gotten in the car. 'You're out, aren't you?'

Mother sighed. 'At breakfast the women elected me top dog – now I won't be there to enjoy it.'

I grunted. 'Don't dismay. If Mark's statement doesn't hold up, you'll be back inside soon enough.'

'Don't try to cheer me up.'

Sarcasm never worked on her.

The jailbird emitted another sigh. 'I am going to *miss* those girls.'

I gawked at her. 'Are you kidding? You only knew them for two days!'

'Twenty-seven hours and fifteen minutes.'

'What, no seconds?'

'Plenty of time,' she said, ever immune to sarcasm, 'to make new friends.'

And for them to make it onto her Christmas card list, from which the only escape is death, because Mother will track a person down if they move. Prison should be so forgiving.

Mother continued wistfully, 'After lunch, the girls threw me such a nice going-away party. I couldn't help but linger.'

I twisted toward her. 'You mean, you could've gotten out earlier?'

'Oh, yes. About an hour ago. Patty even delayed lockdown, we were having such a lovely time.'

I was, as Popeye once said, disgustipated. 'You left me waiting in the parking lot, out in the cold, for a jailhouse frolic?'

She flicked me a frown. 'That car has a heater, doesn't it? Besides, it would've been impolite to depart any sooner. There was even a cake.'

I started the engine. 'Cake, huh? You were already getting out, so you didn't need a file in it . . . Don't suppose you thought to bring me a piece.' Not sarcasm – cake was always a weakness of mine.

At home, while Mother showered upstairs, I prepared a celebratory dinner – or supper, as the last meal of the day is known in the Midwest.

Sushi's initial excitement at having our top dog back in the pack quickly evaporated once I began clanging pots and pans in preparing one of Mother's favorite dishes, a 'cultural appropriation' she lifted while on a visit to the Stockholm Royal Swedish Opera House, dining at Operakällaren Restaurant, where world-famous Hans Kegik was chef. (Was the Muppets' Swedish chef based on him?)

For *your* dining pleasure – and to fill pages because the editor said our books needed to be longer – here is the recipe:

Lobster Curry à la Operakällaren

Ingredients

1 large lobster or 2 small ones (I got tails from the meat counter at our HyVee grocery store)
1 small carrot
1 stalk celery
2 small onions
1 apple (whatever's on hand)
2 tblsp. olive oil
½ cup cognac
⅔ cup white wine (whatever's on hand)

⅔ cup boiling water
1 cup hot cream
2 tblsp. butter
2 tblsp. flour
½ tsp. salt
½ tsp. pepper
1½ tblsp. curry powder
½ cup heavy cream, whipped
3 tblsp. cold butter

Cook lobster, and tear or cut into chunks. Chop the carrot and celery (scraped), onions (skinned), and apple (cored) into fine pieces. Heat the oil in a frying pan, and add the vegetables, but don't brown. Add the lobster pieces, shaking the pan to cover the meat. Add the cognac, and light with a match to flame it, then put out the flame by covering the frying pan with a lid. Add the wine and boiling water, and cover again and let the sauce simmer for 20 minutes. Remove the lobster meat and put into another pan, pour the hot cream over the meat to keep it warm, setting aside. Reduce the sauce in the frying pan one half by boiling it rapidly. Strain the sauce, reheat, add the 2 tablespoons butter, sir and add the flour. Mix smoothly, season with salt and pepper, add curry powder and remove from the heat. Stir in the whipped cream and the 3 tablespoons of cold butter. When ready to eat place the warm lobster meat on plates and cover with the warm sauce. Serve with white rice – or put on top of the rice, as I do. Makes 4 to 6 servings.

I set the Duncan Phyfe table with our best china (Haviland Limoges Rose) and crystal goblets (Waterford Lismore), and then sent Sushi upstairs to fetch Mother.

After we were seated with the meal before us, my fork loaded with lobster on its way to my mouth, Mother stated, 'I do think a feast this grand requires us to say grace.'

I placed the fork on my plate. Gently. It was the Haviland, after all.

We hadn't given grace for decades, and then it was a simple prayer Mother had learned from her mother. This is how little Brandy said it:

Lord, bless this foodwich (a type of sandwich apparently) *now we take and make a sign, for Jesus' sake* (using crayons, I guess).

Made perfect sense to a three-year-old.

'Maybe,' I said, 'you should taste the dish first before you give thanks for it.'

Really, I was fishing for praise for my effort.

Mother studied her plate clinically. 'Perhaps you're right, dear.'

She took a bite, chewed, swallowed. 'Did you scrape the carrot and celery?'

'No.'

'Did you flambé the cognac?'

'No.'

'Did you strain the sauce?'

'No.'

'Did you use real whipped cream?'

'No.'

A long pause. 'They say it's the thought that counts.'

'Personally, I'm thinking it would be better poured on your head.'

Mother bestowed me a patronizing smile. 'No need to be unpleasant, dear.'

The doorbell rang. Someone calling on Archie Goodwin, mayhap?

Fuming, I left the table.

Tony stood on the porch, trench coat buttoned, collar pulled up against the icy wind.

'You look fit to be tied,' he said.

'Not at all! Everything's just peachy-keen.'

'I can come back . . .'

'No,' I said, stepping aside. 'We can always use a referee around here.'

'That bad, huh?' he asked, crossing the threshold.

Mother entered from the dining room.

Tony asked, 'Hope I'm not interrupting a celebratory meal.'

'No,' she replied, 'we're finished with our repast.'

'Oh, yeah,' I responded, 'we're past it, all right.'

Tony eyed us warily. 'I wanted to discuss Clare Shields . . . but it can wait.'

'No!' Mother said quickly. 'Now is fine, right, Brandy?'

'Yes.' I *was* interested.

She and I sat on the Victorian couch while Tony overwhelmed an armless Queen Anne needlepoint chair.

He began with me. 'You said you sensed Clare was in love with Nicole, but also that the feeling didn't seem to be mutual. Do you have proof of that?'

'Not really. As I said . . . just a feeling.'

His eyes narrowed. 'It was nothing Clare confided in you about?'

'Only that Nicole treated her like a second-class citizen.'

Those eyes narrowed further. 'Was Clare incompetent?'

'Not as far as I could see,' I said.

Mother added, 'The Shields woman was clearly more than competent. In my opinion Nicole used the producer as a verbal whipping-boy. Girl.'

Tony looked at Mother. 'You witnessed this?'

Mother nodded. 'After the podcaster and I were seated with microphones on, Nicole uttered several gratuitous derogatory words in response to her underling.'

'Such as?' Tony asked.

Mother shifted on the couch. 'One was an insulting comparison with a female dog, the other a crude term for a female who prefers the romantic company of other females.'

Tony looked to me for confirmation.

I raised two palms. 'I didn't hear either slur.'

'Probably not,' Mother replied, 'as you were across the room. But Clare most certainly would have, through her headset.'

I asked Tony, 'Where was Clare just prior to finding Mother in Nicole's suite?'

'Hunter's.'

Mother asked the chief, 'You've checked out Clare's story?'

Tony nodded. 'Junior Hunter, who was bartending that evening, confirms the woman was there from just before six to a little after seven. And she's seen on the hotel's security camera entering the lobby, a few minutes after you, Vivian.'

'How *much* after?' Mother pressed.

Tony removed a small notebook from an inside pocket, flipped through the pages. 'You arrived at 7:01, talked to the desk clerk and got into the elevator at 7:06. Clare entered the hotel at 7:16.' He flipped the notebook shut. 'I've asked her to remain in Serenity until after the forensics autopsy.'

A more complete examination was being performed at the University of Iowa Hospital, the cause of death necessitating expert attention that could not be provided in small-town Serenity.

I asked, 'Did Clare agree to stick around?'

Tony nodded. 'In fact, she had already re-booked her room . . . said she was staying to do her *own* podcast. Which she'd been planning to start for some time.'

'Let me guess,' Mother said sourly. 'Her first episode would be solving Nicole's murder.'

He nodded, seemed about to say something, but thought better of it.

'Tony,' I said. 'What *is* it?'

He shifted on the small, uncomfortable Queen Anne chair. 'I did do a check on Clare for any prior convictions . . .'

Mother leaned forward. 'And?'

'Some minor charges, but no jail time. However, she *did* file for personal bankruptcy a few years ago.'

Mother said, 'Well, she seems to have found just the right time to go into business for herself . . . She'd better not try to lay Nicole's murder at *my* feet!'

As if it hadn't already been.

I asked Tony, 'Did the techies get anything from Mother's spy camera?'

He shook his head. 'The battery *was* dead.'

'Rats,' Mother said.

He continued, 'But . . . I received some early information from our forensics pathologist. There's some doubt about the weapon thought to have been used on Nicole.'

Mother sat forward. 'You mean, it *wasn't* the bedside phone?'

'Possibly not.'

'What about the blood on the phone?' I asked.

Tony shrugged. 'The headset could have been used to stun the woman – or Vivian might have transferred blood onto it when she called the front desk. But multiple, deeper wounds indicate the murder weapon is composed of something harder than plastic.'

Mother's eyes were slits behind her glasses. 'Has any specific item been put forth as a possibility?'

'Not yet,' he said. 'An expert in such matters has been called in.'

We fell silent.

Finally Mother declared, 'You need to question that Clare woman again. She could have entered the hotel earlier, unde- tected, via another route!'

The chief's jaw muscle flexed. He didn't like being told what to do regarding his job. Not by me, and especially not Mother, who hit him with a flurry of other suggestions through which he sat silently.

'I will take all of that under consideration,' was his curt response.

Which put an end to the conversation.

While Mother retreated to the dining room, I walked Tony to the door, where he grumbled, 'Maybe we'd be better off if she'd stayed in jail. Who knows what that woman will get herself up to.'

'No one,' I admitted. 'But I'll keep an eye on her.'

'Make it both eyes.'

I touched his arm, signaling this wasn't how I wanted us to part.

He found a small smile for me. And a light kiss.

After Tony left, I joined Mother back at the table, where the lobster curry had gone stone cold, but at least the coffee in the carafe remained warmish.

After sipping from her delicate teacup, she said, '*He* may wait to question Clare again, but *I* shall not.'

'Mother . . . let Tony do his job.'

She harrumphed, 'While that man's dragging his feet, Clare will be out there besmirching my good name!'

What was left of her 'good name' to besmirch? But I kept that to myself.

'Look,' I said placatingly, 'maybe Clare *will* find the killer, and save us the trouble. And the danger.'

'That would be a good trick, dear, since *she* is likely *it*. No, she's out to find a way to pin that murder on me and save herself.'

Mother reached for her cell resting on the table, punched in a number.

'Housekeeping, please,' she said. Then a few moments later, 'Lorna, Vivian Borne here. I need you to find out if Clare Shields is in her room for me, discreetly . . . Well, how about by taking her some extra towels? . . . Good. I need to know for certain if she's out. Then get right back to me. That signed David Hasselhoff photo is nearly yours!'

She clicked off.

I stood, hands on hips. 'Mother! You're not thinking about breaking into Clare's room?'

'No, dear,' she said, but nothing further.

While Mother waited for her minion to call back, I cleared the table and dumped the lobster curry down the garbage disposal. Even Sushi, who finds shoes delicious, wasn't interested.

Mother's cell sounded, and I returned to the table.

'Satisfactory,' Mother said to the phone, channeling Nero Wolfe. 'Yes, I'll drop off the photo sometime soon.'

Was there anyone in this town Mother couldn't bribe?

'Clare is out and about,' Mother announced. 'We need to find her and talk to her in person.'

'We?' I asked. 'Oh no, not *me*! I'm in for the night.'

She stood. 'Very well. I'll take my Vespa . . . even though I may freeze to death in this weather.'

I sighed. 'All right, you win. Let it not be said that I let my elderly mother freeze her fanny off.'

'Unkind,' she sniffed.

Anyway, hadn't I just promised Tony I'd keep an eye – or two – on her? 'Where do you want to go first?'

'Let's see if Clare's at Hunter's. And while we're there, we can question Junior further.'

As I walked to the foyer closet for my coat, I texted Tony: *On the move – Hunter's.*

* * *

Contrary to the big city belief that the sidewalks of small Midwestern towns roll up in the evening, plenty of nightlife is to be found in Serenity.

Families could go Midnight Bowling (9 p.m. to midnight) at PlayMore Lanes, where the balls and pins glow under black lights. Moviegoers might take in a flick at the Palms Theater, its outdoor facade featuring a huge neon palm tree beckoning for miles around against a star-flecked sky. And for those who can't make it to Broadway (audience and actors alike) there is the Community Playhouse, currently showing a Christmas comedy, The Elf Rebellion, *featuring Serenity's adored little person, Billy Buckly, whose great-grandfather played one of the Munchkins in the Judy Garland version of* The Wizard of Oz.

Health-conscious but hate aerobics? Shimmy on over to Take It Off, a juice-bar/dance club that opens every afternoon at five with a DJ playing '50s music (for seniors), segueing to '60s at six, '70s at seven, '80s at eight, and so on, the witching hour showcasing alternative rock.

Crave a low-key neighborhood bar atmosphere? Look no farther than The Hilltop Tap, where longtime patrons bask in the latest local gossip and old-timers share long-ago lore, whether you want to hear it or not.

Need to brush up on your golf swing? Grab your clubs and hightail it to Bridgelinks, where you can swig a brew between swings into a simulator screen of the first hole at Augusta.

Thirsty for craft beer? Contrary Brewing with its cement floor, old beer signs, and no-nonsense seating carries twenty of its own concoctions, like 'Cure for Pessimism' and 'Peanut Butter Porter'.

Addicted to sports? Boonies on the Avenue boasts twelve flat screens tuned to whoever is playing whatever on any given night, while serving the best tenderloin sandwiches around, a Midwestern specialty, the size of a hubcap.

Born to be wild? Harley-Davidson afficionados will find like-minded bikers at the rough-and-tumble Golden Spike. But men, heed that you don't get a spike in your head, or women in your drink.

In the mood for upscale companionship? Hook up at Proof

Social, a chic bar/bistro where young professionals hang together not separately, sipping martinis while listening to a jazz combo, and no one expects a follow-up call the day after.

Are you a self-styled hipster? At Cinders, you can sit at the lava-lamp-lighted bar in leopard-print bucket chairs among an eclectic chockablock of collectibles ranging from Elvis to Marilyn to Betty Boop, to life-size standees of the original crew of the Enterprise *while 'Midnight at the Oasis' plays on a vintage jukebox.*

Identify as LGBTQ2+? Head north on River Road to All Inclusive, a new drinking establishment located in a former roadhouse built by bootleggers during Prohibition. No password required at the speakeasy's sliding front door panel.

But the most unusual watering hole of all is Hunter's, its combustible combination of selling hardware and hard liquor causing more than a few trips to the ER after patrons belted back one too many, bought a power tool, then went home to work on a project. The latest casualty, according to a certain local theater diva, is a man who attached his hand to the wall with a nail gun. Other examples, involving a table saw, power drill, and air pressure hose, may be less amusing.

In any event, come to Serenity! Come for the libation and go home with an ablation!

Downtown, I spotted a parking spot on Main Street, beneath a flickering old-fashioned Victorian-style streetlamp, pulled in and we exited the car.

'Let me do the talking,' Mother said, her breath smoking in the frigid night air.

'Fine by me.' I was only along as an observer.

Ensconced in one of dozens of Victorian brick buildings downtown, Hunter's retained its original interior – wood flooring, glazed windows, and tin ceiling – with only its contents keeping pace with progress.

For those readers who aren't familiar with the hardware/bar store, I'll give you some past history as related to my lifetime in Serenity. Others can skip to the paragraph beginning with 'I followed Mother inside . . .'

The building had languished empty for decades when Mary

Hunter and her husband Junior bought it in the early 1990s after vacationing in a southern state surrounded on three sides by water and that often had to worry about hurricanes and sharks. (I'm not being facetious here, just avoiding litigation with the proprietors of a certain talking mouse with big ears.) While there, the couple visited a well-known theme park and took in a new attraction featuring a big ocean fish with very sharp teeth based on a blockbuster movie starring Roy Scheider, Richard Dreyfuss, and Robert Shaw, which, unfortunately for Mary, malfunctioned (the shark not the movie), causing the loss of her lower right appendage.

With the settlement money from the accident, however, Mary and Junior started their hardware/bar business, her selling wares, him dispensing liquor, the latter only too happy to join customers in a round or two, or three.

But after a while, Mary got fed up with most of the bar's proceeds disappearing down her spouse's gullet, and the woman put down her prosthetic leg firmly, demanding the couple sell the building and business, and retire to Arizona.

While the new owners retained the longstanding Hunter's name, and continued selling hardware, they – being opposed to alcohol – turned the bar at the rear into what they assumed would be a trendy coffee shop. Look out, Starbucks! Well, it wasn't long before imbibing regulars – who had before been able to truthfully say to their spouses, 'I'm going to Hunter's for a screwdriver' – began buying their tools elsewhere.

Re-enter Mary, who bought back the building and business (at half the price), having come to the conclusion that Arizona was too blasted hot, and her husband might just as well pickle his liver at a bar they owned rather than somebody else's.

I followed Mother inside, where an accordion-style steel barricade had been stretched into place, sectioning off the hardware area during its off-hours. Junior – whose advancing age now called his name into question – was behind the scarred bar, polishing a glass, a few patrons keeping him company. As we took stools at one end, Junior drifted over.

'Well, Vivian!' he said. 'I *heard* you got released.'

He was a rheumy-eyed, mottle-nosed man, wearing a plaid flannel shirt whose buttons strained over his midsection.

'You can't keep a good man down,' Mother said, 'and you best not keep an innocent woman locked up.'

Junior seemed to commit that advice to memory (what was left of it) before saying, 'What'll you ladies have?'

'Any white wine,' I said, making it easy.

Mother said, 'A hot toddy, but hold the toddy.'

Her usual fare, which was hot water, honey, and lemon, minus the whisky. She'd learned that alcohol on top of her medication wasn't wise after once arriving in Kalamazoo without knowing how she'd gotten there. (The incident remains an unsolved mystery. Maybe next time.)

While Junior prepared our concoctions, Henry – a barfly who'd buzzed in after the reopening – moved to the stool next to Mother. Slender, with silver hair and beaky nose, he'd been a prominent surgeon before botching an operation decades ago, having taken a shot of whisky to steady his nerves before-hand. The patient lived, but the doctor's career did not.

Henry also used to be Mother's premiere snitch, a barely noticed presence seated quietly at the bar all day, ignored by other patrons who spoke freely in front of him, while he soaked up more spilled gossip than Junior's bar rag mopped up liquor. The problem with Henry was making sense of his slurred words, although Mother seemed to have mastered his unusual, unique dialect.

Henry uttered what sounded to me like, 'Fine ham?'

'Not yet,' Mother replied. 'But I am confident I'll find him – or her. Killers know no gender!'

'Artie . . .' Hiccup. '. . . Fix.'

Mother arched an eyebrow. 'Dear, Arthur Fix died several years ago at Sunnyside Up nursing home, after a tryst with a dietitian, sunny side down.'

Henry tried again. 'Allie . . .' Hiccup. '. . . Knight.'

Mother sighed. 'Allison Knight is one hundred and one if she's a day, and confined to a wheelchair, and a most unlikely suspect . . . but thank you, dear, for your suggestions.'

I gave Mother the fisheye; apparently, hapless Henry had lost one too many brain cells in the interim since she'd last consulted him.

Mother took a sip of her toddy-less hot toddy, then turned

her attention to Junior. 'I understand Clare Shields was here the evening of Nicole Chatterton's murder.'

'That's what I told Chief Cassato,' Junior replied.

'From when to when?'

He frowned. 'From when to when what?'

'*Time*, dear. It waits for no man! Or woman.' Her irritation, so apparent to me, seemed lost on him.

'Oh,' Junior said. 'Well. That's easy. During happy hour – six to seven.'

'Was she here the entire time?'

Junior's rheumy eyes rolled up toward his forehead, searching for the answer, like fruit in an ancient slot machine. 'Best as I can remember.'

Mother pressed, 'Could Clare have made her exit before seven? Or even left and come back?'

He shrugged. 'Maybe. I get pretty busy pouring drinks, y'know.'

One for a customer, one for himself.

Henry slurred, 'Bottle.'

Mother swiveled toward him. 'When?'

'Foreclosing.'

'What was it?'

'Slap her.'

What did a bottle, a foreclosing, and slapping some woman – Clare? – have to do with anything? But Mother did seem to be following him now.

She said slowly, 'So Clare bought a tool before the hardware section closed at six, and that tool was a slapper.'

Henry hiccoughed an affirmation.

'What in the world,' I asked, 'is a slapper?'

'A flat metal bar with a handle,' Mother said, excitedly. 'Which could be the murder weapon!' She slid off her stool. 'Come, dear – we must double our efforts to find that woman.'

But on her way out, she wheeled to Junior, making him jump a little. 'Did Clare ever mention any *other* Serenity watering holes?'

Again, the man's eyes searched for his forehead; it had to be up there somewhere. 'She *did* ask me about that new place on River Road.'

'Many thanks,' Mother said, generously, as she strolled away, sticking me with the tab.

River Road was a scenic delight during the daytime, but at night the hilly twisty-turny two-lane could be a real nail-biter, especially if a deer darted across, giving a driver three split-second choices: stay the course and hit the creature, careen down the steep embankment on the right into the Mississippi, or swerve into a deep ditch on the left, which at times was supplanted by a wall of limestone.

So I drove carefully.

Mother was saying, 'I'm ecstatic Henry has returned to Hunter's – even though he's only firing on half his cylinders. Still, as snitches go, I do miss Nona.'

Nona Honts had been Mother's go-to informant for the past few cases – or rather that informant was Nona's invisible friend, Zelda, who gave Mother information through Nona, who was a 'tulpa'. Nona had a condition called tulpamancy, in which a person will summon an imaginary companion, not unlike a child who may go through an invisible friend phase.

For tulpas, however, these attachments do not disappear with age, but only grow stronger. This aberration is seen by some as a form of mental illness, while others believe it's a paranormal manifestation. Either way, these imaginary companions often have a positive influence in a tulpa's life, providing companionship and conversation – albeit to anyone within earshot, their dialogues seem decidedly one-sided.

Sad to say, for some reason Nona's friend Zelda had disappeared, so to speak.

'To Henry's credit,' I said, 'he *did* tell you about the tool Clare bought.'

'Well,' Mother responded, 'we're about to find out if that's true – there's her white van.'

The bar materialized out of the gloom on our left and I pulled our vehicle alongside Clare's.

The clientele inside All Inclusive was skimpy on this wintery weekday night, a few same-sex couples seated at the bar, a handful of others making use of beer barrel tables with up-ended crates for chairs, keeping the speakeasy theme going.

A few sat by themselves in the comfort of a setting where they weren't judged. Mildly raised voices provided a friendly vibe of laughter and conversation while speakers played Kate Bush doing 'Running Up That Hill'.

Mother pointed to a corner barrel where Clare sat in the company of a bottle of beer and complimentary bucket of peanuts. As we approached her, our feet crunched on the empty shells that had been routinely swept from tabletops onto the floor.

'What do *you* want?' Clare asked, unpleasantly.

'A word,' Mother said pleasantly.

Clare snorted. 'With Vivian Borne, I doubt it'll be *a* word.'

'I will require more than one word,' Mother admitted, 'but nonetheless this shouldn't take long.'

'It better not.'

While I remained standing, Mother pulled up a crate. 'I hear you're starting your own podcast.'

'I am.'

'And you plan on solving Nicole's murder?'

'That's right.' Clare cocked her head. 'You may be on the outside for now, but you're not off the hook.'

'Neither are you,' I interjected.

The producer looked my way. 'What are you implying? That *I* killed Nicole?'

'Do you deny a romantic interest in her?' I asked, adding, 'And that she didn't reciprocate? That her interest in you was strictly professional?'

'What business is it of yours?' Clare asked sourly.

'It certainly provides a motive,' I replied. 'Especially after the thoughtless way she treated you.'

Clare raised a defiant chin. 'I was at Hunter's until shortly after seven. If you don't believe me, ask that stupid bartender.'

Mother said, 'We indeed did ask that stupid bartender. And while it's true you were there, Junior couldn't be sure *exactly* when you'd left. You could have made tracks earlier, returned to the hotel via an entrance not covered by a security camera, taken the back stairs to Nicole's suite, eliminated her, and left the way you'd come. Knowing I had an appointment with Nicole, you might have watched for me to arrive, then entered the lobby yourself a few minutes later, knowing full well I would have found her body by then.'

Clare snorted. 'Sounds like one of your outlandish books.'

'Hey, lady!' I said. 'Those are non-fiction!'

Mother asked, 'Why did you buy the slapper?'

Clare looked like she'd been zapped by Mother's Taser. (Which by the way, I have been, playing her unwitting guinea pig back when she was first testing the non-lethal weapon out.)

Flustered for a moment, Clare recovered and demanded, 'How did you know about that?'

Ignoring the question, Mother remarked, 'Seems like a good weapon to hit someone with – certainly tricky to identify.'

Clare swallowed. 'I needed it to straighten out a bent cucol-oris. That's a—'

'I know what it is, dear,' Mother interrupted. 'A metal light modifier used to make patterns on the wall. And I suppose you can prove that?'

Clare got to her feet, jostling the barrel, spilling what was left of her beer. 'I don't have to prove *anything* to you! *Either* of you!' She grabbed the coat she'd been sitting on, and strode off in a huff, heading to the door.

Our voices had attracted attention, including the owner's.

'Everything all right?' Michelle asked, coming over. Tall, with raven-black hair cut in a shoulder-length pageboy, wearing over-the-top makeup, the trans woman looked drop-dead gorgeous.

'Yes, dear,' Mother responded.

'Good to hear,' Michelle said. 'Because I like to keep things friendly here.' She pointed to a sign on the wall which read: BE NICE OR LEAVE. Threats seldom came more positive.

I said, 'We're nice, but we're leaving.'

Michelle nodded, then moved on to speak with customers at another barrel.

On our way, I noticed someone standing at the bar, getting a drink.

'Isn't that Nona?' I asked.

Mother squinted. 'Couldn't be . . . she looks too happy.'

'No, it *is* her.'

'Nona?' I asked the slender young woman just as she turned away from the counter, a glass of red wine in hand.

Her red silk blouse and black leggings were a departure from the usual oversized brown leather bomber jacket, short red-and-tan plaid skirt, ripped black tights, and combat boots. She also was no longer brunette, but blonde. But this was Nona, all right.

The young woman's smile transformed her formerly gloomy face into joy. 'Brandy! Mrs Borne!'

'My dear, it is you!' Mother exclaimed, then asked hopefully, 'Has Zelda returned?'

'No. But I'm doing fine. I've made a lot of new friends. *Real* ones.'

Maybe Zelda had sensed Nona didn't need her anymore, and moved on.

Mother's reply of, 'How nice,' fell flat, colored as it was by the knowledge that she had no further access to Zelda.

'Mrs Borne,' Nona said, 'I'm so glad to run into you because, before she disappeared, Zelda asked me to relay a message.'

Mother perked up. 'And what was that, dear?'

The woman frowned. 'Oh, heck . . . I can't remember now.'

'Do try,' Mother coaxed. 'It may be important.'

'Some kind of quote or something from Edgar Allan Poe . . . about a grave and not everything being lost. Sounded kind of negative to me, which is probably why I put it out of my mind. I'm all about staying positive, now.'

'Thank you, Nona,' Mother replied, 'I'm familiar with the Poe work in question.' She turned to me. 'We should toddle, Brandy.'

Outside, the cold air felt refreshing – at least for a moment or two. As we walked to our car, I asked Mother which poem Nona – or Zelda – was referring to.

'Not a poem, dear – a story. "The Pit and the Pendulum".' She threw back her head. '"In death, no! even in the grave all is not lost."'

To Mother, all the world's a stage, including a gravel parking lot in below-freezing temperature.

'Rather morbid for a last goodbye,' I commented.

Mother stopped short.

'What's the matter?' I asked.

'Clare's van is still parked next to ours.'

As I moved closer to the vehicles, a shadow began to form on the ground between them, and I turned on my cell light.

Clare lay sprawled on the gravel, her head battered and bloodied.

Mother came up behind me. 'It's Clare!'

'It sure is.'

'Is she dead?'

'So it would seem.'

'I'll get a closer look.' Mother tried to push past me, but I extended a stopping-guard arm.

'Dear,' she said, her patience strained, 'you know full well I've seen dead bodies before.'

'It's not that.' I aimed my light at an object on the ground next to the woman.

Mother peered. 'Looks like an antique wood potato masher.'

'It is. With our store's red sticker on the handle.'

Brandy's Trash 'n' Treasures Tip

Protect your sports memorabilia from theft, fire, damage, or loss by purchasing an 'all-risks' insurance policy which also covers those items whether they are at your home, in transit, or stored in a unit somewhere. At the very least get a policy that covers your memorabilia at home, but if you can't afford that, at least make sure to turn off the iron and stove, and lock all doors and windows before you leave.

SEVEN

On the Ropes

After finding Clare's body in the parking lot of All Inclusive, I called 911, while Mother went back into the bar to give owner Michelle the unpleasant news that police would be arriving, and that her customers would have to stay and be questioned.

'How did she take it?' I asked Mother upon her return.

'Not terribly well, dear. But Michelle understands she needs to keep everyone inside.'

By now sirens could be heard in the distance, growing louder, then earsplitting as two tailgating squad cars swerved into the gravel lot, coming to an abrupt stop side by side and cutting their sirens but with their lights still flashing.

Officers Munson and Monroe quickly exited the cars, the former heading to secure the roadhouse, the latter approaching Mother and me.

Shawntea, her police windbreaker not nearly warm enough for the weather, asked crossly, 'Can't you two stay out of trouble?'

'Apparently not,' I said.

The officer bathed the prone figure in her mag light. 'Who is this?'

I'd only told the dispatcher we'd found a body in the parking lot of All Inclusive.

'Clare Shields,' Mother said. 'She's the producer on a prominent podcast out of Chicago . . . or, I should say, was.'

The officer, looking put-upon to have Vivian Borne deliver her yet another murder victim, ordered us to stand over by the squad cars and wait for further questioning.

An emergency truck screamed in, two paramedics disembarking, Shawntea directing them to the body.

Shortly, Tony arrived in his own vehicle, a coat thrown over casual clothes, summoned from his cabin home just west of River Road.

Looking none too happy, the chief approached us near the squad cars. I could smell the fragrance of burning hickory logs from his fireplace. How I wished he and I were snuggled up in front of it right now.

Tony had yet to speak when Mother said, 'Before you embarrass yourself by flying off the handle, I can explain.'

'Save it,' the chief said sharply. He crossed to Shawntea, where they spoke for a few minutes, then he returned to us.

'You'll be going to the station with me,' he said, gesturing to his vehicle. 'You'll have to leave your car here.'

No doubt forensics would be going over our SUV as well as Clare's.

I asked, 'Is that really necessary?'

He almost growled, 'Just because you two are old hands at this doesn't make it any easier.'

Normally, my place was in the front passenger seat, but that's when I wasn't a suspect, which both Mother and I seemed to be. She and I climbed into the back; at least Tony's personal car didn't have a dividing screen.

Not a word was said on the way to the station – not a peep out of the chief until we were seated in the conference room. (Or Mother either, which was remarkable.)

'All right, you two,' Tony said. 'What happened after you left Hunter's?'

Mother glared at me. 'Benedict Arnold.'

I groveled: 'I only texted him once where we were.'

Interesting fact about Mr Arnold: before his name became associated with being a traitor after selling secrets to the British, he was a hero of the American Revolution who built one of the first US naval fleets.

'Vivian?' Tony prompted. 'Care to fill me in?'

Mother said, 'After Junior confirmed Clare had been at Hunter's that evening, we decided—'

'*You* decided,' I corrected.

'*I* decided to find Clare and ask her about a tool she'd bought just before the hardware section closed, a slapper, which seemed to be the type of makeshift weapon that might have been used to inflict Nicole's injuries.'

To his credit, Tony accepted that with no comment other than, 'Go on.'

'Clare claimed the slapper – you're familiar with the tool? – was needed to straighten a piece of metal she used during filming. Still, you really should look into that.'

'I'm always happy,' he said, 'to receive an expert opinion.'

That made Mother smile. She really didn't quite get sarcasm.

Tony's cell sounded. I could only hear his side of the conversation, which was minimal – a few 'all rights' and 'uh-huhs'. I gathered the caller was either Munson or Shawntea with information from the crime scene.

When he'd clicked off, the chief looked at Mother. 'So – you had an altercation with Clare?'

She waved that away. 'I would call it was more of . . . a disagreement.'

'What did you disagree about?'

Mother sighed. 'Well. Thinking back . . . I *may* have accused her of killing Nicole, and she may have denied it. But hear me out, Chief! I *know* how Clare did it.'

Tony did not take the bait. 'According to the owner at Hunter's, Clare left first, then you and Brandy followed a few minutes later, after speaking briefly to someone at the bar. Would you like to explain the potato masher with your shop's sticker on it?'

'Well,' Mother said helpfully, 'red indicates one of our items and white a consignment one.'

He closed his eyes, then opened them again. 'Not what I meant. Explain the sticker's presence on the apparent murder weapon.'

She threw up her hands. '*That* I can't explain.'

I said, 'Tony, you don't believe either one of us killed Clare with the masher, and then were stupid enough to leave it behind?'

'Yes,' Mother said, trying to be helpful, 'we would never kill anybody and leave the murder weapon behind!'

I glared at her.

The chief sat back in his chair, frowning as if something else was gnawing at him.

'What is it?' I asked.

He leaned forward, elbows on the table. 'Vivian, when I saw you at the jail to tell you the spy necklace hadn't recorded, you mentioned some threatening letters you'd received . . .'

Mother tossed her head. 'I hardly think a few poison-pen letters are the priority here. We should be trying to find out who is attempting to frame me with two murders.'

'Quiet, Mother,' I interjected. Then to Tony, 'You think they're connected?'

A curt nod. 'I believe it's the same person – just upping the ante. And, furthermore, this individual doesn't care if Vivian is convicted of murder or not – this is someone who wants to ruin Vivian's life, one way or another.'

Mother was nodding. 'Hence the sloppy planting of evidence.'

Tony addressed her. 'It doesn't help your cause that you're playing into the poison-pen writer's hands with your actions.'

I said, 'Or maybe the writer *knows* Mother well enough to either observe her actions or predict her reactions . . . and take advantage.'

'Then it's someone close to me,' Mother deduced.

'Not necessarily,' Tony countered. 'It could be a criminal you've helped convict but who's out now, and wants to get even . . . or someone who feels you've impacted their life in such a negative way that they're willing to go to extremes.'

I asked, 'What do you want us to do?'

He turned a narrow-eyed gaze on both of us. 'I assume you keep a fairly regular inventory of the items in your shop.'

'I took one a few weeks ago,' I said.

'See if that potato masher was listed,' Tony said. 'And if so, who would have had an opportunity to shoplift it.'

I nodded. 'I'll start with the names on receipts dated after the inventory, and also try to remember who came in but didn't buy anything.'

'That would be helpful,' Tony said. 'While you're doing that, I'll check into any released convicts associated with

Vivian's sleuthing activities – I think we can rule out anyone who's inside.'

Mother, obviously not loving the way Tony and I had taken over, said rather meekly, 'Am I going to be arrested again?'

'No,' Tony said. 'Not yet, anyway. I'll release a statement that this latest death is under investigation, and keep the potato masher under wraps.'

Mother straightened, as if once again taking command. 'Very good. To recap . . . Brandy's going to check the inventory list . . . you're going to look into any recently sprung convicts . . . What would you have me do?'

Tony seemed to be thinking about the rich possibilities for answers to that question.

But what he said, sternly, was, 'Stay home.'

'You can trust me,' she said, standing.

As if either of us would.

Vivian taking back the writing reins (lovely punning there, don't you think?). But before I dive headlong into what was revealing itself to be one of our most dangerous, devious cases, I must point out that a previous chapter written by Brandy went over five thousand words . . . with nary a discouraging word from our editor!

So, dear readers, if you would like to hear more from me in these accounts, please contact our publishing company via social media or snail mail to have my word count increased. You will not regret it!

The following morning, I awoke to find our car in the driveway and a note from Tony stuck under the front door saying the keys were in the glove compartment. Brandy was planning to work at the shop today, but was still asleep, so I took the opportunity to go off on my own and confront those who thought I had done them wrong.

While I admit being tempted to use the vehicle myself, we had enough problems without adding driving without a license to the mix. And it was a tad crisp out for the Vespa. So it was a little after eight when I ventured outside to catch the gas-converted trolley car that made a stop a block from our house.

My feet were nice and toasty in Brandy's Uggs, which

she surely would miss when she left later – but I needed them more than her because she'd be inside most of the day, while I'd be out pounding the cold sidewalks. (Once, to deter me from wearing the boots, Brandy inserted pine needles in the toes, then forgot about it and later slipped in her *own* bare feet. Did she ever howl! Sometimes that child is her own worst enemy.)

The trolley – my usual mode of non-Brandy, non-Vespa mechanized transportation – was provided free by the Downtown Merchants Association to encourage denizens of our fair city to shop with them rather than the competition, the Serenity Mall on the outskirts of town. And on the off-chance occasion that I needed to go elsewhere other than downtown, I was usually able to convince the driver to veer off his or her main route by using (first) flattery, (second) pleading, and (third) blackmail. The third was the least palatable, if the most effective, which is why I made it my business to know everything I could about the various drivers.

Good practice for sleuthing!

I must pause a moment to say that I have been unfairly depicted by others as a gossip. I do not gossip. I *hear* gossip, yes. And that's the difference, a *big* one. Like Miss Marple, I sit quietly and absorb conversation around me, taking note of tidbits I can use. (Margaret Rutherford is still my favorite actress to embody the character; while her depiction may not be the smartest or the most accurate to the text, she nonetheless captures the essence of Agatha's sleuth.)

As the trolley pulled up to the curb, it appeared empty on this early frosty morning; even with the high price of gas these days, folks would rather pay extra at the pump than sit in a drafty old trolley car with no heat. The irony, of course, is that the more people ride, the more heat gets generated.

The latest driver, Mary McBride, was at the helm, not to be confused with Mary Hunter, she of the prosthetic leg. McBride was a bottle-blonde in her forties, bundled up against the cold. So far I had nothing much on her – but everyone has a secret or two.

After clambering aboard, I cheerfully asked, 'And how is Mary on this bright brisk morning?'

She eyed me warily, aware of what others (other than me) view as my past trolley indiscretions, which are too numerous to detail. (See *Antiques Liquidation* for a complete listing.)

'Fine, I guess,' was her guarded response.

'Dear, I must impose upon you to deliver me a trifle off the beaten path.'

'You know that's against the rules, Mrs Borne.'

I stood my ground. 'If you put the pedal to the metal, you could be back on track in less time than it takes to argue the point.'

Now I took a gamble knowing she'd recently spent a week in Las Vegas with some girlfriends; only a scrap of blackmail fodder, but a scrap is a scrap.

'Otherwise,' I said sweetly, 'what happened in Vegas may not stay in Vegas.'

Her eyes narrowed. 'Where to?'

I gave her the address.

'Three blocks away from there,' she said, 'is the furthest I'll go.'

'Farthest, dear, which refers to distance. Further means more.'

'Do you want my offer or not?' she snapped.

Some people simply do not know how to handle constructive criticism!

'I'll take it,' I said with a nod.

With that negotiation settled, I settled into the seat behind her. (Sometimes word repetition can be clever!)

A short time later, I disembarked into a neighborhood of rental homes, most of which were rundown – the landlords wouldn't fix them up as long as the structures continued to attract renters, and the renters themselves saw no point in spending their own money on something they didn't own. Stalemate!

I walked the several blocks to a stucco duplex and went up the cracked sidewalk. A knock at a well-worn door summoned a man in undershirt and sweatpants.

'What do *you* want?' Daniel Riswold asked flatly.

In his mid-forties, his salt-and-pepper beard matching an unruly head of hair, to say he appeared unkempt would be both unkind and understated . . . so let's just assume I had caught him in the morning before he'd had a chance to complete his *articles de toilette.*

'May I step inside, Mr Riswold? It is rather cold out here – for both of us.'

He moved aside.

He motioned me to follow him, which I did, down a corridor to a kitchen that hadn't been updated since linoleum was all the rage.

'Is that coffee I smell?' I asked pleasantly.

He muttered something I didn't catch due to my wax-plugged ears (a doctor's visit would remedy that quickly, but I prefer the drops that crackle and pop, giving me something to listen to while it softens the wax). Soon we were seated, without coffee, at a round oak table that had seen better days.

'Well?' Daniel said.

'I'd like to apologize for that little incident that happened on the trolley last year when you were the driver.'

'Incident? You mean when you sat behind me, and suddenly shouted in my ear, and I swerved off the street, ran over a fire hydrant spraying water everywhere, then hit an electrical pole that tipped over onto a dry-cleaning store and the roof burst into flames? *That* little incident?'

'You zeroed right in!'

He grunted. 'That didn't "happen", lady. *You* happened.'

In a calm, self-controlled voice, I said, 'In my defense, I wasn't shouting, I was singing. It was such a beautiful spring day that I couldn't help bursting into the rousing and obviously appropriate chorus of "The Trolley Song" – the one Judy Garland sang in the movie *Meet Me in St. Louis*? Granted, I may have been a teensy bit too rousing with the clanging, dinging, and zinging, and the chugging, bumping, and thumping . . . but I was also trying to raise your spirits, as you seemed to be down in the dumps when I boarded. So you see, I feel rather responsible that your life went downhill after that.'

His eyes were lidded. 'Are you referring to my "teensy bit" of a nervous breakdown, the divorce, losing my job and my house?'

I nodded. 'From one small snowball, an avalanche can . . . happen.'

He was staring past me into something, or maybe nothing. 'While you did contribute to the breakdown, Mrs Borne, my wife had already served me with divorce papers, and I was about to quit as a trolley driver, anyway. As far as the house goes, it was mortgaged to the hilt. So you might say I was headed for the edge anyway . . . you just gave me the final push.'

'More like accidentally brushed by you,' I said cheerfully, adding, 'What are you up to these days?'

Daniel gestured around the unfortunate kitchen. 'Just livin' the dream. I get by doing odd jobs as a carpenter, and jack of all trades.'

I raised a forefinger. 'I may have a permanent job for you that would combine all those skills.'

His eyes narrowed onto me. 'I'm listening.'

'As you probably know,' I said, 'I'm the director of the Playhouse, and have a say in the hiring of staff. With the conclusion of the current Christmas production, *The Elf Rebellion*, the assistant stage manager is departing, and I will be needing a replacement. It doesn't provide much of a livelihood, but you could also continue doing other jobs, as long as they didn't interfere with your stage duties.'

He cocked his head, not displeased with the offer but suspicious. 'Why are you really here, Vivian? Does it have anything to do with the murder of that podcaster you were charged with? And I heard on my police scanner that the producer died last night.'

I told Daniel of the threatening letters I'd been receiving, and that the killings might be connected to the writer.

He laughed dryly. 'And you think *I'm* this person?'

'You're a possibility.'

'Threatening letters are written by cowards. And I'm certainly not capable of murder.'

I believed him.

'Thank you,' I said. 'What about the job offer?'

He thought for a moment. 'You want some coffee?'

'I'd be delighted.'

We discussed his new job responsibilities for fifteen or

twenty minutes and then I took my leave. I might not be exiting with a new friend, but I had filled that assistant stage manager position (and eliminated a suspect to my satisfaction).

After leaving the duplex, I headed back to catch the trolley again, disembarking ten minutes later in front of the court-house, the ride's final stop.

Along the way, I'd had a bit of a think, coming to the conclusion it was a waste of time questioning everyone who might have felt wronged by me – after all, there were only so many job positions at the theater I could use to make amends. The poison-pen suspect might even include the ROMEOs group (Retired Old Men Eating Out). While their numbers had dwindled over the years due to the grim reaper, and relocating to warmer climes, of the four remaining original members, each had – at one time or another – unsuccessfully invited me to accompany him to the altar.

Perhaps carrying a burning torch of desire for Vivian Borne's remarkably enduring beauty had caused an addled brain or two to go haywire. Had one of them felt spurned? But since these men couldn't bend over to tie their orthopedic sneakers, let alone have the strength to bludgeon two women to death, I set them aside as improbable suspects for now.

Besides which, I had an itch regarding something else, and I knew just the person who could scratch it.

Gate-crashing past reception, I found Gladys Gooch in her cubbyhole office at the First National Bank. A curvy, quiet, rather plain woman in her twenties, Gladys could transform herself from someone who would rate nary a glance to a brilliant, vibrant, sensuous woman. Of course, thus far this had happened only when she stepped onto a stage, in full makeup and costume (preferably with generous décolletage). At such times, Gladys Gooch was Meryl Streep on steroids.

The hitch with Gladys was, she could not make this metamorphosis without being hypnotized first – a discovery I made in desperation after offering her the lead as the femme fatale in *Voice of the Turtle*. This role I'd offered in exchange for financial information I needed to crack a prior case, never dreaming the timid girl would hold me to my side of the bargain.

Enter Tilda Tompkins, Serenity's new age guru, hypnotist, death doula, and teacher of all things mantra and mudra. And while this therapeutic arrangement worked for a while, the effects began to wear off before the first act curtain, necessitating Tilda to re-hypnotize Gladys backstage during intermission. Fortunately, community theater plays were never long-running. Some of mine haven't made it past Act One on the opening night.

Gladys looked up from her computer and her face blossomed into a smile that hinted of what a full transformation would bring. 'Mrs Borne!'

'Vivian, dear,' I corrected, taking a seat in front of the desk.

'I was going to visit you at the jail,' she said, leaning forward, 'after I heard about that podcaster, but by the time I got off work, you'd been released. Thankfully!'

'How sweet of you. Are you ready to tread the boards once again?'

Her big brown eyes began to twinkle, like Sushi when a doggie treat was dangled before her. 'Just tell me what you need,' Gladys said.

Isn't it refreshing when a quid-pro-quo relationship is understood, without the usual quibbling over who gets the quid and who gets the quo?

'Dear, I'd like to know of any large cash withdrawals from your customers in the past few days.'

If Clare had declared bankruptcy some years back, as Tony said, then where was she getting the start-up cash for her own podcast?

'Personal or business accounts?' asked Gladys.

'Both.'

'That shouldn't be too difficult,' the financial officer replied, 'since we're required to keep a record of any withdrawals of ten thousand dollars or over. How soon do you want it?'

'ASAP, dear.'

'And the role?'

'Ulla, in *The Producers*.'

'Oh, wonderful! "Bialystock und Bloo-um! Bialystock und Bloo-um!" When?'

'This spring, dear.'

My cell trilled. Usually when I ventured off investigating on my own, I left the phone behind, not wanting to be bothered – or tracked by Brandy via her cell or computer. Phone ID said Chief Cassato was calling – following up our interview, most likely.

'What's up, Chiefie?' I asked.

His reply came grunted. 'My office. Now.'

He must already have information on the status of the criminals I'd helped put away.

I bade adieu to Gladys, who'd promised to get me the information I'd requested, and I hit the pavement again.

On the way, I walked by All Sports Artifacts, where a sign posted inside on the glass door said the shop was closed while Mark was away attending the National Sports Collectors Convention in Chicago.

Inside the station, receptionist Sarah waved me toward the inner sanctum door and buzzed me through. Then down the corridor of past history trod I, where the gum-infused picture frame was holding fast.

The chief, behind his desk, gestured to a chair. Over the years his gallantry upon my arrival had gone from a full stand to a half-stand, to barely a lift-off, to remaining fully seated. Perhaps next he'd crawl under the desk.

He handed me a spreadsheet consisting of the criminals' names, dates of sentencing, locations of incarceration, current status, release dates, and addresses.

'My goodness,' I said. 'You compiled all of this just this morning?'

'I was here all night.'

I hadn't noticed the unshaven face, loose tie, rolled-up sleeves, and collection of Styrofoam coffee cups on the desk. Perhaps as an author I should work on my observational skills.

'You do look tuckered, Chiefie,' I admitted.

'I am, and don't call me "Chiefie".'

I splayed a hand to my chest. 'My apologies for the familiarity.' But I didn't say I'd stop. 'I *am* your future mother-in-law, you know.'

His eyes glazed over for a few seconds. How's that for an observation?

Consulting a copy of the printout, he said, 'As you can see, eight received life without parole, six are currently serving prison sentences, four are out on parole, two died while in prison, five chose suicide before capture, and one is institutionalized.'

'I *have* been a busy girl,' I said, thoroughly impressed with my own record.

'We should start with the four on parole,' the chief said.

I tapped the sheet. 'The one institutionalized . . . would that be somewhere with "in and out" privileges?'

'Interesting question. I'll need to look into that.'

'If so, that would make five possible suspects.'

Sarah's voice came over the desk intercom.

'Chief Cassato, sorry to interrupt . . . is Mrs Borne still with you?'

'Yes.'

'Well, that little dog of hers is here – scratching and barking at the front door.'

The chief looked sharply at me, and I spoke what we were both thinking. 'Something's wrong with Brandy!'

He grabbed his coat from a corner rack – I still had mine on – and together we hurried down the corridor to the front waiting room, where, sure enough, Sushi was making a kennel's-worth of noise at the glass door.

Soon Tony was behind the wheel of his car, me in the passenger seat, holding Sushi. As he sped away I tried to reach Brandy on her cell, then again on the landline, with no result.

As we approached the mouth of the alley behind the shop, I could see the back door standing open.

Tony brought his vehicle to an abrupt stop next to our SUV, jumped out, and went inside, gun drawn.

Sushi and I weren't far behind and, upon entering the mudroom, I could see Brandy on the kitchen floor, on her stomach, unconscious face turned toward me, blood pooling around her head. Sushi jumped from my arms.

The chief, kneeling beside her, had fingers on her neck.

'She still has a pulse,' he said. Then: 'Call 911. I'll check the house.'

I already had my cell in hand.

He stood and moved through the kitchen to the front of the house, fanning the gun as he went.

While I spoke urgently to the dispatcher, Sushi was circling her mistress, whimpering, tracking small paw prints through the blood. I noticed then that the little dog was limping, probably hurt trying to protect Brandy, before escaping and going for help.

I dropped to my knees and gently brushed Brandy's hair off her face. She looked so peaceful, not a worry in the world.

'My dear,' I whispered, 'I've caused you so much turmoil over the years. I'll make things right.'

Tony returned. 'Whoever did this is gone.' His face showed fury, but his eyes were moist.

The chief crossed to the mudroom to wait for the first responder; and, perhaps, to compose himself.

In the emergency waiting room, Tony paced while I sat holding Sushi, the staff allowing a no-pets exception because of the little dog's injury, or possibly due to the presence of the chief.

The air hung heavy with the accusation that Brandy's condition was my fault.

After a stretch of silence, I said, 'Tony, I—'

But he interrupted. 'Not now, Vivian. There'll be time for that later.'

I nodded. 'You're right, of course. We must think only of Brandy.'

Sushi had settled in my lap.

A doctor approached us, his expression unreadable.

'She's still unconscious,' he said, looking from me to Tony. 'She had a blow to the back of the skull, and due to the swelling of the brain, she has to be kept in an induced coma.'

I swallowed and asked, 'For how long?'

'Unknown.'

Tony asked, 'What is the prognosis?'

'Touch and go,' he said. 'And, should she regain consciousness, there's no guarantee there won't be brain damage.'

Tony moved to a chair, sat down, and covered his face.

'Where's my daughter now?' I asked.

'She's been moved to intensive care.'

'May I see her?'

He hesitated. 'Only for a few minutes.'

I stood, and handed Sushi to Tony.

Behind a drawn curtain, Brandy seemed so small in the bed, so helpless hooked up to a myriad of devices, while monitors beeped out of sync with each other.

I approached and looked down at her.

'Darling,' I said, 'I love you so very much. I know I don't say it often enough. And I know the sacrifices you've made for me and my ways. Please forgive me for what I'm about to do, but I see no other alternative. I have to protect you and others I love.'

I bent and kissed Brandy's forehead.

Such was my goodbye.

Vivian's Trash 'n' Treasures Tip

Not all sports collectibles need to be old to be valuable. Consider the lucky fan who waited patiently in the leftfield stand of Globe Life stadium on October 4, 2022, and caught Aaron Judge's American League record-shattering sixty-second home run ball, estimated at being worth millions. While I'm happy for the ballplayer, it does make my 1962 Topps Roger Marris card less valuable . . . should I ever find it.

EIGHT
Sudden Death

I came out of a haze and saw my fourteen-year-old son slouched in a chair, sleeping. He had my face and fair hair. Was I dreaming this? Jake was in Chicago with his dad.

'Jake . . .?'

His eyes came open. 'Mom!'

'Where am I?' I asked, my mouth dry as cotton. I soon realized, from the tubes running in and out of me, that the answer was a hospital room. But I didn't know how I'd gotten there, or why.

Jake was standing over me now, tears filling his eyes. 'Do you remember anything?'

I tried. 'Just . . . going into the shop through the alley, and . . .'

There my recollection ended.

Jake filled in for me: 'Someone hit you on the back of your head.'

Which explained the head bandage, anyway.

'Is Sushi all right?' I asked.

Jake nodded. 'She got a leg hurt protecting you, but managed to go for help. When Grandma and Chief Cassato found you, the back door at Trash 'n' Treasures was open.'

'How long have I been out?'

'Six days.'

'*That* long?'

'The doctor kept you in a coma because your brain was swollen. You were moved out of intensive care to this private room yesterday.' He looked behind him. 'Aunt Peggy! She's awake.'

My sister was here? I must have been in trouble for her to come from DC, where she lived with her husband, Senator Edward Clark, while Congress was in session.

Peggy Sue crossed the room to join her nephew. Only . . .
Jake was really her grandson, and she was my natural mother,
and Mother was my grandmother, who raised me. It's a long
story. See . . . a whole bunch of *Antiques* books.

But here's a quick recap.

Pretty, pretty Peggy Sue (as Buddy Holly put it) was
seventeen, just out of high school, when the summer before
college she went to work for then-State Representative
Clark's campaign. They had an affair and she got pregnant
with me; but since he was married and the scandal would
have ended his career, Peggy didn't tell him. That fall Mother
took Peg on a six-month tour of Europe, and they returned
with me, Mother's 'surprise' later-in-life baby. (It was easier
to fool people before the Internet and social media became
omniscient.)

I'd only discovered my true parentage after I relocated back
home a few years ago, after my divorce. By that time, the
senator's wife had died, and he and Peg had reunited well
after the fact.

Happy ending? Not for me, who maintained a strained
relationship with both my natural parents, having told Peggy
Sue that Mother would remain my mother, while she – my
sister, while I was growing up, and Senator Clark, a man she
finally married – had given up any other rights.

Peggy Sue was asking, 'How do you feel?'

At fifty, Peg was still a stunner, with her sleek brunette hair,
blue eyes, pert nose, full lips, and slender curves, all wrapped
up in a designer suit, a Van Cleef and Arpels four-leaf-clover
necklace upping the ante.

'Like I got hit by a Mack truck,' I said. 'When's my next
dose of painkiller due?'

'I'm afraid they don't have you on any.'

'But that,' I joked, 'is the only good thing about being in a
hospital.'

My 'sister' said, 'The senator is sorry he isn't here – there's
an important vote taking place before Congress adjourns for
the holidays.'

That was fine with me. I got along with him, but it wasn't
like we'd developed a warm daughter/father relationship.

'But,' Peggy Sue added, 'he's been calling every day to ask about your condition.'

'Where's Mother, anyway?' I asked. 'Downstairs sneaking around the morgue looking for clues?'

Two pairs of solemn eyes stared at me.

Peggy Sue said, her voice quavering, 'She's . . . not coming, Brandy.'

I frowned. 'You mean . . . not today? Well, I guess after all this time since I was admitted, she's probably taking a break.'

'Not coming today . . . or ever.' Peg's perfect makeup began to stream, the tears flowing. And I had never seen Jake look so glum, not even when I told him as a little boy that his father and I were splitting up.

'I don't believe it,' I said. 'That's not like her.'

Jake touched my shoulder. 'It's true, Mom. She . . . she took her life.'

Suicide?

Mother? Impossible! La Diva Borne thought far too much of herself for that.

'That's *really* not like her,' I said, managing a shrug. 'It's a stunt. It's a ploy.'

But something played inside my head, her voice sounding far away: *'Please forgive me for what I'm about to do, but I see no other alternative. I have to protect you and others I love.'*

I tried to sit up but was constricted by the tubes, then the room began to whirl and I fell back against the pillow.

'You're not supposed to move, Mom,' Jake said, then to Peggy Sue, 'Maybe you should get the doctor . . .'

When Peg left, I asked Jake, 'You wouldn't lie to me, would you, for some reason? About Mother?'

'No. It's true.'

I could hardly get the words out. 'How . . . how did she . . .?'

'She . . . she took an overdose of her medication.'

'Who . . . who found her?'

'All I know is a reporter went to the house to confirm an obituary Grandma had written that the newspaper received, and ran into the coroner, who she'd sent the same obit to.'

I cried and laughed at once. 'Her self-penned obit, huh? I bet that's a doozy.'

'Oh, yeah. I've got a copy if you want to see it.'

'Maybe later.'

Maybe not.

Peggy Sue returned. 'The doctor will be here soon.'

Could this be true? Really and truly true*? Had my nearly dying at the hands of one of her . . . our . . . enemies driven her to something rash, even for her?*

'So,' I got out somehow, 'Mother's at a funeral home?'

Aunt and nephew exchanged looks.

'What?' I asked.

'She's . . . at home,' Peggy Sue said. '*Her* home, *your* home.'

I tried to make sense of that. This couldn't be true. Too absurd, even for her. 'What, like, in a casket with ice dripping into a bucket? Wasn't the Playhouse available?'

'No, Brandy,' Peg went on. 'She's in an urn.'

Now I did sit up, tubes be damned. 'Mother was *cremated*? And you didn't wait for an opinion from *me*?'

'We didn't know when – or if,' Peggy Sue said, 'you might wake up.'

It was just like Peggy Sue to step in and take things into her own hands.

'She would *never* want to be cremated!' I replied angrily. 'Mother had a plot and headstone, and a casket already picked out . . . already *paid* for! She'd even set aside what clothes in her closet she wanted to wear. She would rather have *given* her body to science. She *hated* the idea that we might split her ashes between us – a leg in DC, an arm in Chicago, her head here – or put her in a glass paperweight like Aunt Olive, only to end up in a landfill generations from now. No, this has to be a ruse, can't you see?'

Peggy Sue, distraught, said, 'Brandy, both Jake and I went to the morgue to identify her.'

I looked to my son for confirmation.

'It *was* Grandma, mom. They had her in one of those . . . refrigerator drawers.'

I pulled in a breath and let it out. 'Look, not long ago, she and I broke into the morgue looking for a report, and Mother hid in one of those coolers when a cleaning woman came in! See, that's what she did to *fool* you.'

Peg said, 'Brandy, Jake and I attended the cremation at Dunn's Crematorium. We saw her in that cremation coffin just before . . .' She couldn't finish, her voice cracking.

I asked, 'Was Ned Dunn there? The owner?'

'Yes,' Jake said.

'He and Mother were friends. She could have finagled him into helping her. He could have switched the coffin with an empty one at the last minute!'

'Brandy, *please*!' Peggy Sue begged. 'You're making this so much harder.'

I spoke through clenched teeth. 'She *didn't* die, I tell you!'

A doctor entered the room, accompanied by a nurse.

'She's all upset,' Peg told them, painfully earnest, 'insisting Vivian isn't dead. You've got to settle her down, before she gets out of bed.'

The doctor nodded to the nurse, who moved to the IV pole, a syringe in one hand.

'What are you doing?' I demanded.

The needle entered a port in the dangling tube.

'No! I don't want to go to sleep!' I cried. 'I'm *tired* of sleeping!' I suddenly started unintentionally invoking Colin Clive in *Frankenstein*. 'She's alive, I tell you . . . she's *alive*!'

Fade quickly to black.

When I next opened my eyes, Tony was seated next to the bed, looking weary and worried.

'How are you doing?' he asked, leaning forward.

How did he *think* I was doing? But if I answered in the negative, would that nurse just put me to sleep again?

I summoned a tiny smile. 'I'm OK. I just . . . just didn't take the news about Mother very well.'

He nodded. 'I know it's hard to accept, but after your brush with . . .'

'Death?'

'. . . Vivian must have felt it was the only way to protect you and the others she loved.'

Nearly her exact words.

Could I actually imagine that the chief of police, the coroner, the funeral director, my sister, and my son were all tied up together in a conspiracy? Had I joined the Tinfoil Hat brigade? Or was I really just as paranoid as I'd been sounding?

Tony put a bear-paw hand on my IV-bandaged one. 'Brandy . . . I thought I'd lost you.'

'I'm all right,' I said stiffly. 'This has just been hard to process, is all.'

'Do you think you're up to a few questions?'

'. . . Sure.'

'Tell me what you remember. To the best of your ability.'

I explained how I arrived at the shop and parked in my usual spot off the alley. After unlocking the back door, I put Sushi down, stepped into the mudroom, and turned off the alarm.

'I remember heading into the kitchen,' I said, 'but nothing after that. He must've come in right after me.'

'He . . . or she?'

'Don't know,' I admitted.

Tony nodded. 'Was there another car in the alley?'

'No.'

'So your assailant must've been hiding behind a dumpster,' Tony said. 'Could Sushi identify this attacker, do you think?'

I nodded just a little; more would have hurt too much. 'Possibly. She's done it before, but in that instance the man wore a scented aftershave.'

'And this person probably had on a ski-mask, in case you got a look at him . . . or her.'

I asked, 'What progress is being made on the murder cases?'

The chief told me about his meeting with Mother, to go over a list of perpetrators she'd helped put away, with an emphasis on those who were on the outside, either having completed their sentences or released early on good conduct.

'Of those five,' Tony went on, 'three are reporting to parole officers in other states, one died, and the last is in a secure mental institution.'

'Has someone checked the shop's inventory for that potato masher?'

Tony nodded. 'Jake did, and it *was* listed as in stock.' A tiny smile. 'Your son, by the way, said you might want to come up with a stronger password than his birthday. Anyway, there are still receipts to go through since the inventory, as well as your recollections of who came in but didn't buy anything.'

I shifted a little in the bed. 'Do you know when I get to leave?'

He shrugged. 'That's up to the doctor.'

'But you'll tell him I'm all right? Ready to be released?'

'Are you?'

'Of course.'

'It might be safer for you here,' Tony said, head to one side. 'Your mother wasn't the only amateur sleuth in this, who got a bunch of miscreants jailed.'

'No, I was just Watson. She was Holmes.' I would never have admitted that, had she been breathing.

Tony said, 'Well, I've had an officer stationed in the hallway, who could hang around a while longer.'

'Nonsense,' I stated, channeling Mother. 'Whoever is behind these killings, and harming me, got what he or she wanted – maybe even more than expected.'

We fell silent.

'Tony? I want to have a memorial service for Mother while Peg and Jake are still in town. I won't be robbed of saying goodbye to her.'

'I think that's a great idea.'

'And there's another reason,' I said. 'You *know* he'll be there.'

'Or she,' Tony said, one eyebrow hiked.

'Some rotten murderer of some gender.'

The following noon, after an MRI test revealed the swelling around my brain had gone down, I was released from the hospital. Peggy Sue wheel-chaired me out of my room (according to the facility's policy) and drove us home, where Jake was waiting with a huge hug, Sushi pawing at my legs, wanting her share of attention, too.

I knew it would be hard coming back to the house without Mother there, and was grateful Peg and Jake were around to help fill the void, or at least distract me. Jake had made his

favorite Danish dish that his grandmother would fix when he
came to visit.

Små Karbonadepolser i Hvidvinssauce
(small frankfurters in white wine sauce)

Ingredients

1 pound small frankfurters (or cocktail wieners)
2 tblsp. butter
2 tblsp. flour
1 cup dry white wine
1 cup heavy cream
6 pieces toasted white bread
⅓ cup chopped parsley
6 slices of bacon, cooked

Directions
Prick frankfurters with a fork to prevent bursting during
cooking. Heat the butter in skillet and brown the frankfurters. Sprinkle with the flour. Stir in the white wine
and heat the frankfurters thoroughly. Stir in the cream.
Heat but do not boil. Spoon mixture over the toasted
white bread, sprinkle with the parsley, and garnish with
the bacon slices. Serves six people.

While Peggy Sue, Jake, and I sat at the Duncan Phyfe table,
with Sushi below on the lookout for anything we fumbled, we
reminisced about a few of Mother's funnier escapades.

That's what people do, isn't it? Reminisce. Keep people
alive through memories. Only, to have any benefit of relief
or distraction, the memories had to have been shared, which
really wasn't the case with us three. Peggy Sue was eighteen
years older than me, so I don't know what her life had been
like with Mother before I came along, before Vivian Bipolar
Borne was diagnosed and properly medicated . . . but it
couldn't have been a picnic. Well, maybe one with ants.

As for Jake, he lived in Chicago with his father, after all,
only visiting a few times a year, and frankly, some of those

trips were frightening – like the time he'd been kidnapped. Therefore, our reminiscing didn't go on very long before the conversation turned to what kind of memorial service we were going to have.

'It should be at your church,' Peggy Sue said, picking at her food; she just wasn't a cocktail weenie kind of gal. 'With Pastor Tutor presiding, and the choir, scriptures, sermon, and maybe a few *selected* testimonials.'

Mother and I had wound up as members of New Hope – which I'd dubbed 'The Church of Common Sense' – after we spent years sampling every place of worship in town (my vote was synagogue after tasting the matzo ball soup served after Shabbat service). Mother had finally settled on the non-denominational New Hope, comprised of folks like us who couldn't make up their minds.

Peggy was saying, 'I'll select the scriptures.'

Some words about scriptures: tread carefully what you pick for a funeral. I once attended the service of a beloved former teacher who was the kindest, most patient, caring woman in the world, and whoever led the sermon selected scripture from the Book of Genesis, basically stating that everyone deserves to die because of original sin.

Just what sin had this teacher ever committed? Being born? And how comforting to the mourners was that? When I got home, I put band aids on my palms where my nails had dug in. Or were they stigmata?

Apologies if I've offended anyone – I wasn't quite myself. Or was this the real me? Unencumbered by Mother? Not having to be the sane one.

And I found myself compelled to pick up the threads of Mother's investigation – finding her killer was the best way to keep her alive . . . until the he – or she – responsible was brought to justice.

Sis was frowning. 'Well? What do you think?'

I was surprised she asked me. 'About the funeral?'

'Yes, about the funeral.'

'Well. Mother wouldn't have wanted a solemn church service. I think a celebration of life at some classy but fun venue would be far more appropriate.'

'I agree,' Jake said, grinning. 'Grandma would want a party!'

Peggy Sue made a face that dampened her beauty. 'A "party" isn't exactly in keeping with suicide.'

'Two against one,' Jake replied.

'Fine,' Peg acquiesced. Then she added, with some easily detectable bitterness, 'I guess you both knew her better than I.'

Ignoring that, I asked Peg, 'Do you have a copy of the directives Mother gave to the funeral home?'

'Yes,' she said. 'It's in the folder the funeral director gave us, along with the bill for cremation . . . I'll get it.'

After she'd left the room, I told Jake, 'Thanks for backing me up.'

He shrugged. 'Grandma *would* want a party. She even talked to me once about how after she was gone, she didn't want people being sad. Grandma was very specific about it.'

'Really?'

'Yeah. Grandma said she wanted it held in the ballroom at the Merrill, with appetizers like lobster rolls, crab cake poppers, cucumber canapés, fried calamari, and stuffed mushrooms. And CDs of big band music playing, like Duke Ellington, Benny Goodman, Glenn Miller, Artie Shaw, and Ella Fitzgerald. Plus lots and lots of photos on display, especially ones of her in plays.'

'That's awfully specific.'

Jake shrugged. 'I have a good memory.'

Peggy Sue returned and handed me the letter Mother had written and delivered to Ned Dunn, the director/owner of Dunn's Cremation and Burial, just before her death.

I studied the three-paragraph directive (boy, had he gotten off easy!), dated the day after I'd been hospitalized. The writing was in Mother's distinct cursive, as was the signature, reversing her previous burial wishes.

Instead of embalming, her body was indeed to be cremated; rather than interred in the plot she'd bought at Greenwood Cemetery, her remains were to be encased in an urn. He was to sell her casket ('Like New! Gently used!').

'There's no mention of any service or memorial,' I pointed out, 'so I guess that was left up to us.'

'I still think it should be at the church,' Peggy Sue said, in a last-ditch effort to get her way.

'Nope,' I replied. 'It's decided. And Jake just told me what his grandmother once said she wanted – I don't know if you overheard that.'

'I caught snatches of it,' Peg said. 'Something about Glenn Miller and lots of photos. All right, I'm in. But I'd like this to happen rather quickly, if at all possible. And remember, this is the holiday season when most venues are booked.'

Jake said, 'I did some recon, and the ballroom at the Merrill had a wedding reception cancelled for this Sunday afternoon, 'cause the couple broke up, and it's already decorated. Even comes with a cake. We can just take the little bride and groom thingies off.'

How convenient. I wondered if they had pre-ordered lobster rolls, crab cake poppers, cucumber canapés, fried calamari, and stuffed mushrooms for hors d'oeuvres. Mother, wedding planner from beyond!

Peg was complaining, 'That's just a couple of days! We can't get everything done by then! *And* get the word out.'

'I've already started on the photo presentation,' Jake replied.

'And if I tell Norma Crumley,' I said, 'the entire town will know in under an hour.'

Peggy Sue looked on the verge of crumbling herself. 'That doesn't leave much time for out-of-town relatives to get here!'

I frowned. 'Who would that be? Mother only has one living relative that I know of – a brother in Oregon named Otto, who I've never met.'

'Oh?' Sis said, rather grandly. 'I get a Christmas letter from him every year.'

Well, la-de-da.

She went on, 'I know Otto and Mom didn't exactly get along famously – he was a year older – because, frankly, they were just too much alike.'

That was a slightly frightening thought, though I meant no offense to my late mother.

'Anyway,' Peg continued, 'the day after Mom died, I called

him with the news, and Otto said he was coming to stay for a few days.'

'When?' I asked. 'Here with us?'

Peg shook her head. 'No, he's booked at the Merrill. I thought he'd be in town by now. I'll call his cell, and let him know about the memorial celebration.'

'What does he do?' Jake asked.

'He's a professor,' Peggy Sue said proudly, 'at Portland State University.'

'Professor of what?' I asked.

'Medieval Literature,' she responded.

'Cool,' Jake said. 'But what can you do with that kind of degree?'

'Teach, apparently,' I said. 'Turn out other professors of Medieval Literature.'

Peg gave her head a haughty toss. 'Otto *also* has published books on literary criticism and theory.'

Those who can't write, criticize those who can (editors excluded, of course).

Jake was saying, 'Grandma once read me *Beowulf* as a bedtime story, which I thought was great. It's full of swamp monsters and dragons.'

'How old were you?' I asked.

'Oh. Three?' He shrugged. 'Anyway, she said we were related to the Danish prince.'

'Not sure he was real, Jake,' I said, adding, 'but maybe she'd met him in a former life.'

He laughed at that, but not Peg, who had been consulting her cell, and thrust the screen toward me. 'Here's a picture of Otto on one of the book jackets.'

There was a strong resemblance – this could be Mother, if she had bushy eyebrows and a handlebar mustache.

I asked, 'Where is she?'

Peg frowned. 'Who?'

'Mother. Her . . . remains.'

Jake said softly, 'In the library.'

I rose from the table.

On a shelf of Christie novels, including some first editions from the '50s and '60s, doubling as a bookend was a brass urn with an Egyptian cat head as a lid, and a hieroglyphic motif circling the base. Jake must have picked the receptacle out in a nod to his grandmother's tale of having once been reincarnated as Cleopatra's handmaiden, her chief bottle-washer and asp-handler. Keeping Mother company was Aunt Olive the Paperweight.

No, I wouldn't cry. Not yet. Not as long as there was a chance the urn held the ashes of a goat.

I turned toward the old upright piano, behind which was stored an antique school blackboard on wheels that Mother used to compile her suspects lists.

I rolled it out, selected a piece of white chalk from the lip, and printed on the left side:

THE MURDER OF NICOLE CHATTERTON

Suspect   Motive   Opportunity

And, on the right side:

THE MURDER OF CLARE SHIELDS

Suspect   Motive   Opportunity

Then, on the reverse side of the board (Mother always forgot to duck as she swung it down from the top), I put the headings:

CUSTOMER RECEIPTS   NON-BUYING CUSTOMERS
AFTER INVENTORY

Name: Name:

Jake spoke from behind me. 'I brought these from the shop, since I figured it would be closed for a while.'

I turned and looked at the box of receipts he was holding.

'Would you like me to help?' he offered.

I nodded.

He sat on the piano bench with the box in his lap. 'I'll read the names, and you write them.'

'How many receipts are there?'

'One hundred and four.'

I either needed another blackboard, or would have to print tiny. Still, the non-buying customer list would be comparatively small, because I had to rely on my memory, which could be spotty.

We had started on the receipts when – with him reading, me writing – through the library window, facing the street, came an unfamiliar car slowly up our driveway.

The four-door black sedan stopped behind our SUV, and after a moment a man with white hair and a lavish handlebar mustache from another era (both man and mustache) got out. He wore a three-piece brown tweed suit with brown and beige striped tie and had a tan trench coat over one arm.

'I think Otto has arrived,' I said with a tiny smile.

Who did Mother think she was fooling? And how dare she put us all through this charade?

The doorbell rang.

Was Pete Roeder on Archie Goodwin's doorstep? (Reference for Rex Stout fans only.)

'I'll get it,' I announced, hurrying to the front door, where I flung it open to face our guest.

'You must be Brandy,' the man said in a sonorous baritone.

'And *you* must be Uncle Otto,' I replied.

I grabbed one tail of the fluttering-in-the-wind mustache, and gave it a *rip*, yelling, 'Say uncle!'

Brandy's Trash 'n' Treasures Tip

Play the waiting game. If you buy everything at once to complete a collection, you'll end up over-paying. Besides, half the fun is the hunt for a bargain. Like a cashmere sweater that finally goes on sale.

NINE
Dead Ringer

B ut Uncle Otto's handlebar mustache was no rip-off –
that is, it did *not* rip off.

'*Owww!*' he yelled, touching his upper lip. 'Young
lady, what have I done to deserve such a rude welcome? And
I use the word "welcome" with considerable irony.'

Mortified, I said, 'You aren't my mother.'

'No. I would assume I am your uncle, and based upon
information shared by your late, lamented mother, prior to
her becoming late and lamented, your behavior makes you
Brandy, my niece.'

I said, shamefacedly, 'I am so sorry. Please come in. I
mistook you for Mother in one of her masquerades. Accepting
that she's really deceased isn't easy for me.'

His white head tilted back, and a gold upper incisor winked.
'Ah . . . I believe I understand. I grew up with Vivian and
know all about her deceptive and sometimes theatrical ways.
And we do have similar physical traits . . . but I assure you,
I am most definitely *not* her.'

I stepped aside for him to enter.

In the foyer, Otto handed me his coat, which I hung on a
hook before ushering him into the living room, where Peggy
Sue and Jake were waiting.

'*Uncle Otto!*' Peg blurted enthusiastically, rushing forward
to give him a hug. 'It's so wonderful to see you.'

'It does feel as though an eon has passed,' the man remarked.
He held her at arm's length. 'But time has been atypically
kind – you are just as fetching as ever!'

Schoolgirl Peg giggled. Fifty-year-old schoolgirl Peg,
that is.

Me, I suppressed a shudder. That warm mutual welcome
seemed just a tad creepy to me . . .

Otto's eyes went to Jake. 'And this fine young man must be Brandy's son.'

'Pleased to meet you, sir. Sorry it had to be this way.'

'Do call me Uncle Otto.'

Jake tried it out. 'Uncle Otto.'

Sushi, standoffish at first, pawed at our visitor's pants legs, perhaps instinctively knowing he was related to Mother.

Otto rubbed his hands together. 'Dreadful weather you have here. No wonder I left the Midwest! Perhaps you have something to take off the chill?'

Peggy shrugged. 'I can make a fresh pot of coffee.'

The mustache twitched. 'I was contemplating something a bit stronger than caffeine . . .'

'There's always cooking sherry,' I said.

Peggy shot me a look. 'Brandy!'

'It's all we have in the house,' I said, defensive. 'Ever since Mother's trip to Kalamazoo, we haven't kept anything around but rubbing alcohol.'

'I *prefer* port,' Otto said, 'but brandy *would* suffice.'

'I would suffice to do what?' I asked.

Jake squelched a smile. Peg looked pained.

I snapped my fingers. 'How about some Old Admiral?' I'd just remembered the bottle I'd hidden in an upper kitchen cabinet for a nip now and then, when Mother really got on my nerves. Not the first bottle.

'That would *indeed* suffice,' he responded.

So Brandy sufficed, returning a few minutes later to set a tray on the coffee table with the bottle and three crystal snifters plus a can of Coca Cola for Jake, then joined Peggy Sue and Otto on the couch. Jake was in the nearby needlepoint chair.

As Otto poured golden liquid into the three small glasses, he said, 'Let us have a toast.'

We picked up our snifters.

Raising his glass, Otto said, 'To dearly departed Vivian Jensen Borne, *at drekkia minni!*'

Whatever that meant. I downed my glass, as did Otto, Jake swigging some Coke. Peggy Sue faked a sip – her lips were sealed, as the Go-Go's once said.

'It's really not necessary for you to stay at the Merrill,' I said. 'You're welcome here with us.' There were only three bedrooms, but Peg and I could double up.

Peggy Sue agreed, however her breakdown of sleeping arrangements was different. 'Yes, please do – I'm sure Brandy wouldn't mind sleeping on the couch.'

'No, no,' Otto said. 'I am already quite settled in at the Merrill Hotel.'

Jake said, 'That'll come in handy.'

'How so?' Uncle Otto inquired.

'That's where we're having the party for Grandma on Sunday afternoon.'

Otto's bushy eyebrows climbed his forehead. 'How fortuitous that I arrived when I did. Is there anything I can do to help facilitate the festivities?'

Peggy Sue said, 'We might need you to identify people in some of the older photographs.'

'Happy to assist,' Otto replied with a rather grand nod, as if he'd been asked to present the Queen her scepter.

I had a special request. 'Could you tell us exactly how old Mother was? She never would share that information. She said that was on a "Need to Know" basis, and I didn't need to.'

'Yeah,' Jake chimed in. 'Grandma even had her birth certificate reissued. You can't trust the date on *that* piece of paper.'

Otto slapped one knee. 'That *does* sound like Vivian!'

'Mother's age?' I pressed, realizing I'd just witnessed a knee-slapper reaction, something you hear about but rarely see.

Otto stroked his chin. 'Well, now . . . let me ponder . . . I'm a year older than Vivian, so that would make her . . .'

We waited for the big reveal.

'I'm sorry,' he said, shaking his head, his smile tiny under the elaborate mustache, 'but I can't tell you her age without disclosing mine, which like my sister I keep to myself. I admit having, well, fudged the data on certain employment documents, so as not allow ageism to send me to the figurative showers. Unlike Vivian, however, I have never gone to the lengths of revising a legal document.'

So that was a 'no'.

The next hour passed pleasantly enough, then Otto took his

leave. Although I'd warmed to the man, it was disconcerting to look into his eyes and see Mother's gazing back. Even without her thick glasses.

The following days were spent preparing for the celebration of Mother's life – Jake scanning photos for the slide show to be played with big band music; Peggy Sue overseeing the catering and table arrangements; and me getting a notice of the event into the paper for anyone Norma's verbal wire service may not have reached.

I also gathered our extra author copies of the *Trash 'n' Treasures* true-crime books for attendees to help themselves. Sushi got into the act, letting me know, via her barks, which were her favorite covers: *Antiques Wanted*, depicting Sushi dressed as a cowboy; *Antiques Fire Sale*, her driving a toy fire truck; and *Antiques Liquidation*, wearing a witch's hat.

And I performed another task. After a discussion with Peggy Sue and Jake, and obtaining their consent, I purchased a small vault for Mother's Egyptian urn in the newly constructed concrete-and-glass mausoleum at Greenwood Cemetery, where we would gather for a private family interment immediately after the celebration of life.

Late Sunday morning, Jake, Peggy Sue, and I stepped out of the house into an unusually warm and sunny day for December, as if Mother had willed it so. My son had already loaded the back of the SUV with everything we needed for the celebration – except the Egyptian urn, and a Grecian column on which to display it, both to come later. The column had been retrieved by Jake from the prop room at the Playhouse, having been used in Mother's disastrous musical comedy production of *Oedipus Rex*, which she'd claimed Serenity just wasn't quite ready for. Yet.

Soon, on the top floor of the spacious ballroom, with its luxurious art deco patterned carpet, elegant crystal chandeliers, and panoramic view of the sparkling river, we met with the hotel's event planner, Tyler, a pleasant if rather officious young man in a tailored business suit.

Round tables had been spaced throughout the ballroom, each covered in white linen with a lovely fresh flower center-piece, delivered earlier by a local florist. Against one wall was a long serving table holding a variety of elaborate silver chafing dishes, trays, hot drink canisters, silver flatware, stacked white dishes, and folded linen napkins, waiting for the catered food to arrive from the downstairs kitchen.

Even though our newspaper notice requested that, in lieu of flowers, a donation be given to the Playhouse, folks generally did what they wanted to, and the air was filled with the sweet scent of dozens of arrangements. The ballroom looked breathtakingly elegant – fit for the bride and groom who should have been about to celebrate a shared life before them rather than someone else's life in the rearview mirror. Not that Mother had ever bothered looking in a rearview mirror herself, before her license was taken away.

Peggy Sue had moved off with Tyler, no doubt discussing something else she wanted done, and Jake was over in a corner connecting his Mac laptop to a large flatscreen TV on which to play the photos and music.

That left me to unload the boxes of *Antiques* books I'd wheeled up via a hotel brass luggage cart, which would be spread out on a rectangular table just outside the ballroom, between its two sets of double doors. My reasoning was that I didn't want anyone to feel obligated to take one in front of us, just to be polite, only to have the books end up at a Half-Price Books. Yes, I could be that petty, even in this circumstance (although I'm sure Mother would have agreed) (she's where I got the pettiness).

At noon, Peg, Jake and I left the Merrill, and went home for a light lunch – Uncle Otto had been invited, but opted for room service and a nap – then we got dressed for the event.

We had decided to wear colorful clothes, somber black not really appropriate in a setting of a more festive tone. Peggy Sue looked as if she'd stepped off a designer runway in her Chanel gold buttoned kelly-green tweed jacket with matching slender skirt and beige Ferragamo heels, which extended her long legs even longer.

Jake appeared older than I'd ever seen him – a sign of things to come – in a blue shirt and silver tie beneath a burgundy jacket with his private school's crest on the pocket, tan slacks, and brown shoes. I had picked out a pink cashmere sweater that covered my bottom, slimming (I hoped) dark gray slacks, and silver pointy-toed flats.

Mother always chastised me for describing what I was wearing. 'Readers know you're not naked, dear,' she would say. 'They'll put clothes on you.' To which I'd respond, 'But what if the wardrobe they imagine is too tight, or baggy, or a style I don't like?' Certainly, Peggy Sue would dislike being mentally dressed by anyone else, even if (like her) they subscribed to *Vogue* and/or *Harper's Bazaar*.

Peg and I donned coats – hers, designer; mine, don't be silly – Jake warm enough already in his school blazer. We proceeded outside to the car, where Mother and the column were waiting in the hatchback.

I had waffled about bringing Sushi along; she might have been able to identify who had slugged me at the shop, but could also be put in danger by that person, lured by a poison-laced popper or tampered-with tart. And I just couldn't take losing her, too. So Sushi stayed behind.

Since Midwesterners generally arrive early, we planned on having a reception line inside the ballroom to keep guests from converging upon us all at once. After Otto came down from his room – looking dapper in a brown houndstooth three-piece suit – we positioned ourselves against a wall away from the buffet table.

Peggy Sue was first, then me, Jake, Otto, and finally, Mother in her elegant Egyptian urn displayed on the Greek white column. (I'm sure she would have wanted to be first in line, possibly with a pre-recorded message; but she hadn't provided one, and anyway what does a sympathetic mourner say to an urn? I thought that would have been off-putting, and La Diva Borne would probably have wanted to have the final curtain call herself. Best let our guests work up to her.)

Until now, I hadn't realized how many times a grieving relative of the deceased hears, 'I'm so sorry for your loss,' and how many times they reply, 'Thank you.' But there were many nice things people had to say about Mother – whether they *had* to say them or not. And that did feel good.

All of Mother's friends came: her gal pals from the Red-Hatted Mystery Book Club – Alice, Frannie, Cora, and Norma; the

ROMEOs – Harold, Randall, Vern, and Wendell; new age guru/ death doula and hypnotist Tilda Tompkins; Hunter's Hardware owners Mary and Junior; bar-fly Henry; little person Billy Buckly; bank administrator/actress Gladys Gooch; tulpamancer Nona, accompanied by her new 'live' girlfriend; sports store owner Mark Wheeler; crematorium proprietor Ned Dunn; former trolley driver Daniel Riswold, apparently having forgiven Mother for the trolley mishap; and our lawyer Wayne Ekhardt, who managed to stand through the long reception line without falling over once. Or twice, for that matter.

Local dignitaries also arrived to pay their respects: Mayor Goodall (not surprisingly with neither wife Martha nor secretary Gwen); county commissioner Gordon (go ahead and chuckle, but that is his last name); and coroner Hector Hornsby.

Representatives of law enforcement were present: Officer Shawntea Monroe and her three young boys, Trayvon, Kwamie, and Zeffross; Acting Sheriff Chen, a deputy during Mother's brief stint; former sheriff Peter Rudder, who retired because of an ulcer Mother most likely had given him; and, of course, Chief Tony Cassato, keeping a watchful eye on yours truly.

I had a few close friends to console me: my BFF Tina, husband Kevin, and three-year-old BeBe; and Joe Lange, a friend from my community college days, and former Marine, who helped out at the shop when he was on his PTSD meds. The fact that I didn't have more friends, especially new ones since I'd come home, made me realize how tied to Mother I'd been. Or had I preferred it that way?

And there were others – faces I recognized and ones I didn't – all blurring together. And always, at the forefront of my mind, the question: *Could he, or she, be the killer?*

What a terrible way to thank people coming out to express their genuine sympathy.

One surprise guest showed up – Peg's husband, my biological father, Senator Edward Clark (who'd flown into our small municipal airport on a private jet, I learned). He arrived after the reception line had dissipated and we'd begun to mingle among the now boisterous crowd, buoyed by the good food, big band music, and one another's company.

I hadn't seen my father for almost two years, and he'd aged.

He was still very handsome in a tailored black conservative suit, but veering now into the Distinguished Gentleman stage. His years spent in politics – first as a state representative, then congressional senator, and now preparing for a run at the presidency – had taken a toll, adding lines to his forehead, more silver to his hair, and bags beneath his eyes, albeit carry-on size.

The dazzling smile, however, had not changed an iota, factoring in a touch of the bittersweet.

'Hello, Brandy,' he said warmly.

'Senator,' I said, then, 'Ah . . . Father, Dad.' I still hadn't settled on what to call him.

He asked, 'How are you doing since the attack?'

'All right. Apparently I have a hard head.'

The smile turned wry. 'That's what my wife has always said. But I think Peg meant it metaphorically, not literally.'

There were only two people on earth who could call my sister Peg – me, and him – without getting corrected by her.

The senator was saying, 'I hope Chief Cassato catches whoever is responsible for that, and probably those disturbing murders Peg told me about.'

'He will.'

'Not that any murder isn't disturbing.' He brightened slightly. 'Have you two set a date for the wedding? I'd love to be there, if I could.'

'No exact date,' I replied. 'Sometime in early spring. Although, don't be surprised if it happens on the spur of the moment at the County Recorder's Office.'

'Peg *would* be disappointed not being involved in the wedding plans.' He gave me a discreet wink. 'But perhaps that would be for the best.'

My thoughts exactly.

He said, strangely shy, 'But if you do go the more formal route . . . would you . . . consider allowing me to give the bride away?'

Here we were at Mother's funeral, essentially, and only now was I tearing up.

'Absolutely,' I said. I tried to hide my awkwardness with a question. 'When will you be heading back to DC?'

I'd noticed Peg packing her bags this morning, and assumed she'd be leaving with him.

'Right after the interment, I'm afraid. Big vote coming up.'

I was going to lose Jake, too. His father would be coming from Chicago later today to pick him up.

'I should mingle,' I said, adding, 'and it wouldn't hurt for you to shake a few hands. The votes are out there just waiting for you to snag.'

The senator chuckled, nodded, and we moved apart.

Across the room, Peggy Sue was examining a huge floral wreath on a stand. I crossed to join her.

'Will you *look* at this thing?' she whispered. 'You'd think our mother had won the Kentucky Derby.'

Pretty funny coming from Peg, who generally was humorless.

She was checking out the attached card. 'It's just signed, "Don". I suppose he's one of her many Lotharios who preferred not to use his last name.'

Mother *had* spent a night with this distant mourner (*Antiques Con*), but swore she and her host only ate clam linguine and played Scrabble at the retirement home where the old gent resided.

'Not *just* Don,' I said. '*The* Don. As in the New Jersey Godfather?'

Peg's eyes widened. 'Do I want to hear more?'

'Best not.'

She didn't read our books.

Uncle Otto approached, dabbing his nose with a white handkerchief. 'This is a lovely event, even if it does challenge any notion of good taste.'

'Thank you?' I said.

'I seem to have developed a severe case of the sniffles, my dears. If you'll excuse me for a few minutes while I return to my room for a fresh *mouchoir*.'

Whatever that was.

I moved on – the last thing I needed was to catch a winter cold – then crossed paths with Mark Wheeler.

'I'm going to miss Vivian,' he said with a sad smile. 'She was a big help more than once.'

He referred, of course, to the faux sports merchandise in his store Mother had brought to his attention.

'You'd been a great help to her, as well,' I replied with a raised eyebrow, meaning the alibi he'd provided Mother for Nicole's murder.

'I only learned about the death of that producer,' he said, 'and the attack on you, after I got back from the convention in Chicago last week. What terrible news to come home to. How are you holding up?'

'I'm doing all right.'

'Good. Good for you.'

Jake joined us. 'Hello, Mr Wheeler.'

The man smiled at my son. 'Please, call me Mark.'

'I overheard you went to the National Sports Collectors Convention,' Jake said excitedly. 'Did they display that record-breaking ball Aaron Judge hit? I'd have *loved* to see that!'

'They sure did.'

Jake asked, 'Do you think the guy who caught it should've given the ball back to Judge?'

Mark shrugged. 'And give up a million-plus dollars? That's a pretty hard thing to do, Jake.'

'Yeah, I guess it would be. Sure hate to be in that position.'

I left the pair to discuss the moral dilemma, glad to have Jake distracted from thoughts of the grandmother he so dearly loved.

Milling around, I noticed Uncle Otto had returned and was having his second run at the buffet table, piling a plate high. Also, at some point, Tony had slipped discreetly out after asking me if I wanted his support at the cemetery, which I told him wouldn't be necessary.

At three thirty, the guests had begun to leave, and by four, the only people remaining, apart from hotel staff, were family.

Previous arrangements had been made with the event planner to transport the leftover food to the Heart of Hearts building, a temporary housing facility for the homeless; the flowers were to be distributed to various nursing homes; and the remaining books boxed up for me to pick up at a later date, along with the Grecian column.

While Jake retrieved his laptop, and Peggy Sue took

possession of the urn, Uncle Otto returned to his room for a topcoat. Then we left for the cemetery, Peg, Jake, myself, and the senator in the SUV, with Uncle Otto following in his rental car.

Greenwood was the oldest and largest cemetery in Serenity, set among towering oaks and whispering pines with a view of the Mississippi in the distance. Unlike the more modern Memorial Park – which required all kinds of rules and regulations, such as approving only flat-plate headstones and how high a shepherd staff might rise (and what color and how many hooks) – Greenwood had character, and history.

City founders were buried here, many entombed in ornate stone crypts with stained-glass windows, small doors, and iron gates . . . tiny houses for dead people to live in. In the oldest section of the cemetery one could find humorous writings on the leaning headstones, like: *Mary Brown lived each day as if it were her last, especially this one,* and *Here rests good old Fred, a big rock fell upon his head.*

Plus there was an area that had been set aside long ago for children from the old orphanage who had succumbed due to various childhood diseases, now curable, the small plots with simple marble crosses watched over by a trio of winged angel statues.

But we were going to the newest section, where a modern mausoleum had been erected, a brick-and-glass structure with cathedral roof, large enough to contain dozens of vaults in both coffin and urn size, which had quickly sold out to Serenity's hoity-toity, who preferred to be above ground instead of below. Were they expecting a suntan?

I had been able to acquire a small vault only because the previous owner was a rabid Iowa Hawkeye fan and decided to have his ashes distributed (unlawfully) over the Kinnick Stadium football field – or at least so the rumor went – even though the artificial turf was regularly cleaned and disinfected. Did I mention rabid?

A private drive led to the mausoleum where I parked the SUV off to one side half on the grass, Otto drawing his rental up behind me.

The unseasonably warm and sunny day had turned cold and

blustery, gray clouds swirling overhead, beginning to spit a combination of rain and snow as we exited the vehicles, and made a dash for the brick-and-glass shelter.

Inside, our footsteps echoed on the marble floor as I led the way past cement benches to an empty compartment midway up the wall, its marble cover – a brass plate as yet unmarked – leaning against the base.

Since the Egyptian urn with cat's head was too tall for the height of the opening, Peg gently laid Mother on her side. Well, who wanted to stand up through eternity, anyway?

Then Peggy Sue, Senator Clark, Otto, Jake, and I stood facing the vault as my tearful sister read a passage from the family Bible (which I really didn't hear), before segueing into the Lord's Prayer (which I recited rotely). I still couldn't accept that Mother was gone.

Afterward, when everyone moved to the front of the mausoleum, I announced I would be staying behind until the vault was sealed.

'Do you want me with you?' Jake asked.

I looked at my son's earnest, wet-eyed face. 'No. I'd like some time alone with Mother.'

Otto offered to take Jake to our house after driving Peggy Sue and Senator Clark to the airport.

'That would be nice,' I told him.

'I'll probably be gone by the time you get back,' Jake said. 'Dad texted me he's already there.'

That was just as well. I didn't want to hear any false words of sympathy from my ex, who had never gotten along with Mother.

Otto touched my arm. 'Dear, would you like to sup with me later this evening? I noticed you didn't partake of anything at the celebration, and you need nourishment.'

He'd certainly 'partaken', chowing down royally.

'Thank you, but no,' I demurred. 'I just want a hot bath and some canned soup. But will I see you before you leave town?'

He smiled, displaying the gold incisor. 'Indeed. I'll be around for the next few days. This local group of yours, of retired men – the ROMEOs? – have invited me to take luncheon with them.'

'I think you'll enjoy their company.'

Otto smiled and nodded, then asked, 'What plans does my niece have for the morrow?'

Or, in human talk, *What are you doing tomorrow?*

'Since the shop is closed on Mondays,' I said, 'I'll be staying home and writing thank you notes.'

'Ah – an unenviable task that must be performed.'

A dirty job, but somebody has to do it.

After a round of hugs, and tearful goodbyes, Peggy Sue, Senator Clark, Jake, and Otto went outside, where the wind had died down, sleet having turned to snow, blanketing the ground and graves, cocooning bare branches and boughs.

I watched from behind the glass door until Otto's car drove off into the serene landscape.

Then I returned to Mother.

What was I going to say, among a mixture of sorrow and anger? That I never told her enough how much I loved her? Or scold her for leaving me so abruptly in such a cowardly fashion?

But I didn't get to voice any of that, because the door opened and a male cemetery worker entered, along with a flurry of snow. Wearing a parka and cap with ear flaps, and carrying a tool kit, the man stomped off his boots, then spotted me.

'Oh! I'm sorry,' he said. 'I can come back.'

'No, you're fine. I just wanted to make sure the vault was, you know . . .'

Final nail in the coffin sort of thing.

'I understand,' he said, approaching. 'It won't take long.'

I sat on a nearby bench while the man picked up the vault's marble cover and fitted it into the aperture. Then, from the tool kit, he used a canister of clear liquid rubber with a long tip (Flex Seal, clear) to glue the seams of the cover shut. (One more use for its product the company could advertise, besides plugging a hole in a boat or making a screen door float.)

With his task finished, he said goodbye with a nod, and left us.

I was still seated on the bench when my cell sounded. Expecting Jake or Peggy Sue – or Tony checking on me – I was surprised the caller ID window said: Matilda Tompkins.

Tilda, as everyone called the new age guru, lived directly across from Greenwood Cemetery in her white two-story clapboard house, which one might call shabby chic; from there she performed her hypnosis and taught mystical classes.

'What's up, Tilda?' I asked.

'I can see your car from my house.'

'. . . OK . . .'

'So you're still at the mausoleum,' she deduced.

'Yes, I'm there. Here.'

Where was this going?

'Well, Brandy, *she's* not.'

'She's not what?' I asked.

'There.'

'Who?'

Was I in an Abbott and Costello routine?

'Vivian.'

I got to my feet. 'Then where is she?'

'With me.'

My heart was in my throat. 'You mean, Mother faked her death and she's been staying with *you*?'

'No, no, no, I don't mean that at all.'

Hope turned to annoyance. 'I don't understand.'

'Vivian turned up on my porch a few minutes ago as a cat.'

For those not in the know, Tilda believed that the many felines showing up regularly on her doorstep after a burial at Greenwood were in fact reincarnations of real people whose spirits, for one reason or another, hadn't 'moved on' yet.

Oh . . . my . . . God.

Mother reincarnated as a cat? What a comedown from her former lives as Iras, handmaiden to Cleopatra, in charge of the Queen's asps; not to mention Matoaka, younger sister of Pocahontas and the true love of Captain John Smith; or Myles Carter, personal attendant to King George III, who had convinced the monarch that any talk of revolution by the American colonists was empty 'poppycock', among others.

'I'll be right over,' I said.

A few minutes later, Tilda met me at her door. Fortysomething, slender, with long golden-red hair, translucent skin, and a scattering of youthful freckles across the bridge of her nose, she wore the same Age of Aquarius clothes she'd had on at the celebration: white long-sleeved blouse, velvet patch-work long skirt, and Birkenstock sandals with socks.

I stepped out of the snow into a modest living room that doubled as a waiting area for clients, a mystic shrine of soothing candles, healing crystals, and swirling mobiles of plants and stars, incense hanging in the air like a fragrant curtain. It was also a hellhole for anyone allergic to cats, the comforting ambiance compromised by the ever-growing horde of cats lounging everywhere – floor, couch, various chairs, and all the windowsills.

'Which one is Mother?' I asked, my eyes already itching. Yes, I was allergic to cats.

Tilda, who called each cat by the real person's entire name, said, 'On the couch in between Eugene Lyle Wilkenson and Franklin Ellis Upshaw.' She was pointing to a matted, mangy, skinny gray one.

'Are you positive?' I asked, my eyes widening.

Tilda, wide-eyed, nodded solemnly. 'Vivian's was the only burial in Greenwood today.'

Oh my. Mother would be horrified to find herself stuck in that cat.

'I suppose . . . I suppose I should take her.'

'Her is a him.'

Doubly horrified!

Since I hadn't arrived prepared to adopt a cat, Tilda put together a box of canned food and a bag of kitty litter, and helped me out to my snow-covered car, where I put 'Mother' in the front passenger seat.

The drive home consisted of the two of us warily eyeing each other. Well, at least cats were popular in books. I'd probably write up this last case myself, right? (Isn't that what I've done?)

After struggling inside the house with both the Cat Care Package and Mother, she jumped from my arms, and came face to face with Sushi.

Neither looked happy about it, Sushi emitting a low, clenched-teeth growl, Mother arching her/his back and hissing.

I dropped to my knees to come between them, if necessary.

'Now, Sushi, be nice,' I said, as if the dog could understand me. More often than not, she seemed to. 'This is Mother, and you'll just have to get along with her.'

And to the cat, 'And Mother, you will have to respect Sushi's space . . . this is *her* house, too.'

Sushi's response was to turn her back and trot away.

And Mother's reaction?

She/he sprayed me with urine!

Exhausted, demoralized, and miserable, I marched upstairs to the bathroom, removed my stinking clothes, and had a long hot soak. Afterwards, I took two sleeping pills from the medicine cabinet, got into pajamas, and crawled into bed.

Then, and only then, did I finally begin coming to terms with Mother's death, and cried myself to sleep.

I dreamed she came into my room, sat on the edge of the bed, and said, 'Dear, don't despair. Everything will be all right. You must trust me. And, please return the cat to Tilda before it wrecks my Queen Anne furniture – that feline is *not* me.'

I woke up with a start. The dream seemed so real that I threw off the covers, and went into her room.

'Mother?'

No answer.

Shaken, and groggy from the sleeping pills – which must have triggered the dream – I returned to my bed, where Sushi and the cat were sleeping at the footboard, having made a tentative truce.

Brandy's Trash 'n' Treasures Tip

Joining a forum or blog dedicated to the types of sports memorabilia you like to collect is a good way to connect with others who share your passion, and gather information. You can learn from their mistakes, and they from yours.

TEN
Pinch Hitter

Dearest ones! This is Vivian speaking to you from beyond the grave . . . *not!* I wouldn't dream of trying to fool my audience, who are the smartest and cleverest and most astute of mystery readers. Not to mention your obvious good taste.

How did I fake my demise? I thought you'd never ask . . .

Immediately after leaving Brandy lying helpless in intensive care – not knowing if she would live or die – I approached Tony about an idea to feign my passing, inspired by Rex Stout's *In the Best Families*, a novel in which Nero Wolfe disappears to avoid certain death by his evil nemesis, Arnold Zeck.

Of course, Nero Wolfe had me at a disadvantage – I did not know who *my* evil nemesis was . . . just that he or she was endangering the lives of those I love.

The chief, due to the viciousness of my foe – and with the attempt on the life of his fiancée no small consideration – acquiesced to my plan, despite initial misgivings. He then approached two major players essential to the scheme: Hector Hornsby, who agreed to release to the media his coroner's report stating my cause of death as suicide (but not filing it so as to break the law or his oath of office); and crematorium owner Ned Dunn, who consented to switch my casket (during Peggy Sue and Jake's viewing I was chilled and holding my breath in the refrigeration locker) with a burnable empty one, which provided the ashes for the urn.

I also brought my grandson Jake into my confidence, knowing he would handle himself well and not give the plan away. Plus, I needed him to carry out certain directives while also keeping an eye on his mother's fragile psyche, as the girl is simply rudderless without me to steer her.

Peggy Sue was kept in the dark, as I didn't trust her to play any part very well (she had been simply dreadful as Guinevere in a high-school production of *Camelot*). Of course Brandy's acting experience was zero – she had even bobbled the non-speaking role of hat-handler in my one-woman production of the Scottish play.

Indeed, Brandy was the major problem. I agonized over my ultimate decision to exclude her, well aware of how hard she would take my death, but also realizing how effective and convincing she could be if she truly believed I was gone.

My dear brother Otto was instrumental to the success of the ruse, agreeing to come a great distance so I could become his doppelganger, allowing me freedom to move undetected among suspects when the time was right. We'd had our problems, Otto and I, but this situation united us and, I think, rather excited him as a break from that dull academic life of his.

The fact that Otto and I looked so much alike was both a plus and a minus. The pluses were obvious, the main minus being that someone might believe it was me dressed as my sibling (as when Brandy tried to painfully pull off Otto's mustache!). Therefore we took great caution for me not to emerge in my starring role too soon.

Also, when impersonating Otto, I had a hollow gold tooth that slipped over mine, and wore my contact lenses (which, when I was alive, I'd only used theatrically) since he didn't wear glasses. The rest was left to good theatrical makeup – wig, bushy eyebrows, mustache – great acting, vocal training in lowering my voice, and wearing an identical suit (with padding).

By the way, what was your opinion of Otto? Quite full of himself, I'm afraid. We do love each other, but I've discovered that affection is best displayed at a distance. On the other hand, he and I are there for each other when needs must. (A delightful British turn of phrase, that! Needs must!)

As to the celebration itself, kudos to Jake for carrying out my directives. The ballroom was lovely, the flowers beautiful – especially the wreath from 'Don' (I'll never tell) – and the food delicious. I was glad to be able to partake, as my meals had been few and far between, since my passing. And didn't

I look exquisite in the Egyptian urn, displayed on that Grecian column! (By the way, my production of *Oedipus Rex* was not the disaster Brandy claimed. I had a full house for the Prologue . . . it's just by the Exodus, people had exited.)

While I was, in general, pleased with the turnout for my celebration, I noted a few people absent. Although I will not name names, they know who they are, and can expect to be removed from my Christmas letter list forthwith. (Unless they were in the hospital or had died. A good excuse is a good excuse.)

You may ask how I was aware of such intimate details, as if I myself had attended the celebration? It's because, like Tom Sawyer, I did! But so did Otto. Do you recall when my brother told Brandy he was returning to his room for a fresh handkerchief? That was when we made a switch for the first time, so that I could test my impersonation (and get some mileage out of the food I was paying for). Then, a short while later, I returned to the room to get an overcoat for the trip to the cemetery, but it was *Otto* who went, not *moi*.

Isn't stagecraft simply magical?

And now, to address the break-up of the bride and groom who had booked the ballroom only to bail, thus freeing it up for my party. Did I, or did I not, have anything to do with that? Well, you're sitting there in my head – you tell me. Short answer: yes. Longer answer: I'd found out the presumptive groom was still 'seeing' an old girlfriend on the side. Nothing wrong with maintaining old friendships, you say? At the Shady Rest Motel? (The almost bride will eventually thank me – after all, I did cover all her expenses. Win win! And, anyway, the cake was to die for.)

Since Brandy had informed Otto she planned to stay home this Monday, writing thank you notes, I wouldn't have to worry about encountering the girl while out and about in disguise, conducting my investigation. Also, to avoid any happenstance wherein two 'Ottos' might be seen at different locations at the same time, my brother pledged to remain in his hotel room, not answering the door, and letting the room phone ring.

(I was to take his cell, and to further the illusion, use his rental car. *Whoopee!* Back behind the wheel once again. And I didn't hit a single mailbox and was not at all tempted to make a shortcut through a cornfield.)

My first stop on this snowy Monday morning was to pay a visit to Gladys Gooch, the bank officer who'd promised to provide a list of customers who'd withdrawn a substantial amount of cash after Nicole's death and prior to Clare's demise.

I was working on the assumption that someone on that list had killed Nicole to frame me, and been seen by Clare leaving the suite just before my arrival. Clare, rather than going to the police, likely blackmailed the killer in order to finance her own podcast, and in so doing sealed her fate. Karma's a bee!

While parallel parking in front of the bank, I may have run into a teensy-weensy spot of trouble, admittedly being out of practice, and might have put a weensy-teensy itsy-bitsy dent in the rental car. So I hoped Otto had opted for the added insurance.

Inside the bank, a female receptionist escorted me to Gladys' office, where I entered to find the woman standing behind her desk.

Usually prim and proper, Gladys looked a tad disheveled this morning, suit rumpled, hair somewhat askew, face puffy, the child undoubtedly taking my death hard.

'Mr Jensen, I'm so sorry about Vivian,' Gladys said, extending a hand, which I took briefly, suddenly aware that perhaps I should have applied some faux hair to my fingers.

'Yes,' I said, easing into one of two client chairs. 'Such a terrible blow. Vivian was quite a magnificent person . . . a great detective, accomplished actor, superb former sheriff . . . one of the most illustrious denizens of this fair city. Perhaps *theee* most illustrious.'

Gladys, seated now, reached for a tissue on her desk. 'You . . . you sound just *like* her . . .'

Not *too* much like her, I hoped! Was my voice not low enough? Still, Gladys seemed to be swallowing my impersonation, hook, line, and sinker. Of course, she was something of a dope.

Gladys went on, 'Vivian used to describe herself in those very words.'

The woman daubed her eyes, then blew her nose – *honk!*

'Gladys,' I said, 'I must ask a favor, one that would be kept just between us girr . . . folks.'

'Of course,' she sniffled, 'if I can.'

'The list, dear. Do you have it? The one you were to give dear Vivian, regarding large cash withdrawals?'

She goggled at me. 'Mrs Borne *told* you about that?'

'We kept no secrets from each other.'

Gladys fidgeted in her chair. 'Well, I don't know. It was risky enough before, but . . .'

'Don't you think Vivian would want me to carry on in her stead?' I asked, sitting forward forcefully. 'To find the killer who drove my poor sister to such terrible depths as to take her own life? Depriving Serenity, indeed the *world*, of one of its most fascinating inhabitants?'

'But . . . well . . . it could cost me my job if someone found out.' She was shaking her head. 'I'm sorry, Mr Jensen, I just can't take that chance. Giving the list to her was one thing, but after all . . . I don't really *know* you.'

(My God, the woman had scruples after all! Who could have anticipated that?)

'I see,' I said. 'There is nothing I can say to make you change your mind?'

Her chin lifted. 'I'm afraid not.'

I needed that list! Without it, my investigation was kaput! Zip, zally, zilch, no advancement, nothing.

I stood, then moved to the open office door and closed it.

Seated once again, I leaned forward. 'Gladys . . . I'm going to take you into my confidence because Vivian informed me of what a great actress you are.'

'She said that?'

'Indeed.' Well, when hypnotized by Tilda, anyway.

Gladys smiled. 'Golly. That sure means a lot to me.'

To think I was having difficulty getting something out of a woman who said, 'Golly!'

'So,' I continued, 'I need you to remember your training.'

'OK.' She squinted hard.

'Ready?'

'Yes.'

Slowly I removed the handlebar mustache.

She frowned, befuddled. 'If you wish to wear a fake mustache, Mr Jensen, that's between you and your conscience. You needn't worry – your secret is safe with me.'

And you thought I was being harsh, calling her a dope!

'No, Gladys,' I said firmly but quietly. 'It is *I* – me . . . Vivian.'

Confusion crossed her face. 'But isn't Vivian . . . dead?'

Obviously not!

'Gladys,' I said using my own voice, 'if you don't give me that list I'm going to tell everyone what you did for me in the town of Antiqua. *And* I'll give that part in *The Producers* to some *other* actress.'

Her eyes grew huge, and her mouth opened wide, and it was only thanks to my new hips that I managed to lunge forward across the desk in time to stifle her squeal with my inadequately hairy hand.

'Now, Gladys,' I said, 'you must promise to be quiet.'

She nodded, and I removed my hand.

I returned to my chair.

'It . . . it really *is* you,' Gladys said, still confused but happy.

'Yes, dear.'

'But how . . .?'

'There will be time enough for that later. It's enough to know that I've gone deep undercover. Right now I have a killer to catch. The *list*, dear.'

She opened a drawer, drew out a sheet of printer paper, and placed it in front of me.

My contact-lens-covered eyes – one designed to see up-close; the other distance – slowly scanned the printout. Three names stood out: each had withdrawn the same amount of cash, ten thousand dollars, the day after Nicole's death.

Borrowing a pen from the desk, I circled the bank account numbers attached to the three names.

'Gladys,' I said, pushing the paper toward her, 'was the money withdrawn from these accounts ever *redeposited*, say within a week?'

Her fingers clicked across her computer keyboard. Less than a minute later, Gladys – having changed into a thorough professional, like Clark Kent emerging from a phone booth as Superman – said, 'As a matter of fact, yes.'

By the way, George Reeves will *always* be Superman to me.

I asked, 'Which of the accounts?'

Her eyebrows rose. 'Actually . . . all three.'

'The same amount for each withdrawal?'

'Oh yes – ten thousand. Is that helpful?'

I beamed at her. Or at least a mustache-less Otto did. 'Oh, yes, dear. Very.'

'Is there anything else you want to know?' Gladys inquired.

'That information should be quite sufficient.' I had my suspects now. 'Thank you, dear – I'll forever be in your debt.' Then, in the voice of Ulla in *The Producers*, I said, '*Go to vork!*'

Tears formed in her eyes again, happy ones this time. 'I'm so glad you're alive.'

'As am I.'

Now all I needed to do was keep it that way.

I was moving toward the closed door when the woman called out, 'Oh, Vivian!'

I turned.

'Don't forget your mustache!'

She was holding it out, like a hairy centipede.

'Oh, my,' I said. 'That would have made quite the blooper.'

Moments later, having reapplied the mustache with some spirit gum stashed in my suitcoat pocket for just such a contingency, I made my exit.

I had finagled an invitation to meet the ROMEOs (Retired Old Men Eating Out) for a late lunch at the Riverside Café, set for the uncivilized hour of eleven a.m., just so they could get the early-bird discount on the luncheon Blue Plate Special. Since the diner was directly across the street from the bank, I left the mildly dented rental vehicle parked where it was.

Arriving in the café at ten thirty, in order to get my bearings, I was surprised to discover the men already seated at their usual round table in the back . . . or perhaps they'd been here for hours, taking breakfast as a prelude to their early lunch, and lingering over coffee.

The café, with its Mississippi River theme, was a popular eatery in Serenity – the food was good, came fast, and was reasonably priced. At peak times – nine for breakfast, twelve for lunch – it could be hard to get in, but at the moment, the long narrow room was only half-filled.

I made my way past the booths, each overseen by a framed nostalgic wall photo of life on the Mississippi River – steamboats, barges, tugs, fishermen harvesting mussel shells with long poles (an illegal practice now) – and wound my way through the tables to reach the ROMEOs.

Quite a few of the old boys had flown south for the winter, but present this morning, by happenstance, were the four (surviving) founding members.

Harold was an ex-army sergeant somewhat resembling the older Bob Hope, right down to the ski-ramp nose, jutting chin, and thinning hair. Some years ago, after both our spouses had passed, he proposed marriage. But since I had no desire to be assigned permanent KP duty, I'd declined. (I also didn't respond to 'Hup-two-three-four' terribly well.)

Randall was a former hog-farmer who might best be described as an unsophisticated Sydney Greenstreet. In the past, I avoided sitting next to him, or even downdraft. But since then, he had leased his vast land to corn and soybean growers, while still living in the farmhouse and tending a large vegetable garden, giving himself time to shed his porcine bouquet. But the sense memory lingered. Randall, too, once asked me to the altar, but, as with Harold, I demurred.

Vern reminded me of the suave if vaguely villainous movie star Zachary Scott, particularly when I wasn't wearing my glasses. The retired chiropractor had also wooed me, but I discouraged him; he had a habit of cracking his neck that over time would have gotten on my nerves, although free adjustments was a consideration in his favor.

And then there was Wendell, a doppelganger for Leo Gorcey (that's what Google is for, young people!), and a one-time riverboat captain whose career was cut short when he fell asleep at the wheel and t-boned a barge. Wendell owns a small working replica of the steamboat *Delta Queen* with a capacity for a hundred people, which he will take out on short tours for a hefty price. And, yes, he also proposed, but Tugboat Annie is one role I can't picture myself in.

I must admit I'd once overheard a discussion of Viagra among this group, and the thought of an elderly gent locked and loaded and chasing me around his house or farm or boat did not appeal to my finer instincts.

As a rule, women were not welcome to join in on their conversations, but I was an exception, something akin to the way the Rat Pack let Shirley MacLaine hang with them back in *Ocean's 11* days. But even she, like myself, was given only so much latitude from the boys – which included information.

You see, the ROMEOs had the best dirt on who did what to whom and where and how in Serenity, putting any female kitchen-clatter cluster to shame, which was my reasoning for accepting the invitation to join them this morning. Even though an outsider, 'Otto' might hear something pertinent to the murders; and as an outsider, not involved with the community, scheduled to soon return home a thousand miles away, he (me!) would be taking any shared secrets along.

Now you might be asking yourself, why not be (almost) forthright with these men? Tell them that I (Otto) am picking up the investigative mantle for Vivian, and looking into the murders? Seeking whoever attacked Brandy, and trying to learn what caused my sister to take her life? That might seem the easiest and most direct way to gather information.

Ah! But two of my three suspects were not only men of means and influence in the community, but friends of the ROMEOs. While not yet retired, those two possible killers were viewed as the coming wave of new oldster members for this group, and casting any aspersions upon them might well be met with stony silence, the men closing ranks.

Regarding my third suspect, a female, she also was well entrenched into the community, with a wicked tongue that could (and has) cut many a man down to her size (5' 4"). I've witnessed more than a few ROMEOs jaywalk across a busy street, hobbling with their three-pronged canes and risking life and limb, just to avoid her.

No, the best tactic for Otto was the one Vivian always used: trick them. Deceive.

Usually, when I approached this group, I gave them my best Mae West impression of 'Hello, boys,' which I almost did, but caught myself just in the nick of time.

Instead I gave them W. C. Fields: 'I spent a year in Serenity once – I think it was on a Sunday. Just jesting, gentlemen!'

They smiled and welcomed me and gestured to a waiting chair.

'Thank you for the invitation,' I said as Otto.

After receiving a variety of greetings, I filled the empty chair between Randall and Vern.

I wasn't too worried about being in rather close proximity of the gents, where my disguise might be examined more thoroughly; they all wore glasses with preposterous prescriptions, and had complained about how hard it was to focus with their multi-graduated lenses.

I started right in buttering them up: 'Vivian always spoke so highly of your group.'

'She certainly was one of a kind,' replied Harold, nodding.

'There'll never be another quite like her,' responded Randall.

While these comments from the ex-sergeant and former pig-farmer might sound well and good, they could be taken in a negative way, as in, 'She was one of a kind. *Thank God!*' and, 'There'll never be another like her. *Fingers crossed!*' These were the kind of ambiguous assertions one often heard backstage at Playhouse performances.

Thinking Vivian deserving of more respect – where was the effusive adulation? – I repeated what I'd said to Gladys: 'Vivian was quite a magnificent person . . . a great detective, accomplished actor, superb former sheriff . . . one of the most illustrious denizens of this fair city. Perhaps *theee* most illustrious.'

'Vivian did think highly of herself,' Vern said, cracking his neck.

'More than *anyone* else did,' added Wendell with a chuckle.

What next? Deny ever asking me to marry them?

'You know what I'll miss?' Harold asked. 'Viv angling for a wedding ring.'

The others nodded and laughed.

Where was the management of this establishment? Someone needed to inform him his restaurant was infested with vermin!

I was beginning to think it wasn't such a good idea to pretend to be dead, and be subjected to what others really thought of you.

A waitress appeared to take our orders, the men choosing today's Blue Plate Special – meatloaf, mashed potatoes, and green beans – with me opting for a dinner salad with no dressing, which wouldn't compromise my mustache.

After the waitress departed, Harold said, 'You must forgive us, Otto, for having some fun at Vivian's expense.'

When I couldn't defend myself!

The ex-sergeant went on, 'But so often she got the better of us.'

Former chiropractor Vern smiled. 'That's right. We'd try to worm information out of her, but she'd always manage to turn the tables.'

Former hog-farmer Randall added, 'If she shared anything with us, it was stale old gossip we already knew.'

Mini-steamboat owner Wendell nodded. 'We never figured that out until *after* we'd picked up her check and she was gone.'

That brought laughs all around, including from me.

Across the table, spokesman Harold leaned forward. 'Can I – *we* – assume you are resuming the investigation where Vivian left off?'

Busted. 'I am.'

Vern, next to me, said, 'Our group was very fond of your sister. She brightened our otherwise dull lives with her escapades, and it pains us that someone tried to frame her for two murders, and attacked her daughter, leading Vivian to take her life.'

Harold, on the other side of me, asked, 'So how can we help?'

Without implicating Gladys, I told the ROMEOs that I'd obtained information on three people who had each withdrawn ten thousand dollars from their bank accounts right before Clare's death, then redeposited the money soon after. Wasn't

it possible one or more of these three were being
blackmailed?

'After all,' I concluded, 'so many motives for extortion are
available here – poison-pen letters, an attack on my niece, and
two murders? Was the same person responsible in each
instance, or do we have a multiplicity of miscreants?'

'Who are these three?' Harold asked.

The others gazed at me intently.

I said, 'Mark Wheeler, Robert Goodall, and Norma Crumley.'

Wendell shook his head. 'Well, you can pretty well eliminate
Mark. He always takes a substantial amount of cash to sports
shows to get a better deal.'

He must not have done much wheeling and dealing, because
the money had been redeposited, post-convention.

Vern spoke softly, 'The mayor seems like he might be a
good candidate for blackmail.'

I said, 'You're referring to the affair with his secretary.'

The retired chiropractor raised an eyebrow. 'Robert had
another ill-advised affair some years ago before he became
mayor. And that podcaster – Nicole? – could have found out
and threatened to reveal it in her podcast.'

Clare, as producer, would likely also have had this information, which she could have then used for blackmail . . . putting
herself in a murderer's sights.

I frowned. 'But the podcast was supposed to be about, uh,
my sister. And the plentitude of murderers she apprehended.'

'That was only part of it,' Harold replied. 'Nicole also
intended to paint a very ugly picture of our town and
citizens.'

For someone who prided herself on being in the know, I
seemed to have had my head buried in the sand lately!

'Still,' I said, 'the mayor would have weathered that bit of
scandal, if it was consensual.'

Randall leaned toward me to speak in my ear. 'Maybe so,
but rumor is, that long-ago affair? The girl was underage.'

That storm he couldn't have weathered.

'What about Norma?' I asked, almost as an afterthought,
thinking I knew everything there was to know about my
Red-Hatted Mystery Book Club friend.

The men exchanged looks.

I waited.

'All right,' Harold sighed, 'but you didn't hear this from me.' His voice dropped to a whisper. 'Did Vivian tell you Norma had been the social director of the country club since, I don't know, forever?'

'Yes,' I said. 'She mentioned that . . . also that the woman recently stepped down from the position.'

Harold asked, 'Do you know *why*?'

I didn't, and shook my head.

Harold continued, sotto voce, 'Because she embezzled funds from the social account – oh, the money was returned once it was discovered missing, and everything got hushed up . . . but *that* is the reason for her sudden "retirement".'

What a fool I'd been, not leveling with the ROMEOs in the past. I needed to disguise myself as a man more often!

Our food arrived, but I was in no frame of mind for even one small bite of my salad.

'Gentlemen,' I said, 'you must forgive me, but I must take my leave.'

'We understand,' Harold said.

'You have a lot to think about,' replied Vern.

'And a killer to catch,' responded Wendell.

'Gonna take that salad?' asked Randall.

I pushed it toward him, and stood.

'Thank you, gentlemen. Vivian couldn't have had any finer friends than you.'

And I meant it.

I had misjudged the ROMEOs, seeing the group as an obstacle to overcome. Oh, they could be irascible and contrary old codgers; but, ultimately, these men had good hearts.

But I still didn't want to marry any of them.

I doubted as Vivian I'd ever change my approach with this not so-wild bunch. At their age, they would miss the cerebral jousting, and the chance – however slim – to get the upper hand with me.

And what of the readers? Who doesn't smile when Lucy Van Pelt once again tricks Charlie Brown into trying to kick the football, only to have her pull the ball away at the last second?

Outside, the cold air felt refreshing, reinvigorating, as I mentally prepared myself for the greatest challenge of my life: to expose my own Moriarty.

My own Arnold Zeck.

Vivian's Trash 'n' Treasures Tip

Cash usually goes further than any other form of payment at a trade show. The seller doesn't have to worry about a check bouncing, or putting up with an added credit-card charge. Plus, there's something irresistible about the immediacy of real money being flashed in someone's face – as they say, 'Cash is King.' And heaven help the dealer who tries to out-negotiate Queen Vivian.

ELEVEN
Home Stretch

That's right, dear reader! 'Otto' (which is to say me, Vivian Borne) is back, to continue reporting on my/our undercover operation.

After my informative lunch with the ROMEOs, I drove several blocks to All Sports Artifacts, where my parallel parking acumen appeared to have restored itself. What a pleasure to be behind the wheel again! A pity it took masquerading as a man to be able to do so. The enduring prejudice against female drivers is unforgivable.

Within the shop, Mark Wheeler was not behind the long glass counter as usual, but the aroma of a microwave meal greeted me and indicated the owner's backroom presence.

I cleared my throat loudly, in a most male fashion, and moments later the handsome proprietor came from the back through a curtained doorway, dabbing his mouth with a paper napkin.

'With apologies, sir,' I said, 'for disturbing your lunch.'

'That's quite all right, Otto,' Mark replied, the wadded-up napkin disappearing into a jeans pocket. He had met the genuine article uncle at the celebration of my life, and apparently they were on familiar terms. 'I have to grab a bite whenever it gets slow.'

'Salisbury steak?' I inquired, sniffing the air.

He smiled. 'Yeah – Hungry Man.'

'I much prefer Stouffer's,' I said. 'Especially their tuna noodle casserole.'

'Ha! I believe I detect a fellow connoisseur of frozen dinners.'

'As a bachelor with limited cooking skills,' I admitted, 'I have to be.'

We both chuckled.

Mark's face turned somber. 'That was a very nice celebration for Vivian yesterday. Glad I got back in time to attend.'

I nodded. 'I feel certain my esteemed sister would have been pleased that you did. And delighted with the event in general.'

He paused, small talk exhausted. 'Is there something can I do for you, Otto?'

'Indeed. I would like to get Vivian's grandson Jake something for Christmas that might help cheer the boy up. This has hit him rather hard, you know. He adored that wonderful grandmother of his.'

'I'm sure that's so.'

I leaned against the glass of the counter. 'He'd mentioned you'd gone to a sports convention in Chicago. Perhaps you purchased some merchandise of interest?'

'Unfortunately, no,' Mark said. 'The prices are really getting out of hand. Truth is, I returned empty-handed – a wasted trip, really.'

Hence the reason for redepositing his ten thousand dollars.

'How very disappointing,' I said.

'Very is right. To stay in business, it's necessary to add a profitable amount for re-sale, which would have made anything I'd bought at the show beyond most customers' reach.'

'I quite understand.'

Mark glanced around. 'If I recall correctly, the last time Jake was in my store – which I believe was some time this past summer – he'd been eyeing a Gale Sayers autographed football.'

'How much might that run?' I asked.

'Five hundred.'

Now, I – Vivian, not Otto – happened to know as a die-hard Chicago Bears fan that the legendary Hall of Fame running-back had signed a plentitude of footballs, especially near the end of his life, so this pigskin seemed over-priced. Plus, I'd just spent a lot of money on a very expensive if well-earned celebration of life.

Still, I needed to buy something to justify dropping by.

'While I *am* fond of Jake,' I hedged, 'I hesitate to spoil the boy.'

Mark scratched his trim beard. 'Tell you what, since Vivian meant a great deal to all of us . . . how 'bout I sell you the football for half the price?'

Now that *was* a good deal, and a wonderful way for me to thank Jake for his help.

I smiled, a nice opportunity to show off my gold-capped tooth ('Love Potion #9,' anyone?). 'Done!'

After paying for the item, I returned with it to Otto's car, then drove three blocks to the Heart of Hearts building, which had diagonal parking in front, meaning no fender-bendering to worry about (until I backed out into traffic, anyway – these drivers were so much crazier nowadays than in my prime!).

The building used to be an old YMCA, but after a new state-of-the art facility was erected on the outskirts of town, the city purchased the brick structure to use its dorm-style rooms as temporary housing for the destitute and those fleeing domestic violence.

Residents were offered one hot meal a day – lunch – and I knew Norma was scheduled on Mondays to help serve it up. Perhaps, after her recent financial indiscretion, the normally not-prone-to-volunteer-for-anything female may have been trying to whitewash her soiled reputation.

Inside, two wide staircases offered a choice of ascending or descending. The up staircase led to the main floor with a hotel-type reception counter, a communal room for watching TV, a small library with donated books, and private sitting areas where residents could meet with visitors as the dorm rooms were off-limits to guests.

The down staircase – which I took – went to the basement where the pool had been covered over and transformed into a large dining area with long tables (not retractable as in *It's a Wonderful Life* – isn't that a delightful scene when Jimmy Stewart and Donna Reed fall into the pool?). The adjacent locker room had become the kitchen, volunteers dispensing food on trays at a large open window, in a chamber not haunted, one would hope, by the dripping wet ghosts of naked men and boys. (Apologies for my vivid imagination.)

Most tables were nearly full, the crowd consisting of more than just the residents, word having gotten around to others in need of a meal that today's offering was special: in addition to the usual bland, fattening fare were such delicacies as lobster rolls, crab cake poppers, cucumber canapés, fried calamari, and stuffed mushrooms, all donated out of the generosity of the late Vivian Borne.

I spotted Norma flitting amongst the tables, carrying a carafe of coffee, refilling empty cups – no behind-the-kitchen-counter role for her, requiring a hairnet to ruin that costly coiffe, or apron to cover her designer attire – this waitress bore arms and neck bejeweled and baguetted, completely tone deaf as to the circumstances.

'Well, welcome, Mr Jensen,' she said as I approached. 'Wonderful turnout, isn't it? We had a little prayer for Vivian before the meal.'

'How thoughtful,' I replied. Then: 'Might I have a private word, my dear?'

'Certainly,' Norma smiled, her Shalimar perfume dueling to a tie with mystery meat gravy.

She handed off the carafe to another server, then I led us over to one side, just beyond the tables.

'More private,' I said.

'Oh! I understand,' she responded, batting the spidery fake eyelashes. 'Come with me.'

Good grief! Did the woman think Otto could possibly be interested in becoming husband number four?

I followed Norma through the kitchen and into the pantry, garnering quizzical looks from the kitchen staff.

She turned to me and purred, 'What can I do for you, Otto?' No 'Mr Jensen' now!

I got to the point. 'I'm assuming the role of chief unofficial investigator into the murders of Nicole Chatterton and Clare Shields . . . and of course the brutal attack on my niece Brandy.'

Norma's face fell, or would have, but for a recent facelift. 'Oh. Well, good luck on that effort.'

'So, naturally, I have a few questions for you.'

She frowned. 'What about? I'm sure I can't tell you anything you haven't heard or don't already know.'

'Shall we start with ten thousand dollars withdrawn from

your bank account to pay Clare for not disseminating information regarding a certain indiscretion of yours?'

Norma's eyes grew large with alarm, confirming my supposition correct. She took a step back. 'How . . . how do you know about that?'

'About which? The blackmail payoff? Or the embezzlement?'

She summoned some outrage. 'How *dare* you! I don't have to speak to you any further. You're even worse than your late sister!'

I didn't think an insult like *that* was necessary, although I *was* relieved she hadn't seen through my masquerade.

With a shrug, I said, 'Fine. I'm sure Chief Cassato would be interested in my well-founded opinions.'

She considered that.

'All right,' the woman said. She took a deep breath. 'After Nicole was killed—'

'By *you*, you mean?' I interjected.

'No! Why would *I* kill her?'

'Oh, I don't know. Perhaps because she was going to divulge the embezzlement on her podcast.'

Her eyes goggled in their spidery setting. 'But I didn't find out she was planning to do that until later! I just thought Nicole wanted to interview me as a friend of Vivian's. It wasn't until *after* that dreadful woman had been murdered that her associate, Clare, told me Nicole planned to conduct an ambush interview. But all that is irrelevant, Mr Jensen – I have an alibi for the time Nicole died. I was having bridge club at my house. My God, you're a terrible detective! Vivian would have known *all* of that.'

Touché.

I said, 'But then Clare demanded money to keep quiet.'

'She did.'

'Which is why you killed her.'

'No!' She shook her head emphatically. 'I did no such thing . . . I was going to pay Clare off, all right, but not the way *you're* saying. No, I even had the money in hand. But, after thinking it over, I was sure she'd only ask for more. That there would be no end to it. So I never kept our appointment.'

'At All Inclusive.'

She drew in a breath and let it out. 'Yes. Then, the next day when I heard *she'd* been killed, I redeposited the cash.'

'Do you have an alibi for the time Clare died?'

The thrice divorcee shook her well-coiffed head of hair; it didn't move an inch. 'I was home alone that night. So were a lot of people. I didn't know I'd need an alibi.'

Which gave Norma both a motive and the opportunity to, in copycat fashion, dispatch the producer. And she could have planted the potato masher at the crime scene, as her name was on Brandy's blackboard list of people who'd recently been in our shop.

The woman was asking, 'What do you intend to do, Mr Jensen?'

'Nothing for the time being,' I responded. 'I still have another suspect to question.'

'Is that what I am? A suspect?' She touched my arm. 'You have to *believe* me . . . I may have stolen some funds – which I returned, let me remind you. But I am *not* a murderer.'

'You wouldn't have to be a murderer,' I said, 'to have attacked Brandy.'

Her eyes were buggier now than her lashes. '*Of course* I didn't do that! What reason would I have to hurt Brandy? I *like* her! It was *Vivian* I couldn't stand.'

Ouch.

'So that's why,' I said, 'you sent my sister those threatening letters.'

Now her eyes, fringed in black, disappeared into a tight frown. '*What* threatening letters? For heaven's sake, Mr Jensen, even as much of a buffoon as Vivian was, she never accused anyone of something without first knowing the *facts*!'

And, with a little shove, Norma pushed me out of her way.

My next stop was City Hall and the office of Mayor Robert Goodall. The three-story limestone structure was built around the same time as the nearby courthouse, though minus any of the latter's Grecian grandeur. Small, austere, with chugging window air-conditioners, its rooms heated by ancient hissing radiators, City Hall seemed to shout, 'No taxpayers' money wasted here!'

Set back from the street, the building had an odd shape, as if having been square until a toothless giant took a bite out of one corner, the architect allowing for space on the grounds where citizens – cheering or protesting – could gather.

Finding no parking spaces within a block radius, I parked my rental buggy in a loading zone in front and took my chances that my brother wouldn't get a ticket.

A well-salted walkway preventing city lawsuits led me along the snow-covered grounds dotted here and there with small trees and park benches, then past a human-size replica of the Statue of Liberty painted a garish gold. At the wide steps of the front entrance, I ascended to a small two-columned portico where American and Iowa flags fluttered valiantly in the icy wind.

Goodall's office – the largest of them, which wasn't saying much – was up another flight, his door always open (he liked to brag); but first they'd have to get by the lovely if officious Gwen.

I had a pitch ready for her, but the moment I stepped into the reception area, she looked up from the mound of work on her desk and said, 'The mayor is expecting you, Mr Jensen. Please go on in.'

Which told me 1) Goodall had been warned by Norma of my imminent visit, and 2) that they were aware of being mutual victims of Clare's blackmail scheme.

I entered the mayor's personal office, closing the door behind me. Some improvements to the room had been made during various mayoral regimes – new carpeting, modern furniture, custom-made bookcases. But it still retained that temporary feeling, like an apartment from which the current inhabitant might be ousted at any time, and it was prudent that all personal items might fit in a single cardboard box.

Goodall, his suit impeccable, his grooming glistening, rose behind an uncluttered desk with a polite smile. This was the type of administrator who passed tasks on to his secretary, leaving him free to glad-hand.

'Please take a chair, Mr Jensen,' the man said in a monotone.

I did.

He resumed his seat, then leaned forward, elbows on the desk, tenting his hands. 'First and foremost, my sincere condolences on the death of your sister. No matter what I may have thought of her—'

'Would that have been negative in any way?' I interrupted, wanting to know.

The tent folded, and Goodall sat back. 'Since you asked – I found Vivian Borne arrogant, intrusive, maddening, and overbearing.'

I was *not* arrogant!

He continued, 'But, as I was saying, no matter what I might've thought of her, it distresses me that she was driven to take her own life. Vivian did have some admirable qualities.'

'I like to think so. What would you say those qualities were?' I needed some ointment for the sting, and would settle for just about anything, no matter how insincere.

His eyebrows went up and his gaze went down. 'I would say, uh . . . she was honest, forthright, and, in her own way, well-meaning.'

I came to my sister's defense. 'You forgot to mention that if it weren't for Vivian, there would be a multitude of murderers running around your fair town.'

Goodall nodded. 'There is at least a grain of truth in that . . . although the notoriety that brought to Serenity was rather more negative than positive.'

'Like attracting the attention of Nicole Chatterton, for example?'

'Yes. Like that. And I'd like to address that subject without further interruption, if I might.'

'You have the floor.'

His eyes met mine and were unblinking. 'I did not kill Nicole or Clare. Neither did I attack Brandy, nor send threatening letters to Vivian . . . please!' He raised a palm. 'I said no interruptions.'

I shut my mouth.

'Yes, Norma called to tell me you were investigating. And yes, I knew she was being blackmailed by Clare because, as it happens, we were at the bank at the same time, withdrawing the exact amount of cash – ten thousand dollars. But, unlike Norma, no specific time had been set for my payoff, so – after hearing Clare had been killed – I redeposited the money. Regarding Nicole, I *was* at the Merrill with Gwen the evening the podcaster was murdered, but was provided an alibi by Vivian when she spoke to us as we left our room.'

That much was true. I'd given the mayor an alibi, just as Mark had provided me with one.

Goodall went on: 'The night of Clare's death, I was one of several speakers at a charity dinner at the Country Club, and there are dozens of people who can swear I never left the dais.' He paused. 'Now, Mr Jensen, that's all I'm going to say without my lawyer present. So I wish you a good day . . . and hope to see you return home soon.'

The door suddenly swung open, as if Gwen had been listening on her intercom and heard her cue. Maybe she had.

Discouraged, demoralized, deflated, I departed City Hall (lovely use of alliteration, don't you think?) (but I forgot despondent!) and returned to Otto's rental where a yellow parking ticket had been left under a windshield wiper. He could afford it.

I needed to go somewhere to think. To mull this through – somewhere I wouldn't be bothered in the early afternoon's chill, where I could get a hot drink.

Fuming, I abandoned the car where it was, and hoofed the short distance to Hunter's.

Were my detecting days over? Had I finally met my match? Or was this disguise weighing me down? It was hard enough just being Vivian Borne!

Inside the store/bar, holiday shoppers were keeping Mary busy in the hardware section, but the rear was nearly deserted, except for several farmers at a table discussing whether to plant corn or soybeans come spring. Hapless Henry, however, was (unsurprisingly) seated at the bar.

Junior, spotting me, called out, 'Otto ol' boy! What say a drink on the house in honor of Vivian?'

I took a stool one down from Henry.

'What'll ya have?' asked Junior, having had plenty himself.

About to tell him the usual hot toddy without the toddy, I

caught myself – Otto would hardly order Vivian's specialty. Nor her back-up, a Shirley Temple. Not a man's drink, that.

'Port wine,' I said.

Junior looked at me as if I had cauliflower growing out of my ears. 'Sorry – only beer and hard liquor.'

'Whisky, neat,' I said, strategizing only to have a few sips. Still, perhaps I should use Otto's cell and check if any Greyhound buses were leaving Serenity for Kalamazoo any time soon.

While Junior turned away to tend to my drink, I swiveled to the former surgeon, a tumbler in front of him.

'And how are *you* doing, my good man?' I inquired. '"Henry", isn't it?'

He looked at me, shockingly clear-eyed. 'Just fine, Mr Jensen. May I offer my condolences on Vivian's passing?'

Well, dear reader, I nearly toppled off my stool!

'Henry,' I said, dumbfounded. 'You're . . . you're . . . you're *sober*!'

'I am at that. Strictly a ginger ale tippler these days. Ginger and Seven, hold the Seven.'

I'd been trying to get him off the sauce for years, with no luck.

'How did you manage it?' I asked.

'With the encouraging help of a new friend,' he said.

Who didn't seem to be with him at the moment.

'Well, congratulations, Henry,' I replied. 'Vivian would be so proud of you.'

He nodded. 'I'm only sorry I hadn't been of any help to her in catching the murderer.'

To keep our conversation more private, I closed the gap between us.

'You *did* give Vivian some rather strange leads,' I said.

'Did I?'

I nodded. 'You said the killer was Arthur Fax, when Artie died several years ago. Then you claimed it was Allison Knight, and Allie is a hundred and one if she's a day.'

Henry frowned. 'I didn't say any of that. What I said was "artifacts", as in All Sports Artifacts, because I couldn't remember the owner's name. Then I said, "in the alley that night", because that's where the All Sports fella was seen, behind the Merrill Hotel.'

Good Lord! Mark Wheeler was the killer?

But how could this be? He was talking on his cell to Nicole from his home only minutes before the podcaster was bludgeoned to death in her hotel room. And Mark was at a convention in Chicago when Clare was killed and Brandy attacked. Also, what possible reason would the sports store owner have in sending me those threatening letters?

I needed to know the exact time Henry had seen Mark in the hotel alley the night Nicole died, so I asked him.

'Oh,' Henry replied, 'it wasn't *me* who saw him.'

'Who was it, then?'

'My new friend.'

'Where can I find this friend?' I slid off my stool, ready to roll.

Henry pointed to the vacant one on his other side.

'She's sitting right there. Her name is Zelda.'

A major if interesting set-back. Imaginary friends could not give testimony in court. Still, Zelda had always been accurate.

Henry was saying, 'Zelda says "Hi," by the way, and congrat-ulates you for getting the meaning of her "The Pit and the Pendulum" reference.' Henry whispered: 'We're both relieved that you aren't dead, and your performance as your brother is quite impressive.'

I quietly addressed both Henry and the empty stool. 'Thank you, dears, but it seems faking my death has been for naught.'

Otto's cell sounded and I answered.

'Is it OK to talk?' Jake asked.

Walking a few paces away, I replied in my natural voice, 'Yes. Go ahead.'

'Grandma, I've been doing some checking back here in Chicago, because, well, when I talked to that Mark guy at your party about the sports convention, he said something that didn't line up quite right.'

My pulse quickened. 'Go ahead.'

'He said they showed Aaron Judge's record-breaking home-run ball . . . but the guy who'd caught it changed his mind

about bringing the ball at the last minute. And that's not all
. . . I went to the security company that keeps track of when
each person uses their badge to get into the convention. See,
you walk through these gates kinda like metal detectors except
they record the radio frequency identifications in the badges
and—'

'Cut to the chase, dear.'

'Mark's badge was never used . . . so he never went! He
didn't attend that convention at all.'

My bad knees nearly buckled.

'Jake, you are the salvation of my deteriorating career as
a detective!'

'I did good, huh?'

'Better than good.'

'Grandma? I think *I* started this whole thing,' he said, his
voice cracking, whether from emotion or emerging manhood,
I couldn't be sure. 'Accidentally.'

'How so?'

'That time I told you about the fake Air Jordan 2 OG tennis
shoes that guy was passing off as the real deal, he must've
got real mad at you. But hid it.'

'Jake,' I said sternly, 'you are not responsible for that man's
actions.'

'. . . OK. But he just had to be the one who wrote you those
terrible letters. Listen. I love you, Grandma. I'm really glad
you're not dead.'

'I love you, too. And I am very happy you are alive.'

No sooner had I ended the call than a second one came
through, with no ID. But I recognized the number.

'Mr Jensen?' Tony said in a businesslike manner. 'This is
Chief Cassato. Could you come over to my office?'

'You can drop the pretext,' I replied.

A pause. 'The forensics specialist has identified the weapon
used on Nicole and Clare . . . and Brandy.'

'What was it?'

'A golf club. An *iron* to be specific.'

Mark Wheeler sold autographed golf clubs! And one specifically came to mind: a driving iron Brandy had commented on,
signed by Patty Berg who had used it to win the 1946 US

Open Championship, priced at a ridiculous two thousand dollars, ensuring it wouldn't sell. The irony that Brandy and I had employed the same tactic of overpricing merchandise we wanted to keep was not lost on Vivian Borne. (Nor is the cleverness of juxtaposing 'iron' and 'irony'.)

'Chief, I have news for you, as well,' I said. 'I will be there toot sweet.' Then, recalling too many movies where a witness waits to divulge the killer to authorities in person, only to be murdered before he or she can, I added, 'Mark Wheeler is our man.'

Since the police station was closer than going back to Otto's car, I hurried on foot – my breath puffing white like a steam-engine stack (that was a good one!) – where soon one loud rap on the back door brought Tony.

I followed the chief into his office, where he shut the door.

Seated in front of his desk, the chief now behind it, I shared Jake's intel that Mark had not attended the sports convention.

Tony nodded. 'So he had the opportunity to kill Clare, *and* attack Brandy.'

'Indeed so.'

He frowned. 'But not Nicole, as he was talking on his cell with her moments before she was murdered.'

I arched one of Otto's hairy eyebrows. The left one. 'But *was* he?'

The chief gestured open-handed. 'The call history of both cellphones indicates as such.'

Suddenly, clues began tumbling into place, like colors aligning on a Rubik's Cube (although I never could solve one of those things).

Leaning forward, I said, 'Mark discovered – or strongly believed – that Nicole was going to confront him with selling faux merchandise during their interview, and decided to silence the podcaster. When he heard from Clare – who was at Hunter's at the same time as Mark that evening – that I had an appointment with Nicole at seven thirty, Mark thought he'd found a perfect opportunity to frame me for the deed.'

Tony nodded and listened.

I continued: 'Mark left Hunter's earlier than he claimed,

entering the hotel through a service door in the alley to avoid security cameras, and going up the back steps to Nicole's suite to knock on her door. She answered, he entered, using the pretext of confirming their filming. When Nicole went into the bedroom for her briefcase, he followed, and hit her with the room phone. Stunned, she was unable to fight off his further assault with the short driving iron he'd concealed beneath his overcoat . . . one I believe is displayed in his store.'

Tony was taking this all in.

I said, 'To give himself an alibi, Mark took Nicole's cell-phone, called it with his, answered hers, and – playing out a short conversation – made it appear they were talking. No one really knocked, cutting short their non-existent exchange – that was meant to put me in his debt. Then his plan was to leave the front door of the suite ajar with the dead bolt, so I would enter, find the body, and be accused of doing the foul deed.'

His forehead tensed. 'But you arrived early . . .'

'I did, right after Mark had turned the dead bolt and cracked the door, but before he'd had a chance to leave. Now, how he avoided exposure by me is supposition. He could have slipped into Clare's adjoining room as the two women prob-ably kept that door unlocked . . . or he could have hidden behind the curtain in the outer room and waited until I entered the bedroom, before he slipped out. One thing is clear: in exiting either the suite or Clare's room, he was seen heading to the back staircase by Clare as she came out of the elevator.'

Tony took over. 'After Mark gave you an alibi – to clear himself, he had to clear *you* – Clare then knew who'd murdered her employer. But she didn't turn Mark in.'

I shrugged. 'Why would she? Mark had done Clare a favor, giving her the opportunity to take over a very popular podcast. And Clare needed money. From there, it was an easy step for Mark to dispatch the blackmailing Clare using the same golf iron, but planting an antique potato masher at the scene taken from our shop to incriminate me once again.'

Tony sat back. 'It all fits.'

I felt redeemed.

The chief asked, 'You say the golf iron is in his store?'

'It was a few hours ago when I – rather, "*Otto*" – was there.'

Tony smiled a little. 'Perhaps Otto should buy it.'

'Mark wouldn't risk selling it to anyone, that's why it has a high price tag, remember.' I smiled. 'But I have a plan on how to get it.'

'Does it involve breaking and entering?' the chief asked wryly.

'No. It involves a white robe, angel wings, a harpsichord, and a lookalike golf iron.'

The chief sighed. 'Spare me the scenario until later. Right now we have a more pressing matter to deal with.'

I nodded. 'Telling Brandy I'm alive.'

'I don't know who she's going to be madder at,' Tony said. 'You or me.'

'Might be a tie on the ol' scoreboard,' I said glumly.

Vivian's Trash 'n' Treasures Tip

Collecting autographs of athletes inducted into the Sports Hall of Fame is generally a good investment, whether the honor took place while the athlete was playing, or sometime after retirement. Of course, it matters *what* they sign, an actual baseball being better than the hurried scribble I got on a greasy empty single pizza container after spotting Ernie Banks coming out of a men's room at O'Hare Airport in 1996.

TWELVE
Down to the Wire

I had spent the morning and early afternoon at the Duncan Phyfe table writing 'thank you' notes to those who had sent flowers, or given a donation to the Playhouse, or added more than just their signature to their sympathy cards for Mother's passing.

Sushi lay curled at my feet while the cat had taken over the living room couch, the truce between the animals coming to an abrupt end during breakfast – specifically, a squabble over sausages after I'd given each one, with Sushi thinking she should have seniority rights over both. Henceforth commenced a lot of barking and hissing, which ended when Sushi got sprayed, forcing me to pause in my work to give the pooch a bath, adding insult to her injury.

After my hand cramped and penmanship became close to illegible, I broke for a late lunch to select a casserole from the many covered dishes (each with a thoughtful note of support) left on the porch while I was at the cemetery.

Casseroles – a staple of Midwestern potlucks and funerals – were always a gamble; you never knew for sure what lay beneath that layer of cheese or breadcrumbs. Could be comfort food, or culinary discomfort.

I was about to withdraw one of these mysteries from the fridge when my cell, abandoned on the table, sounded. I returned to my chair and answered it. Jake was calling, probably to check up on me, and I put the cell on speaker.

'Hi, Mom,' Jake said.

'I'm doing fine,' I said, preemptively.

There came a long pause. 'I have something to tell you.'

He sounded troubled, but not *in* trouble.

'Go ahead,' I said. He'd probably had a fight with his father.

'Are you sitting down?' Jake asked.

'Yes.' Must've been a doozy of a blow-up! Both my ex and our son could be stubborn.

The deep breath Jake took was clearly audible over the line. 'Grandma's alive. I just talked to her.'

For a few moments his words didn't register. Then I gasped for air. 'Uh . . . wha? What . . . uh?' Repeat. Rinse. Repeat.

Jake waited a bit for me to calm down. 'You have to know I wanted to tell you sooner,' he said.

'Really?' I managed to ask through sobbing. Indignation was already setting in. 'How *much* sooner?'

A long pause. 'Pretty much right after you woke up in the hospital.'

That much sooner.

This was Mother's work, obviously!

'She says,' Jake said, 'it was a necessary "ruse".'

'Who else knew?' I demanded. 'Peggy Sue?'

'No. No, she thought Grandma was dead, too.'

Somehow that was a consolation. Small, but a consolation.

'Did *Tony* know?' I pressed.

'Uh . . . yeah. He's the one who kinda gave the plan an OK . . .'

My cheeks burned. How could the man who claimed to love me put me through such mental and even physical torture?

Stiffly I said, 'Anyone else?'

'Well, Uncle Otto. He was in on it from the git-go, so Grandma could pretend to be him after the trip to the cemetery, and do her investigating. Oh. And the coroner, you know, to make it look official . . . who else? The man who runs the crematorium, so he could switch Grandma's coffin with an empty one.'

Now I was seething. 'So, then, not *everyone* at the "Celebration of Life" was in on it. There were others like me, left out.'

Jake continued, 'Mom, it was important you believed Grandma's suicide was real, to fool the murderer, and keep you and, really, all of the rest of us safe. And it worked.'

'What do you mean, it worked?'

'Grandma has cracked the case. She's sure it's that guy who runs the sports collectibles shop.'

Mark Wheeler? With my mind already a jumble, I had difficulty making a murderer out of that affable individual.

The doorbell buzzed.

'Someone's here,' I said.

'That's probably Tony to tell you about Grandma,' Jake said, adding quickly, 'Mom, please don't be mad at him. He loves you a lot.'

'Right,' I said.

I ended the call, and looked at the hundreds of thank-you notes culminating in hours of work spread out before me, each now in need of a postscript: So sorry, false alarm . . . here's your check back. At least the envelopes hadn't been sealed.

On my way to the foyer, the couch cat lackadaisically stretched its body, paws showing sharp claws that had already done enough damage.

'As for you, "Mother",' I muttered. 'It's back to Tilda's, first chance I get.'

As soon as I opened the door, I could see Tony realized I knew Mother was alive.

'Jake called you,' he said.

I nodded. 'At least *someone* in this thing had a conscience.'

I looked beyond Tony to the figure in the front passenger seat of his car. 'Is that the real Otto or the faux one?'

'It's Vivian.'

'Get her in here.'

Tony signaled to Mother, who got out of the vehicle, wearing the same suit Otto had worn at the celebration – or one just like it, perhaps altered to fit her a little.

Joining us in the entryway, she removed the short white wig, bushy eyebrows, and handlebar mustache, standing there an actor only partly still in costume. 'I would imagine, dear, that you must be terribly put out with me.'

Understatement alert!

Terribly, horribly put out. Angry beyond words. But the anger evaporated, and I threw my arms around her, and held myself to her and her to me and cried on her shoulder.

'There, there,' Mother said soothingly, patting my back like she used to do when I was little and had hurt myself. And I'd been just clumsy enough for that to be a somewhat regular occurrence. 'Everything's going to be all right.'

Sniffling snot, I pulled back and spoke through clenched teeth. 'Don't you think for one minute I'm *ever* going to forgive you.'

'Yes, dear, I quite understand,' Mother said. 'We *are* rather prone to holding grudges in this family.'

I looked at Tony. 'And that goes for *you*, too, buddy boy.'

He nodded just a little. 'You have every right to be upset with both of us.'

'With *all* of you! Everybody but me in this thing was trusted with this, this . . .'

Mother's eyebrows rose hopefully. 'Magnificent plan?'

'I was thinking,' I said, 'unforgivable insult.'

Sushi, roused by the commotion from her nap beneath the dining-room table, trotted in to investigate and immediately began jumping up at Mother, realizing the Big Dog had returned to the pack. It took all three of us to calm Sushi down.

'Let's talk in the dining room,' Mother said. 'And I could use some coffee.'

I headed to the kitchen, where I already had a fresh pot going, and – moving like a zombie – gathered cups and cream and sugar on a tray. When I joined Tony and Mother a few minutes later, she was seated where I had been, sifting through the stacks of sympathy cards.

'Will you just look at all of these,' she exclaimed, pleased beyond words. 'Such an outpouring of love! And so many checks to the Playhouse!'

Setting the tray on the table with a little too much force, rattling the cups, I said, 'Those checks will have to be returned, of course.'

Mother looked aghast. 'Let's not be hasty, dear. Shouldn't we give people the option to let their donation stand? Perhaps we could suggest we're raising funds to improve our sound system. Personally, I have no problem being heard at the back of the house, but these youngsters simply don't know how to project.'

I looked at Tony, seated next to her, who rolled his eyes.

'That's a hard pass,' I said firmly.

She sighed. 'If only you had already cashed them.'

Mother lives.

Resigned to that fact, I poured coffee into the cups and passed them around, then pulled out the chair across from Tony.

I locked eyes with Mother. 'What's made you zero in on Mark as the killer?'

She laid out her case, Tony interjecting evidence including the report from the forensics expert as to the type of weapon. When they were done, I was convinced.

But I did have a few questions of my own. 'Why didn't Mark finish me off, as he had Nicole and Clare? Could he have panicked after Sushi went for help?'

'I don't think he intended to kill you,' Mother said. 'It was more about inflicting pain on me. He was my Moriarty, and it became clear even before I determined his identity that I had to protect you in any way I could.'

'But what made him your ultimate foe?' I asked. 'What had you ever done to him?'

Her shrug was rather grand, undercut only by the male clothing she still wore. 'I cost Mark money, by pointing out faux merchandise in his store several times. Eventually he knew I'd come to the conclusion that his business may not be legit. Exposing him was only a matter of time, no matter how nice he feigned to be.'

We fell silent. Then, still hurting, I blurted, 'You should have *told* me.' The remark was meant for both Mother and Tony.

Mother said, in a reasonable tone of voice not typical of her, 'You must understand, dear, we did what I felt had to be done to keep you and Jake and little BeBe safe – not to mention myself.'

'Jake told me about the others who you let in on your secret. Who else rated higher than me? Gladys at the bank? Henry at Hunter's? Zelda the Tulpa?'

'She *is* a most insightful person,' Mother said.

'She isn't a person at all!' I felt like I might cry again. Or strangle her. '*I* could've played a part, too.'

Mother's smile was infuriatingly patronizing. 'Ah, but you did, Brandy. You played a very important, crucial role – in fact, you were the lead actor.'

I grunted, and folded my arms. 'I just didn't know I was in a production.'

Mother continued, 'Don't you see the entire ploy hinged upon you believing I was gone? You were convincing because you *were* convinced – your swollen eyes, puffy face, the sniffling when anyone mentioned my name, and the tearful farewell at the cemetery . . .'

'You're not making this better,' I said, 'by making it sound like you enjoyed witnessing my very real grief.'

She waved a hand. 'You must admit you couldn't have given such a stunning performance otherwise.'

Mother was right, of course. I was no actor. I really *had* screwed up the job of hat-handler in the Scottish play.

Tony, who'd wisely not weighed in on this exchange, changed the subject. 'Vivian . . . you mentioned a way to get that golf iron.'

I asked archly, 'Might I be included in the planning this time?'

'Yes, dear, you are included,' Mother said, ignoring my tone, and presented her plan.

Which sounded completely weird and wacky and almost certainly would totally fail. Or be crazy enough not to.

I don't know what Tony thought. His eyes had glazed over.

Vivian here.

I think I handled Brandy quite deftly, don't you? Although (as indicated) we Borne girls do tend to hold a grudge, I'd best check the toes of her Uggs for pine needles before ever wearing them again.

After our confab around the table, the chief returned to the police station to gather some equipment, while Brandy and I – in my Otto persona once again – (accompanied by Sushi) made a trip to the Playhouse.

Situated among cornfields about ten miles west of town, the theater began in a barn where community actors would gather and perform on a makeshift stage to the delight of

family and friends – much in the tradition of Judy Garland
and Mickey Rooney shouting, 'Come on, gang – let's put on
a show and save the farm!' Only not on the MGM payroll.

Over the years the barn had been transformed into a modern
performance facility, with new additions, periodic remodeling,
and a state-of-the-art auditorium – thanks to my relentless
haranguing for donations from Serenity's well-heeled residents who supported the arts, and others just glad to get rid
of me. (What a fine sound system those Celebration of Life
donations would buy!)

But now the old barn's roof needed replacing, resulting in
buckets being placed hither and yon whenever there came a
hard rain. Only a few weeks ago, during opening night of
The Elf Rebellion, moments before the curtain rose inside,
thunder cracked outside, and before the stage manager could
rush for the pails, Little Billy Buckly made his entrance
coming down a high slide in Santa's workshop. (Imagine here
the sound of a slide whistle.) Rather than stopping center
stage, he slipped through a puddle, went flying off the apron,
and into the orchestra pit.

Billy came away with nary a bruise, having made a soft
landing in the spacious lap of Mrs Zybarth, the first chair
flutist, and the audience, believing this to be part of the performance, howled with laughter, resulting in a show-stopping
standing ovation. Needless to say, this happy happenstance
was kept in, a child's mattress substituted for Mrs Zybarth's
girth.

Where was I?

This being a Monday, the theater was dark – inside as well
as out – and as Brandy steered our SUV up to the rear stage
door, a security light was triggered.

After disembarking into the icy air, I handed Sushi to Brandy,
which enabled me to use my key in the lock. Once inside, I
halted the alarm countdown, then turned on a few lights, illu-
minating only the areas of the theater we needed: Wardrobe
and Props.

Immediately Sushi jumped from her mistress's arms, and
trotted down the hallway to the prop room, where she relished
sniffing among the thousands of items stored there. And why

not? Where else could a dog find such oddities as a skull to chew on (*Hamlet*), or an alien man-eating plant to bark at (*Little Shop of Horrors*) – not to mention a cornucopia of odd odors that had fermented over years of being trapped in a windowless room.

But my destination was Wardrobe, where I perused the overstuffed racks, searching for a white choir robe as Brandy trailed behind holding open a plastic garbage bag like Santa waiting for the elves to fill it.

'You're going to look ridiculous,' she said, still grouchy about my faked death. 'Especially when you add wings and a harpsichord.'

'That's precisely the point, dear,' I replied, continuing my search.

'I don't get it.'

I turned to Brandy. 'Mark seems to relish a cat-and-mouse game – therefore, the more unrealistic I am the better.'

Since the girl still looked skeptical, I said, 'Use your imagination, dear . . . The man is nestled all snug in his bed, while visions of sugar plums dance in his head. When out on the lawn there comes such a clatter, he springs from his bed to see what's the matter.'

'I'm familiar with the poem,' she said testily. But a faint smile forming on her lips spurred me on.

I gesticulated to really sell it. 'Away to the window he flies like a flash, tears open the window and throws up the sash!' My words came quicker and quicker. 'The moon on the breast of the new-fallen snow gives luster of midday to objects below. And what to his wondering eyes doth appear? Why it's Vivian Borne, descending from heaven – or rather, Otto *impersonating* me, impersonating an angel, in some typically daffy Borne-born plan. He watches amused, that is, until a golf iron appears from beneath the white robe. And I disappear as mysteriously as I appeared.'

Brandy's skepticism did her features no favor. 'And I suppose you think Mark will go immediately to his store to see if that golf club is his? The murder weapon?'

'I do indeed.'

She smirked. 'What if he just waits until morning?'

'He won't.'

'Why not?'

'Because, dear, the man won't be able to help himself, once the game is afoot.'

'Mother, he doesn't *know* he's Moriarty!'

Coincidentally, in the adjacent prop room, Sushi was attacking her own foe – a large black toy dog with horns and glowing eyes that had been featured in *The Hound of the Baskervilles*.

Funny story about that production. Whenever possible I like to use live animals in my plays – such as the aforementioned horses that ran across the stage in the Ascot scene of *My Fair Lady* (which may possibly have been a misjudgment) – as they lend realism and the kiddies simply love it. Anyway, I had a big black hound dog named Elvis all decked out, ready to respond to commands from his owner who was hiding behind a rock on stage during the climactic scene. It was simply thrilling to see that animal growling and snarling, pretending to attack Sherlock (probably my best previous male portrayal).

All went well until one matinee when Lila Farnsworth snuck in her miniature French poodle, Mitzi, because the woman couldn't find a sitter, since she never left her dog unattended. Anyway, during the confrontation between hound and Holmes (*moi*), the little dog ran up on stage, and proceeded to chase the hound around with such a ferocity that most of the scenery collapsed, as did the audience in laughter. In the end, Mitzi was captured, and the hound came through unscathed, but that was Elvis's farewell Playhouse performance.

In the children's Christmas prop section, I selected wings – which were nothing like something out of the Victoria's Secret angel ads, but then neither was I – and a toy harpsichord. Brandy added the finishing touch to her elf's bag: a halo made of silver pipe cleaners attached to a headband.

With my task complete, we turned off the lights, turned on the alarm, locked up, and left, prepared to present a very special Christmas pageant.

But back home, I tried on my costume – wearing a white

unitard beneath the robe for warmth – and stood before a full-length mirror in my bedroom and found myself standing there clucking at the glass.

'Not quite the effect I'd been after,' I said, disappointed. The concept had played better in my head, I fear.

'May I suggest a slightly different approach?' Brandy asked. 'Despite my lack of theatrical expertise?'

'Please do.'

She took the harpsichord from my hands, removed the halo, and wings, and tossed them on the bed. After leaving the room – I could hear her rummaging around next door in her closet – Brandy returned with a long white gauzy scarf, which she wrapped around my neck so the ends trailed down my back.

She unpinned my chignon, silver hair cascading in waves to my shoulders, and whitened my face with powder and a puff from the vanity. To create the effect she was after, Brandy dimmed the lights, turned on the ceiling fan, and the breeze blew the ends of the scarf up and out, creating the illusion of wings.

The image in the mirror was startling!

I *was* an angel.

'*Now* you're dead,' Brandy said.

'A heavenly apparition!'

'You're not out to amuse that creep,' Brandy said. 'You need to unsettle him.'

'My dear,' I replied, 'as Henry Higgins proclaimed, "I think you've got it."'

She touched a hand to her chin and gave me an appraisal. 'You should ditch the contacts, though, and wear your glasses, to look more like you.'

Downstairs, the doorbell rang, the chief arriving at the rendezvous hour of ten o'clock.

After a nod of approval from Tony of my Brandy-directed appearance, we convened in the dining room, where he placed a black duffel bag on the table and unzipped it.

'You recall how this works?' Tony asked, extracting the electronic surveillance equipment – transmitters attached to earbuds allowing communication between us three.

'Will I be able to *talk* this time?' Brandy asked, referring to our last use of such gear (*Antiques Liquidation*), when she was allowed only to hear.

'Yes, you can talk,' Tony replied patiently.

'Good,' she responded curtly.

That man was in the doghouse for sure! He already seemed like a whipped puppy.

After the chief wired Brandy and me, he tested the equipment – including his set – to make sure all was working. Then the transmitters were turned off.

'Where is Mark now?' I asked.

'At home,' Tony said. 'Officer Monroe has had him under surveillance since he closed his store this afternoon. She'll call me when the lights go off.'

After going over a few more details, the chief departed.

Brandy and I retired to the living room, where the drapes had been closed, then sat on the couch in the dark, Sushi curled up next to her, the cat on my lap, purring as I gently stroked its fur. Perhaps we could keep it, if I could stop Brandy from calling it 'Mother'.

As Brandy listed and snored, I remained alert with that special excitement I always had waiting in the wings before stepping out onto the stage. And, as usual, my audience had no idea what it was going to get!

A little past midnight, my cell sounded.

'It's a go,' the chief said. 'Don't forget to turn on your transmitters once you get there.'

'Roger Wilco,' I responded. Then to Brandy, who was awake now, 'Showtime, dear. Let's make magic, shall we?'

We donned warm coats. Then I picked up an iron selected earlier from my golf bag, while Brandy gathered a large tote packed with items we needed. We went out into the still of the night (isn't that a lovely song?).

In the middle of Serenity was a wooded area dotted with expensive houses on expansive lots, secluded from one another. Behind the homes lay an access road where Brandy parked the SUV.

After exiting the vehicle, I removed my coat and slid the golf iron beneath my robe, holding it in place from the outside with one hand. Brandy retrieved binoculars from the tote, and we activated our transmitters.

'Testing, one, two,' I said.

The chief's voice came through my earbud. 'I'm in position.'

Tony was to be in his own car, across the street from Mark's residence, but down a ways.

'I have a view of his truck in the driveway,' he continued. 'Brandy? Can you hear me?'

'Yes,' she said, her voice also coming via my earpiece.

'All right, ladies. Good luck.'

The moon – visible through wispy clouds floating by like spirits on a mission – helped guide us through the forest as we walked on the snow, our feet crunching through its hardened crust.

When we came to the clearing behind the rear of Mark's house, Brandy took cover behind a thick tree trunk, binoculars at the ready, while I – doing my best to ignore the chill, in my coatless state – slowly proceeded on.

Whether by lady luck, or divine intervention, large snowflakes began to fall, and a gentle wind blew life into the tails of my scarf. I could have written it myself!

Suddenly, a security light on the patio blazed on.

I halted and backed up.

Some seconds later, the light went off.

I moved forward again, triggering the beam.

Then retreated.

This was not an unintentional reaction of surprise on my part – there was an object to it: getting Mark's attention.

'He's at the window,' Brandy said sharply in my ear.

Once more I activated the beam, but this time stayed in the spotlight.

Brandy was saying, 'He's looking . . . he's looking . . . Do it now!'

I withdrew the iron, and – in my angelic state – swung it back and forth in front of me, like a pendulum.

'What's he doing now?' I whispered.

'He's not laughing, that's for sure,' Brandy replied, then, 'Oh! He's gone from the window.'

The chief's voice came. 'Time to leave.'

Quickly, Brandy and I retreated, retracing our path through the woods to the SUV, where I was glad to put my coat back on.

On the drive downtown, I asked, 'Dear, how did I look?'

'Like a cross between an angel and apparition. The Ghost of Christmas Wackadoodle. I think you pulled it off.'

Rare praise from Brandy – understandable, perhaps, given that I offered her so little kudos in her Watson role.

'Dear,' I said, 'that was a nice idea you had, going the angel route.'

'Thank you.'

'You're welcome.'

That should make up for my past deficiencies!

To conceal our SUV, we parked it among others in a nearby used car lot, then walked through the alleyways to reach the back of his sports shop. We took a page from our unwitting host's playbook, hiding ourselves behind a dumpster, as he had likely done waiting for Brandy to enter our shop when he attacked her in his cowardly fashion.

From the tote bag Brandy removed two blankets – one for sitting, the other for warmth – and a thermos of hot coffee.

I checked in with the chief. 'We're in the alley. Over.'

'You don't have to say "over",' he said.

'Roger that. Any movement?'

'The car's still here. House dark.'

Having left my cell at home, I consulted my wristwatch – one thirty-five.

Minutes dragged on, then hours, causing me to grow disheartened.

My feet were frozen, my tushy sore, and the coffee stone cold.

Then Brandy grabbed my arm, putting a finger to her lips.

At the end of the alley, a figure emerged from the falling snow and was coming toward us.

'Chief,' I whispered, 'I think he's here.'

'But his truck hasn't moved,' he countered.

Brandy whispered back, 'He must've gone through the woods, like we did, and walked here.'

'Listen to me,' the chief said, urgently. 'You are *not* to proceed further. Understand? Wait for back-up. You hear me, Vivian?'

But I didn't answer, having turned off my transmitter.

Vivian's Trash 'n' Treasures Tip

Many factors are taken into account when experts appraise an item: the subject matter, athlete, or team, its history, and the edition number, if there are multiples. Certainly, the rarer or more unusual the piece, the higher its value. For example, how many other single pizza containers signed by Ernie Banks are floating around out there? Who needs a home-run baseball?

THIRTEEN
Time Out

V ivian here, continuing her report.

Huddled behind the dumpster in the shadows Brandy and I watched as Mark Wheeler walked down the alley toward us, looking frankly rather sinister in his navy parka, black slacks, and black tennis shoes. Even his handsome features had taken on an evil air. The owner of All Sports Artifacts paused at the rear door to his store and sent his eyes cautiously around.

We drew back, turtles into their nonexistent shells.

Then came the sound of that rear door opening, then slamming shut and (I assumed) locking again.

Slowly we crawled out of our hiding place, Brandy assisting me to my feet, my replacement hips a marvel of medical science but not without limitations.

Per the plan, before picking the lock, I was to allow enough time for Mark to disable the shop's alarm system and move to the front of his establishment. Like any good burglar, I would perform my task quickly and efficiently with two picks withdrawn from my coat, after which I was to enter with Serenity's police chief as my backup.

Only he hadn't gotten here yet.

Brandy said, 'We should wait until Tony arrives.'

'All right,' I said. 'Let's return to our dumpster.'

'Like good little rats,' she said.

Then, when she turned and started off all hunkered down, I quickly opened the door and slipped inside, making certain my daughter was safely locked out. I hadn't gone to the trouble of pretending to die for naught.

'Sorry, dear,' I said mentally to my absent child. 'This is my Reichenbach Falls.'

I stood in a processing area filled with packing materials,

stacked boxes, and mailing equipment, angular shapes casting long shadows in the darkness, turning moonbeams coming through a window into something ominous.

On a table, I left my lock picks, transmitter, and earbuds, then moved on into a break room that was even darker, with no windows at all; but an illuminated panel on a microwave acted as a nightlight, allowing me to see well enough to avoid stumbling into the table and chairs.

Cautiously I continued forward, drawn toward the curtained doorway where faint light edged around the material. This was no surprise – most retail establishments kept some illumination on during the overnight hours, making the movement of thieves more noticeable to police cars on the prowl or anyone happening to drive by.

Slowly, I drew back the curtain, my performance about to begin.

Mark stood in front of the display of golf clubs, his back to me while he unlocked the security bar that held Patty Berg's iron in place.

As he withdrew the club, I spoke. 'Careful, Mark – that's evidence.'

The iron clattered to the floor as, startled, he whirled around.

'Yes, it's Vivian,' I said, gesturing to my ghostly garb. 'Back from beyond.'

The man forced a laugh. 'You mean Otto – putting on a ridiculous masquerade.'

I walked closer. 'No . . . this is the very real Vivian. Sorry to disappoint, dear, but I'm not dead. I staged my own demise – it was as cleverly phony as is much of your merchandise.'

He blinked several times, then realization spread across his face, reddening it like an instant rash. His eyes widened. 'So that was *you* in my yard, putting on a performance ludicrous even for Vivian Borne.'

He didn't have to be insulting!

'Ludicrous? It was inspiring enough to send you scurrying after your favorite murder weapon – hidden here in plain sight. Consider this a backstage moment, where we can have a little talk.'

His laugh rang hollow. 'You're deluded if you think I'm going to tell you a damn thing. You've been known to wear a wire, after all.'

I moved even closer.

'Not tonight, I'm not,' I said, turning the pockets of my coat inside out. 'You see? No cellphone, either.' I unzipped the choir robe to reveal the front of my form-fitting leotard. 'No wire. It's just you and me. Mano a mano – or should I say nemesis to nemesis?'

Because, after all, to him, that's what I was. And to me, that's what he was . . .

Mark's smile was awful. 'I'm almost disappointed. You're making this far too easy for me.' He picked up the golf iron. '"Officer . . . I happened to be driving past my store when I noticed a burglar inside . . ."'

He sprang forward, swinging the iron one-handed at my head. But I was ready, and jumped aside, the display case behind me taking the blow, shattering the glass in a noisy shower of shards.

'By the way,' I said, backing up a step, 'those letters you sent me? I've received far worse. It is but to laugh!'

'This you won't find funny.' He swung again. But I ducked, and one hand reached under the hem of the robe where my Taser was taped to my ankle.

I straightened. 'Care to take a Mulligan on that? Incidentally, Otto and I thank you for the discounted Gale Sayers football. I hope it's legit.'

Enraged, gripping the iron with both hands, he drew the club back – as if about to make a shot down a fairway and my skull was the ball. 'I should have killed you *first*.'

That was as good a confession as I thought I might get.

And, with his mid-section exposed, I thrust forward and discharged the electrical prongs, which found a soft home in his belly.

Dear reader, would you think less of me if I admitted I enjoyed watching the man writhing on the floor like a hooked fish on a boat deck?

The front door banged open, the chief filling the frame, a battering ram in his hands, an alarmed Brandy visible behind him.

'He may need some medical assistance,' I said. 'He's had quite a bad shock.'

Brandy taking over.

I don't know who was madder at Mother – me or Tony – for deviating from our plan. But Tony was plenty P.O.'d.

'What were you thinking,' he demanded of her, 'turning off your transmitter?'

We were seated in Tony's office, dawn just breaking, and he had already scolded Mother in a general way for the danger she'd put herself into.

'You only die once,' Mother said with a smug shrug. 'And I already did. Anyway, in my defense, Mark never would have incriminated himself if he thought I might be wearing a wire.'

Tony batted at the air in frustration. 'That's not the point! Nothing got recorded. We only have your word that he said he should have killed you first, before Nicole and Clare – with that last part only implied!'

'But it *was* recorded,' Mother said sweetly.

'How?' I asked. 'Not by your cellphone – you left that at home.'

Mother withdrew something from a coat pocket and placed it on the table.

Her spy necklace.

'You weren't wearing that,' I said.

'No. But I had it with me, and just before confronting Mark, I hung the necklace on a wall hook while his back was to me. And, this time, you better believe I made sure the necklace was charged.'

Tony – having little faith in Mother's spy gizmo – looked skeptical, so she handed him the USB cord, which he connected to the necklace and his computer, then downloaded the video footage.

Moments later, we were watching a replay – sight and sound – of what had transpired.

Tony sat back in his chair and let go a sigh that began at his toes. 'Vivian, I stand corrected. This is more damning than anything your transmitter could have provided. Congratulations.'

Mother beamed, basking in the praise. 'Thank you, Chief. If I'd had more time, I might have managed a better camera angle. But I do think this footage has a nice immediacy.'

'What now?' I asked Tony.

He looked at me. 'I'll need detailed statements from both of you about what happened tonight.'

'That'll make good reading,' I said with a chuckle.

Tony went on, 'And, Vivian, I still want those threatening notes Mark sent you . . . there may be some forensic evidence we can get off them to add to the case against him.'

Mother nodded. 'Can do. But right now Brandy and I could use a little shut-eye.'

I yawned in agreement.

'Fine, when you're rested,' the chief said. Then, 'Mark Wheeler is a very lucky man.'

Startled, Mother asked, 'How so?'

Tony said to us both, 'He's lucky we don't have the death penalty in this state. And we'll have to settle for him going away for a very, very long time.'

A few days later I had dinner with Tony at his cabin, taking Sushi along for a Rocky fix. We hadn't spoken since Mother and I were in his office at the PD, and I was anxious to clear the air between us. Which, admittedly, would be mostly a one-sided conversation – my side.

My feeling of having been betrayed hadn't eased at all. If anything, it had grown. And since I couldn't stay mad at Jake because he was my son . . . and Mother, well, because she was Mother . . . that left Tony to take the brunt of my ire.

We were cordial throughout the meal, even chuckling about the episodes we'd been streaming on Netflix of a series called *Murderville*. We had a good laugh imagining Mother as a guest star.

But the after-dinner clean-up was strained, both of us knowing something uncomfortable was coming.

Finally, we retired to the couch in front of the fireplace, where logs crackled and popped and sparks flew as if in a foreshadowing of the conversation to come. Blissfully unaware, Sushi was curled up on the hearth with Rocky.

Tony spoke first, 'I think we should take some time out.'
Talk about a preemptive strike!
Stunned, I asked, 'You're breaking up with me?'
'No, Brandy. I love you. I'll always love you.'
I waited for the 'but'.
'But . . . it's obvious we can't start a marriage until you come to terms with what I put you through. What I did.'
That's what he had to say? Not 'forgive me for what I did'? This was on *me*?
My cheeks grew hot. 'That's not fair! You're making this into something that's my fault! As if I hadn't endured enough. I can expect thoughtlessness from Mother – she can't help herself. But from *you*?'
He went on, 'You need to understand that if I had it to do all over again, I would do the same. And the result would be the same, even if I knew I might lose you. Because I almost *did* lose you in the hospital.'
While Tony's eyes were moist, he did have his pride.
'All right,' I said. 'Let's discuss what "time out" means.' I continued rhetorically: 'I'm to let you know when I've gotten past this. Until then, we don't see each other.'
'Is that the way you want it?' he asked.
'Yes.' I had my pride, too.
He nodded. 'I'll honor that.'
Since there seemed little else to say, I rose from the couch, gathered my coat – along with an irate Sushi having been plucked from her love – and took my leave.
I don't remember driving home, my mind replaying the evening, wondering what I could have done differently, should have said differently. Or was I like him, predestined to take the same actions?
I pulled into the driveway, turned off the engine, and sat in the cold, waiting for the waterworks to come, when my cell sounded.
I looked at the ID, hoping it was Tony asking – no, pleading – for me to come back.
But the caller was my ex.
'Roger,' I answered anxiously, as he only called when something was urgent.

'Jake's all right, Brandy,' he began, his voice sounding weary. 'But this *is* about our son. He's been suspended from school for the second time this year, and they won't have him back.' He paused. 'I'm afraid Jake is heading to a very bad place.'

'What did he do?' I asked, almost afraid to hear.

Roger sighed. 'Same as last time – Jake got into a fight with another boy. And since the school has a zero-tolerance policy in that regard, both boys were expelled.'

A possible solution popped into my head. 'Could you set up a Zoom meeting in an hour, between you and Laura and myself?'

'Yes.'

'Good. And we'll include Mother.'

When Roger started to protest, I cut in, 'She's his grand-mother and has a right to know what's going on.'

Perhaps it was the firmness in my voice that made him respond, albeit reluctantly: 'All right. But tell Vivian to just *listen*. I don't want her weighing in and muddying the waters with her . . . nuttiness.'

I let that pass. 'Fine. You have my email, and I'll send you Mother's, because she'll be on a different computer.'

'One hour,' he said, and ended the call.

Now, you may well wonder, why wait one hour for a confab of such importance? Well, it's because that's how long Mother takes to prepare for a Zoom call, ever since her first experience with a virtual meeting went (as she put it) 'awry'. She had positioned herself with a ceiling fan going behind her, which made it appear that she was wearing a giant beanie with twirling propellers. In addition, the lighting made her look ten years older (whatever that age might be I can't say, because that's on a need-to-know basis and she says I don't need to know).

Her second meeting didn't go terribly well, either. Mother had selected an outer space background on her green screen, then wore a green long-sleeved dress, so what appeared to others on the call were her bobbing head and gesticulating hands floating in the stratosphere. Of course, it did make her look like something out of a 1950s sci-fi movie, which I argued was appropriate. She didn't take that well, either.

Nowadays, for Zoom calls, Mother uses a specific corner of her art nouveau bedroom as a sort of standing set arranged with flattering lighting and arrayed with interesting antiques in the background. Here are her Zoom 'Dos and Don'ts' for the over-fifty crowd, born (pun very much intended) from her missteps.

1) **DO** position the webcam at eye level so that you won't be looking down, which will give you a double chin (or triple, if you start out with a double).
2) **DO** place a light source in front of you to soften your features – an overhead light source will only serve to make you look like Lon Chaney in *The Phantom of the Opera* (unless it's Halloween and a desired effect, of course).
3) **DON'T** lean into the computer screen, which will distort your face, creating a large proboscis (Jimmy Durante impressions meaning nothing to the younger generations).
4) **DO** made sure if you wear glasses and use one of those circular lights, their round reflections won't dance distractingly in your lenses (googly-eyes best reserved as an emoji).
5) **DO** wear a colorful scarf or turtleneck top to hide a crepey *cou de femme*, and also some jewelry to dazzle (I find Swarovski crystals bring just the right amount of bling).

Inside the house, I found Mother tidying up in the kitchen, Sushi at her feet, hoping for any leftover dinner morsels.

'Back already, dear?' she asked, surprised.

'I seem to be.'

She frowned, sensing trouble. 'Everything all right between you and our favorite Chiefie?'

Since I didn't want to get into the break-up right now, I invoked one of her favorite phrases, 'Tickety boo,' and changed the subject to Roger's call and the Zoom meeting coming up in an hour.

I also informed Mother of an idea I was going to suggest,

but advised her that it was imperative she remain mum on the subject if the plan was to succeed.

To the former, she said, 'Splendid proposal!' To the latter, 'I shall do my best,' which was all I could hope for, although admittedly Vivian Borne's 'best' involved a sliding scale – in fact, a scale you could slide right off of like Billy Buckly.

Then, wiping her hands on a dish cloth, she quipped, 'And now . . . I must prepare!'

Refer to her Zoom 'Do's and Don'ts' above for what that would entail.

While the star of her own show disappeared upstairs, I set up my laptop on the Duncan Phyfe table in the dining room, then went into the downstairs toidy to tidy.

At the arranged time, I logged into the meeting. Roger and his wife, Laura, were already onscreen, seated next to each other at a mahogany desk, which I presumed was in his den, files neatly stacked to one side, work brought home from his office in downtown Chicago.

He was looking older than mid-forties, more lines in his face now, brown hair thinning, graying at the sides and temples, but still quite handsome; he wore a blue sweater, the collar of a button-down pale yellow shirt showing at the neck.

Laura, a pediatrician in a suburban hospital, had on a crisp white blouse, her straight blonde hair worn shoulder-length, face pretty but strained with worry. She was a better match for Roger than I, and we got along fine, as far as it went, which admittedly wasn't far. Really, there was only one thing that bothered me about Laura, and it wasn't her fault: she looked a lot like me.

My grainy square on the screen paled in comparison with theirs. Not only did I look bad, the candlesticks on the buffet table behind me made it seem like horns were growing out of my head! Devil Brandy was not the impression I wished to give, but I lacked Mother's stage-management skills.

'Hello, Roger . . . Laura,' I said, adjusting my position.

'Brandy,' they said in lock-step.

'Mother should be along shortly,' I said. No surprise that she would keep an audience waiting. Dramatic entrances were among her many specialties.

Suddenly, like a pop-up ad, the grand dame made her appearance. Wrapped around her neck was a long multi-colored scarf worthy of Isadora Duncan, dressed up further by a plethora of pearl necklaces. But the piece de resistance was the tiara on her head.

Oh brother, Mother . . .

'I, uh,' Laura said, 'hope we're not keeping you from a theatrical performance, Vivian.'

'Yes,' Roger interjected a little too quickly, 'please feel free to go, if you need to.'

Nervously, I said, 'Ah . . . she's just come back from a rehearsal, *right*, Mother?'

Mother, appearing hurt that her outfit selection hadn't been appreciated, responded, 'Yes, that is correct. I'm playing the Witch of the East in *The Wizard of Oz.*'

Avoiding any discussion of whether that was a good or bad witch, I plowed ahead. 'Regarding the trouble Jake has been in with his school, I would like to propose a solution.'

'Which would be what?' Roger asked, dubiously.

I jumped right in, cutting to the chase even as I mixed metaphors. 'That he transfer to Serenity High School for his second freshman semester.'

'You mean . . . live with you?' Roger asked, making it sound as if I had suggested we all move into a commune; and before I could answer, he went on: 'Oh, no. *That's* never going to happen.'

Laura turned to him. 'Roger . . . let's hear Brandy out.'

'Thank you, Laura,' I said.

Roger looked at his wife, then swallowed, and nodded to the camera and his previous wife.

I went on: 'Serenity High is small compared to the school Jake has been attending . . . the teachers are good and work very hard for every student to succeed. Plus, there are a lot of extracurricular activities he could get involved in – sports, chorus, drama. Also, Jake could work at our antiques store on weekends, which would keep him busy while earning himself some money.'

Mother added, 'The boy could even help out at the theater . . . perhaps get a part in a play.' She paused, then continued,

quietly smug: 'It so happens I have an in with the director.'
Meaning herself, of course.

When Roger didn't protest, I pressed on. 'It could be a trial
run to see how he does . . . if his grades are good, and he
stays out of trouble, he could stay on, if he so desired.
Otherwise . . .'

I didn't have an otherwise.

But Roger did: 'Military school.'

I could tell by his expression, and Laura's, that neither
father nor stepmom relished that possibility.

After what seemed like forever, but was only five or ten
seconds, Roger said, 'There's only one problem with that, and
it's a big one.'

He made me ask.

'Jake will be under the influence of Vivian, which –
forgive me, Mrs Borne – has in the past been anything but
healthy.'

Mother couldn't help herself. 'I beg your pardon!'

Roger addressed her directly. 'Do you deny that you recently
sent Jake into a very rough part of Chicago to do some investigating for you at some disreputable antiques shop, putting
him in obvious danger? And that he skipped school in order
to do your questionable bidding?'

Mother blurted, 'How did you know about that?'

'Oh, for pity's sake,' he said. 'It was in your book *Antiques
Fire Sale!*'

'I didn't realize you could be bothered to read our series,'
Mother said, astonished. 'I'm flattered . . . I think.'

'I read the ones that have something to do with Jake,'
Roger snapped. 'I would say I am among those readers who
find nothing amusing about them at all.' Then he turned his
ire on me. 'And Brandy, you're no better than Vivian. In
Antiques Maul, Jake was only twelve when he got involved
in one of your amateur sleuthing escapades . . . only to be
kidnapped! And what did *you* do? You shot the kidnapper
with a gun!'

'That's redundant, dear,' Mother advised him. 'What else
might she have shot him with?'

I groaned inwardly.

Laura touched her husband's arm. 'Roger, please . . . your blood pressure.'

'I just shot him in the foot,' I said defensively, 'so the man would tell me where Jake was. And it worked, didn't it? You *did* want your son rescued, didn't you?'

Roger's face was growing redder by the minute. 'Suppose I grant you that. What about the time Jake was staying with you when you two started poking your noses into an *ax murder*, no less!'

He was referring to *Antiques Chop*.

Mother said somewhat defensively, 'That is a very old crime. And Jake was not directly involved in the present-day aspects of that investigation.'

'Only because I took him back to Chicago,' Roger went on. 'If I hadn't, who knows what would have happened to the boy.'

Laura whispered to him, 'Careful, darling – you'll go into afib again.'

'Roger,' I said, 'remember that while Jake is here, Tony will be a big presence in the boy's life.' Or anyway I hoped he still would be . . .

My ex grunted. 'Well, that *is* one positive element, I grant you. The chief is a good man.' He paused. 'But Vivian would have to promise not to get involved in any new cases while Jake is around . . . and, frankly, I don't think that's possible.'

Mother said, 'Roger, dear, I do promise. Jake's welfare is more important to me than anything. And I guarantee that you won't get a single whiff of murder or mayhem coming from these quarters while my grandson is here. Cross my heart and hope to die.'

'And here I thought you already did die,' Roger said with a smirk.

Unkind as that was, I could tell he was softening, and the fact that he hadn't shut down our proposal immediately made me almost certain Jake would be with us soon.

'At least talk it over with him,' I said. 'He could come after Christmas and settle in before classes start mid-January.'

Roger looked at Laura, who nodded.

'All right,' my ex said, 'we'll discuss the matter with Jake and get back to you.'

'Thank you,' I said.

Their square disappeared, leaving Mother's and mine.

'Boy,' I said. 'It's a good thing *Antiques Foe* won't be published until a year from now, and Roger finds out how much you used Jake.'

Mother, nodding, the tiara blinding me, smiled. 'Yes. And – best of all – *should* a case arise while Jake is here, *that* book won't be published for another *two* years.'

And, with a cackle, she vanished. Bad witch, then.

I would have to watch Mother as she always envisioned her relationship with Jake represented by the end of the classic movie *Auntie Mame* where Rosalind Russell ascends the grand staircase in her Park Avenue apartment with an arm around her grandson while extolling the great adventures they would share together.

But I wouldn't think about that now. I was going to have my son around! One man steps out of my life, another steps in. *C'est la vie*, as Frank Sinatra said. In English.

To be continued . . .

Brandy's Trash 'n' Treasures Tip

Not all sports memorabilia goes up in value over time, so be sure you love what you buy. After my 2009 Grand Slam Tennis video game – reduced to one dollar – had no takers at our shop, I took it home and started playing it again. The game is still fun! And who knows what it might be worth in another twenty-five years?

BARBARA ALLAN

I s a joint pseudonym of husband-and-wife mystery writers, Barbara and Max Allan Collins.

BARBARA COLLINS made her entrance into the mystery field as a highly respected short story writer with appearances in over a dozen top anthologies, including *Murder Most Delicious*, *Women on the Edge*, *Deadly Housewives* and the best-selling *Cat Crimes* series. She was the co-editor of (and a contributor to) the bestselling anthology *Lethal Ladies*, and her stories were selected for inclusion in the first three volumes of *The Year's 25 Finest Crime and Mystery Stories*.

Three acclaimed collections of her work have been published – *Too Many Tomcats* and (with her husband) *Murder – His and Hers* and *Suspense – His and Hers*. The couple's first novel together, the Baby Boomer thriller *Regeneration*, was a paperback bestseller; their second collaborative novel, *Bombshell* – in which Marilyn Monroe saves the world from World War III – was published in hardcover to excellent reviews. Recently they collaborated on the short suspense novel *Cutout*.

Barbara also has been the production manager and/or line producer of several independent film projects.

MAX ALLAN COLLINS was named a Grand Master by the Mystery Writers of America in 2017. He has earned an unprecedented twenty-three Private Eye Writers of America 'Shamus' nominations, many for his Nathan Heller historical thrillers, winning for *True Detective* (1983), *Stolen Away* (1991), and the short story 'So Long, Chief'.

His classic graphic novel *Road to Perdition* is the basis of the Academy Award-winning film. Max's other comics credits include 'Dick Tracy'; 'Batman'; his own 'Ms. Tree'; and 'Wild Dog', featured on the *Arrow* TV series.

Max's body of work includes film criticism, short fiction, songwriting, trading-card sets, and movie/TV tie-in novels, such as the *New York Times* bestseller *Saving Private Ryan*, numerous *USA Today* bestselling CSI novels, and the Scribe Award-winning *American Gangster*. His non-fiction includes *Scarface and the Untouchable: Al Capone, Eliot Ness & the Mad Butcher* (both with A. Brad Schwartz), and *Spillane – King of Pulp Fiction* with James L. Traylor.

An award-winning filmmaker, he wrote and directed the Lifetime movie *Mommy* (1996) and three other features; his produced screenplays include the 1995 HBO World Premiere *The Expert* and *The Last Lullaby* (2008). His 1998 documentary *Mike Hammer's Mickey Spillane* appears on the Criterion Collection release of the acclaimed *film noir Kiss Me Deadly*. The Cinemax TV series *Quarry* is based on his innovative book series.

Max's recent novels include a dozen-plus works begun by his mentor, the late mystery-writing legend, Mickey Spillane, among them *Kill Me If You Can* with Mike Hammer and the Caleb York western novels.

'BARBARA ALLAN' live(s) in Muscatine, Iowa, their Serenity-esque hometown. Son Nathan works as a translator of Japanese to English, with credits including video games, manga, and novels.